Only 5 Days

M.A. Higgins

Only 5 Days

By M.A. Higgins

Paperback edition, 1st printing

Copyright © 2012 Michael A. Higgins

For information, individual orders, movie or television rights, contact

M. A . Higgins

PO Box 874

Buxton, N.C. 27920

www.mahiggins.com

M.A. Higgins is available November – May for book signings and presentations.

Cover Design: Jennifer M. Williams, L.Ac

Text Formatting and Editing: Jennifer M. Williams, L.Ac

Associate Editor: Joshua B. Carver

ISBN-13: 978-1478104858

ISBN-10: 1478104856

DEDICATION

To my mother and father who told me, "You can be a bum, but you will be an educated bum. You will finish school."

Thanks.

CONTENTS

ACKNOWLEDGEMENTS

I am thankful to Mary Hixinbough from Uniontown, Pennsylvania, for her belief in me from the beginning.

I would also like to thank my editors for seeing my vision and having patience.

.

FOREWORD

Hello, my name is Mina. All of the events in this story are true. Based on legal advice, this story had to be published as fiction, even though the names were changed. The locations of the events were not changed. Some of the people in this story are still alive and their accounts of what happened may differ. If you pay close attention, you may be able to figure out who they are. I will simply say that it was inspired by a true story.

There is something quite unusual that happened to my brother, Mika, and me; something that has been documented by physicians all over the world, but never at the same place or at the same time. The strong bond between my brother and me may be the reason this rare phenomena happened to us. When you get to this part of the story, you might not believe it at first. However, let me assure you that it did happen, and just as described.

Liberties were taken concerning some of the dialogue. Knowing the facts and the positions the people held at that time allowed me to presume what their responses might have been. Everything else not witnessed by us was recovered from documents.

This story screamed to be told and I feel privileged to be the one telling it. I guarantee that you will remember it forever. Remember, we were not only witnesses, but participants. You may even wonder how I could know such details that occurred before I was born. Eventually, you will understand everything.

CHAPTER 1

Mika and Mina

April 28, 2005, Berlin, Germany

Only five days until the 60th anniversary of the end of World War II

On the first day of our vacation we stopped at an outdoor café for strudel and coffee. It had looked and smelled so good that we had to stop and have some. This café was somewhere close to where our parents were raised and looked inviting. It had a green canvas awning blowing in the breeze with an assortment of tables and chairs outside.

Mika looked at me with a twinkle in his eye and said, "I hope this trip is more than just a boring family search. I hope we find out everything we want and have some sort of dangerous adventure too. It would make this trip more than what we had planned and dreamed."

"Watch what you wish for Mika." Just as I said those words, we heard a car traveling at a very fast speed and tires screeching. Mika turned to look, and then he turned back to me with fear in his eyes and yelled, "Run Mina, run!"

I woke up in a cold sweat. It had been a bad dream. The discomfort lingered and the hunger had not abated. The car hit us hard. Everything, including tables and chairs, was thrown into the air. We barely had time to scream. When I opened my eyes, they hurt. Dust stung my eyes and coated my face. The filth tore at my nose and throat, and it filled the air – making it hard to see. A woman grabbed my arm, pulling

2

me up off of the street. She called me by my name and with her other arm she picked up a little boy and asked, "Mika, are you alright?"

I realized she was speaking German, not my native language, yet I understood perfectly. Looking stunned and hurt, the little boy explained, also speaking Deutsch, "Um. Yes, except for my hand." He raised a hand, sheepishly displaying a deep cut dripping blood.

While she was speaking to him, a woman in a long black coat grabbed food from a nearby table. She looked directly at me, never saying a word. She picked up what food she could and ran away. When I looked down to scan my body and check for my own injuries, what I saw frightened me further. I was no longer in my adult body. I hadn't noticed before, but I was much shorter than I was just a moment before. I was a child again, garbed in fettered rags and absolutely filthy. I looked again at the little boy. It was my younger brother, Mika, who was no longer an adult either.

The woman then took my little brother and me by our little hands and led us quickly away, back inside the café and down some stairs. It was dark and looked like a basement. There were other people in this cold place. They were all huddled together and looked more frightened than I felt. One of the women noticed Mika's bleeding. She gently cleaned his hand with a dirty rag. She then removed a clean handkerchief from her soiled, dark coat and wrapped his hand. "It is not bad," she assured him, "I will fix it better when we get home."

Again, I understood her perfect German dialect. I had only learned basic German before our trip. First I thought I must have incorporated those lessons into my dream, but some of the words were not so basic. I felt faint and ill. Mika looked like he was in shock. He just stared at me. I held up one finger in front of my lips. He nodded in compliance. I looked around nervously to determine if anyone had noticed my adult gesture in this child's body. The quiet calm and solace of the strangers was comforting. My rapid breathing slowed as I observed more detail.

I slowly looked around, taking notice of everything. There was a smell of human odor. Candles were lit, making shadows dance on the walls. It was musty and damp. The dark plain clothing that the huddled people were wearing was rather odd. The entire scene looked like a

3

vintage bombing raid right out of the history books. I gasped out loud when I suddenly realized that it was exactly what I was witnessing; a bombing raid during World War II!

Getting up and dusting herself off, the kind woman said, "It is over. We can go up now children."

Leading us by our hands, we went outside. My tiny hand was swallowed in the kind woman's bony fingers. My small legs nearly tripped on every obstacle. I wanted to wake from this dream. I felt overwhelmed by the pain and anxiety, but I was also in awe of the graphic details that seemed so real. The weird sounds, smells, voices, and architecture enticed my senses. The buildings looked old with recent damage. Some were in total ruins.

Mika is the History professor. I did not remember learning this amount of detail. I am a Special Education teacher. My focus was on contemporary research, theory, and the future. I did not have an interest in the past, except for my family's history. That is why Mika and I came to Berlin during our spring break. We had questions that we were unable to answer on the Internet. This wasn't a pending trip, we had arrived. The café was our first stop after we left the airport. We had not yet found our hotel. Why did this feel so real?

I wanted to run away. I wanted to wake up. I wanted to eat. I hoped we were being lead to the kind woman's home. My stomach burned with emptiness. I had never felt such hunger in my life. After a quick one-block walk and a left turn, we entered a doorway. We went up one set of stairs, turned left, and then she opened a door. This place, we found out later, was where we lived. As we entered the apartment, everything we looked at and touched was so strange. We were in children's bodies, but I remembered everything from our past, including our graduation from high school and college. From the expression on Mika's face, he remembered too.

He later described his pain and the salty taste of his blood. Looking back and forth at each other's eyes, we began a communication of sorts, without words. We seemed to know what the other was thinking while we were looking around. Sometimes we would raise an eyebrow, give each other a little smile, or just open our eyes a little wider. We used subtle expressions that only we would notice. It seems we were both becoming aware of the significant importance to remember dates and events that we may be about to witness.

Every year since September 11, 2001, Germans have been conflicted about whether to celebrate the end of World War II, or just let it pass. The similarities between the burning of Reichstag and the September 11th attacks concerned many. The Reichstag fire was an arson attack on a government building in Berlin on 27 February 1933. The event is seen as pivotal in the establishment of Nazi Germany. It was later determined that Hitler covertly planned the attack that catapulted him to leadership. Mika and I knew that tensions may be mounting in Europe during our travel, but we were determined to find answers.

Not only would we enjoy the sights, but we would also learn things about our family that no one would tell us. There were many family secrets. By personally going to the region, we could learn more from local newspapers and maybe even personal accounts. There was no guarantee; only hope. We had desperately sought answers to many questions, but were never successful in our endeavor. We had exhausted the use of the Internet and all other resources thus far.

Both of our parents had died several years ago. Whenever we would ask them about what it was like when they were children, they would find a way to gently put us off. When we asked about their parents, they just shrugged it off like it was insignificant. What we did know, was that we were named after our parents. Our grandmother's name was Marion and our grandfather's name was Joseph. We also knew our parents were young children in Germany at the end of World War II, specifically in Berlin. Almost immediately, after the war ended, our entire family relocated to America.

Several rumors whispered by our aunts and uncles intrigued us. The only thing we knew for sure was our family immigrated days after the war to the United States. One rumor was there was incest. Another was that everyone left to keep from being prosecuted for war crimes. The worst was that our family hated Jews so bad that they were afraid of being hunted down and maybe killed for what they had done to some. Then there was the simple story that they left just to have a better life for their children. What our other family members were like and all of the family history was like a puzzle begging to be solved. The only picture of any of our grandparents was one of Joseph in his German uniform carrying his rifle. The picture was in a beautiful antique frame.

I was still trembling. There was no comfort in the stale damp air in this lady's apartment. The blanket she placed on me smelled of cigars and stale bread. I looked around the small room. Little Mika was gazing at a picture across the room. It was of a young German Soldier in uniform with his rifle. Our father had the same picture in the same unique frame.

We moved closer to examine the photograph. Just past the wall where the photograph hung, was a door that led to another room. The room we were in included the kitchen. The sink had dishes in it and a window that overlooked the streets, including the one we had just left. I could clearly see the damaged buildings and the roads in front of our building. The building that was directly in front still had its readable sign: 108 Nine Straße. The building was severely damaged from the bombings and looked as if no one could be possibly still be living there.

The building sat in the center of an intersection shaped like the letter Y. We looked out of the window and had a great view of buildings and all three roads. If one stretched out of the window and looked to the right, he could see the outdoor café about a block away where this whole nightmare started. It looked very much the same as it did when we started this journey. It was slightly damaged by what had just happened and the tables and chairs were all over the place.

The kind woman came over with some small bandages and sat at the table to carefully inspect Mika's wound. She said, "It isn't really that bad." Then she smiled at us. I am sure it was to reassure and keep us calm. The bleeding had stopped and she finished wrapping it up when she said, "Keep this on at all times and keep it clean if you can." She then stood up, walked to the kitchen, and started to wash the dishes. With her back turned we both looked at a newspaper on the table. I read the headlines and Mika looked at something else.

The headline was a desperate call to young boys for military duty. The article stated that it was essential for the defense of the motherland. It also said this call-up was necessary not because of losses, but because of the successes they were having on all fronts. The bombing of Berlin was just an attempt by the enemy to scare the German people and somehow change the course of the war that the allies were losing. Mika was looking at several hand-written letters on the table.

The letters looked as though they had been handled many times. The sides were worn with finger smudges from holding the paper with wet hands, as if she went back and forth between f the letters and housework. Mika clandestinely slid one of the letters over toward him and started reading. I glanced at the woman who was not paying any attention to us. She was washing the dishes and humming a tune. She looked familiar, very similar to our mother. Giving Mika a stern glance, I warned him to be careful. He slightly shrugged his shoulders and gave me a big smile. It almost made me giggle. It was the first relief I experienced since the car crashed into us. He was now about five years old and would not yet be able to read.

As she was finishing the dishes, I wanted Mika to stop "reading" before he was caught. "We need to talk in private and now," I whispered. Then I said something louder so the woman could hear me say in Deutsch, "Let's go in the other room and play."

Without turning around, the woman said, "Don't make a mess in there. I cleaned all morning from your mess yesterday."

We went in and looked around, leaving the door cracked so we could listen and see inside the other room. The room was not much to look at; it was a small room with two beds and little more. On one bed there were toys and a stuffed animal. The other bed was a little bigger and nicely prepared. We figured out that we must sleep in one bed with her in the other. We sat down in the corner behind the door to talk and not be overheard. We could see but not be seen. We took with us a few toys so if she came in to check on us we had something to act like we were playing.

"Did you see the date?" was the first thing Mika said to me.

"I have to say I didn't. So what is it?" I replied.

Mika leaned forward looking straight into my eyes as if it were extremely important and whispered to me, "April 28, 1945. Does that mean anything to you?"

I looked intently at Mika and replied, "Not particularly, except the end of World War II is about to happen. You are the History teacher.

You tell me." Then I added, "Maybe that is why we are here in this place and time? Maybe this has something to do with our search. Do you remember enough history to help us now?"

Mika continued on saying, "There are only five days until the surrender. In some parts of Germany the war is already over. But not around here. Adolph Hitler is alive in his bunker with many of his high-ranking officials not far from us, right now. They are getting everything ready to celebrate his birthday. No one except us knows he will commit suicide in two days. They keep telling the people they are winning. If anyone has any doubts and says so out loud, they can be shot right on the spot; sometimes on the street with everyone watching.

Mika took a deep breath and then continued, "I do not know why we are here now. I do know this; we are in probably the most dangerous time in history for us to be here. Then we heard the woman say to us, "Bedtime, you two need your sleep now. Get ready for bed and I will tuck you in."

Mika smiled at me and said, "I can't remember the last time I was tucked in."

There were no more nearby air raids during that night, and we slept- uninterrupted. Sometime during that night, off in the distance, we could hear what sounded like bombs or shelling. It was so faint that we could not tell the distance or tell the difference between bombs falling or distant thunder. At this time in history, only sixteen miles to the east, there were Russians fighting and pushing hard for victory against their much-hated enemy, which now included us.

*****

April 29, 1945

Only four days until the fall of Berlin

The sun was shining between drifting white clouds, but it was still cold for late April. During the night, we figured out that this woman was our late grandmother Marion and somehow we were our parents as children. Now we would get to know her, as we never had the chance. We would also discover what our parents experienced as children. This was exciting. After breakfast we quickly got ready to leave the apartment. Marion noticed this and reminded us to "Bundle up. You both know the rules."

When we both looked at her with an empty expression, she added, "You can't go any farther than the café on the right. You cannot go the other way at all. If you hear the air raid sirens go directly to our basement and I will be there waiting for you. I should not let you go out, but I do not think I can keep you here all day and night either."

We went out the door, down the steps and to the right toward the cafe. We skipped along as children do, laughing and whispering at each other as we went along. We decided to play a little game of tag. We were quick to learn that hide and seek would allow us to enter and leave anywhere we wished almost unnoticed. Mika said something first, "Some of the Soldiers look so young."

I smiled and replied, "Yes, and the German Soldiers in their uniforms do look quite handsome."

Mika then said, "Control yourself, girl. You are only eight now."

We were saying everything in German and mostly whispering so as not to be overheard. It seemed like everyone was watching us play. They seem to be paying a lot of extra attention to us for some reason. I whispered to Mika, "Don't slip and start speaking English. It might have a devastating effect."

As we were playing, Mika said, "Heck this isn't so bad. I still do not know what is going on. There must be a very important reason for all this to be happening. Maybe more than just one important reason too."

"I do not think the reason is only about our family search. I believe we are going to have to do something extremely important. Something may have been missed in our family's past. Something they wished they had done differently. There are things we may get involved with that will help us understand everything. We need to be ready." I got more serious and continued, "These are just feelings I have. Nothing I can prove yet. We obviously have to be here to help us understand."

"I have the same thoughts, and I think we just need to go with the flow. We need to pay close attention to everything and see where this takes us."

Immediately after we said this, we noticed a young Nazi boy all dressed up in his brown uniform with a red swastika badge on his sleeve. He was about twenty feet away passing out papers. At about the same time, we saw him notice us. I got a bad feeling in my stomach at that moment.

He was wearing his impeccable uniform with pride. His black boots shined in the sunlight. He had several ribbons on his chest. They resembled the same ribbons adult Soldiers wear on uniforms. He appeared to be about fifteen or sixteen years old. At this time in history, seventeen year olds were the youngest that were accepted in the military, so he had to be younger. He gave us a second look. He knew that something was just not right about us.

I said one more thing about him to Mika. "We have to watch out for him and anyone like him. They will be paying a lot closer attention to us than the adults. Every one of them wants to get bonus points for turning people in to the police or Gestapo."

We discussed later that we were risking all of our family; past and future. An entire generation of our family was now in jeopardy because of us. If something bad were to happen to us and we are killed, then we might never be born or our children. Mika ran ahead of me as I caught up with him at the café. We had started playing tag. I looked back and the danger was not in sight anymore. I felt a little better.

We could now play as children and maybe even have some fun. We were able to laugh a little and started whispering funny things about the people around us. All the adults were watching us, two innocent children playing and having fun, totally unaware of what was happening. Or so they all thought. Many tried all kinds of things to get our attention.

Most held out a treat to entice one or both of us to come over. If we went over to them, then we just might have to push the limit and see what else we could get away with. We knew as children this would allow us to do almost anything we wanted. At least for that moment, that was what we were beginning to believe. This was our second mistake.

I could tell Mika really was enjoying being a child again and being the center of attention. He did not have to say a word; just act young and be cute. I had the responsibility of interacting with the adults and having to be the one that would have to correct any problems that arose, some that might even become life threatening.

It was amusing to watch Mika. Mika was staring at a German officer. He was a very high-ranking officer with red patches on his collar and many metals on his chest. I remember seeing the patches on The History Channel. It seemed like years ago, but it was only last week. The documentary presented the very same hat on a table beside this officer. It had all of the historic relics including skull and crossbones. I knew it signified high rank. The officer looked to be in his late sixties and possibly retired.

Mika later told me that he thought the officer was a General, but for some reason he also believed he was not active. Someone so important at this time in history would be working trying to save this country somewhere else and not be where he was right then. Mika suspected somehow that he now was not allowed to be involved in the campaign. He probably was some sort of national hero that the high command did not want helping, but because of his loyalty and past service was allowed certain privileges like wearing his uniform if he wished.

The General smiled at us the whole time we were playing. One could just see in his eyes that he must have children and maybe even grandchildren. Perhaps he was now missing them as he watched us.

Knowing Mika as I did and knowing the deep hatred he had for all Nazis gave me concern. I knew he had studied in detail everything he could get his hands on concerning this time in history. He was fascinated with all of the problems and stories concerning Jewish peoples' plight, especially the inhumanity so many suffered. Mika's own hatred for Nazis festered. These strong feelings coincided with Mika's desperation to understand. There had to be a reason for this burning hatred that was deeper than just reading about it in history books. He now had an opportunity to discover the reason.

It was not just the horrible things that they did that bothered Mika. There was something important, something hidden. He confided this to me later, wondering if this deep-rooted hatred had something to do with us being here. I could see him inching closer and closer to the General. I did not know what Mika was going to do next. However, I did know he was going to do something. The General held out in his hand a piece of candy to entice him to come over. It was chocolate.

I thought that ought to do it. It would have for me. I love chocolate. I also remember thinking quickly that if he eats all of it instead of giving some to me I would turn him in myself. If he knew this, I believed he would still open it up and eat it right in front of me and smile the whole time.

Mika slowly went over took the candy from his hand and softly said "Danka."

The General responded, "Bitta,"

Inspecting the General a little closer, Mika reached out and touched one of his medals. The General saw him doing this and reassured Mika that it was ok. "It is fine, you can touch it."

As Mika was getting a little closer to look, the General suddenly reached out and grabbed Mika by the waist. I almost jumped out of my skin. He surprised both of us. In one quick motion, he lifted up Mika and put him on his lap. One minute everything was calm, and then suddenly there was tension. Even the littlest things could be disastrous for us. A minor detail that got us noticed could become a huge issue. If such an issue was reported to Gestapo or police, then they would have reason to come for us. Everyone, we felt, had this fear.

I believed we needed to go. I slowly walked over to the General, pointed a finger at Mika's heart, and touched him there saying, "Tag you're it."

Mika quickly got up grabbed an orange that was on the General's plate and we both started toward our new home. As we were walking towards the flat, Mika started peeling the orange and dropping the peelings on the ground. We looked back at the General who was smiling at us. We could tell he did not mind Mika taking it. We believed that he liked the little courage this shy boy just showed him. However, this seemingly simple act might just give someone like the General a glimpse into what this little boy was really like. If only he knew the truth. Bravery by men and boys was something everyone in Germany respected. As he was peeling and eating the orange, he smiled at me and said, "This is really good."

Then he said something a little peculiar: "Boy would I love a cigar right now. Now wouldn't that be a sight for everyone to see - a five year old boy smoking a cigar and dropping peelings on the street." Then he added, "If we are stuck growing up again, I know one thing I am definitely going to do."

I just had to ask him, "What would that be?"

He gave me a cocky little smile and said, "I am investing in IBM, Microsoft, or something that will make me rich. That way growing up a second time will be a whole lot more fun. What do you think?"

We started laughing causing Mika to mishandle the sticky orange. He dropped half the orange on the ground. As he went to pick it up, I told him, "Just leave it there, don't pick it up and eat it now."

As we got about ten feet away, we stopped and I bent down to tie his shoe. Suddenly, and without warning a young boy about four or five years old ran from the bombed-out building across our street. He was wearing shorts and a light coat. He had that distinctive yellow Star of David on his coat telling the whole world, including us, that he was Jewish. He stopped and picked up the piece of orange that was on the ground. He looked directly at us. Hair stood up on the back of my neck and I shivered all over. Then the little boy rushed back into the building. I turned toward Mika and asked, "Did I just see what I think I saw, or did I imagine it?"

He stood there for just a moment with his mouth gaping open and replied, "You didn't imagine it. I saw it too. Let's go. I have a bad feeling right now."

We both looked around to see if anyone else saw this. Reassured that no one else did, we started running home. Upon arriving, we quickly ducked into the other room. We had to discuss this new development while not being watched by our caretaker. We deduced that someone had to be helping him; possibly a mother or father. Whoever was helping was also Jewish. How they were able to have survived so long in Berlin was something we would have to find out later. We knew there was just four days left and then everything would change. All they would have to do was remain undiscovered and survive four more days.

Even though we faced real danger, we knew we could not stand by and do nothing. We debated every possibility we could think of. What would our parents have done? Were they faced with this problem in the past? What happens if we are discovered? What does this boy mean to us and are we somehow related to him? So many things we considered that night. It was exhausting. We decided that the risk did not matter. We had to try to help them. All we had to do was assist them just a little; just enough to keep them alive for the last few days.

Our plan was simple. In the morning we would play a game of hide and seek. During the game, we would duck into the building and drop some food. We hoped to do this without being seen by anyone, especially the people that were in hiding. We could do this easily with only a slight risk of being caught. It would mean so much more to them than simply nourishment. It would also give them some sort of extra hope. At the end of our discussion, I smile at Mika and said, "All this is your fault you know? You wished for real danger and it seems that we have it now. I know we are doing the right thing and we will find out tomorrow just how brave we are."

Neither of us slept much that night.

CHAPTER 2

Anna and Max

Berlin Germany, 1939

Anna

Her name was pronounced the old-fashioned German way, *On-a*. Anna was so pretty with her long black hair and round puppy-dog eyes. She could stop a man in his tracks or traffic by simply walking by. She was five feet three inches tall and a petite one hundred ten pounds. She was simply beautiful.

Her beauty was not just from her outward appearance. She was always bouncing around like a young teenager full of life. Whenever she walked, she added a little sway to her step. This was exciting for men to see. Men were captivated and could not help watching her walk away. When she wanted, she could slow down and walk with the grace and style of an experienced well-taught woman. She was fully aware she had grown into a beautiful woman.

Anna was nice to everyone, not conceited in the least. If someone wished to approach her she was amicable. She almost always made them feel comfortable. She wanted to be liked by everyone. She noticed a few years ago how much people wanted to be around her and she loved the attention. It seemed to happen to her all the time since she started college. Both men and women enjoyed the way she looked and the electricity that emulated from her. They simply could not help gravitating toward her.

Public education for Anna was always very easy. She never understood why so many of her friends had trouble learning. She found learning new things to be exciting and she loved sharing what she had just learned with anyone. After high school, Anna became fascinated with the arts, especially sculptures and paintings. In the beginning everything concerning the arts intrigued her. She constantly dreamed of traveling to Italy and France. She wished to experience different cultures, people, customs, and the foreign arts.

She considered herself a student of romance. Her favorite story at the time was Romeo and Juliet by Shakespeare. She often daydreamed that someone as dashing, brave, and romantic as Romeo would come into her life. She was consumed with a passion for learning every aspect of all these new things the school offered. She was in the last few months of her four-year education at the third largest state college for the arts in Germany called The University of Music and Theater in Leipzig. She was so devoted to learning music and drama and enjoying life she had never made time for her own romance.

*****

Max stood six feet two inches high with short blond hair and deep blue eyes. He looked like the picture-perfect German soldier on many recruiting posters. He stood lean and proud with his head held up high even when not on duty. After completing extra officer training in the art of war near Nuremburg, he was ready for some transitory fun. He was scheduled for only one more training school before deployment to his assigned Army unit. He was the only son of a prominent and well-respected German family.

His father died a war hero. He was one of the first pilots to become an ace after single-handedly shooting down twenty-four enemy planes before he was shot down and killed. He lost his life during the last two months of the war. Elsa, his wife and Max's mother, never fully recovered from the loss. She had resentment and hatred for those she blamed for causing that terrible war; anyone of Jewish descent.

Max had natural skills inherited from his father that helped him with his Army career. Leadership and a natural ability for noticing details were two of these inherited traits. He was a quick learner of everything new thrown his way including the most difficult tasks others struggled to learn; very similar to Anna's traits. He was always willing to take on extra duties no matter how busy or difficult that would be for him. This kind of intelligence and ambition propelled him in a short time to lieutenant status in the Army. This allowed him to wear the much vaunted and impressive dress officer's uniform. He was so very handsome in his uniform.

In the early days of Germany's rebirth, considered to be from 1933 until 1939, it was somewhat rare to see an officer in full dress uniform in public. Max knew this, and when allowed to wear the uniform in public, he made sure it looked perfect. It was an honor he respected. When wearing his formal uniform, everyone around him treated him like a national hero. This only fed his conviction to the career in the military he had chosen. He also believed he had become the ultimate German Soldier. Little did he know that a woman would soon change him.

*****

Anna's education became more intense and diverse in her final year, as the school continually updated their schedule with plays and musical performances. For most of the students and faculty it was more than just a college; it was life at its best. The first two years were spent with the proper foundation to build real talents. The next two years involved the deeper meaning in music and drama, thus highlighting each individual student's unique interests and abilities. Anna was at the top of her class.

The school was very good at helping its students obtain what they desired out of their education. This public college was well respected in Germany and most of the European continent. After the war, branches of this university spread out as far as the United States of America. It is still respected to this date.

Anna figured out early that she adored the stage. She truly loved performing. She once told her parents about the thrill and excitement after pleasing an audience. She even found ways to enjoy aspects others disliked. She seemed to like everything concerning the theater. She looked forward to getting up every day. She enjoyed the excitement of doing something different almost every day and conquering new challenges.

One of her instructors insisted that Anna learn the piano. The teacher knew it would be a match made in heaven and she was right. However, this challenge almost beat her. She struggled and struggled with the piano lessons, which was totally unusual for her. The endless practicing on the piano and seemingly not making progress was boring to her. Then something happened that changed everything. She was practicing Beethoven's Ninth symphony and after months of endless practicing it just happened. As she was practicing, everything seemed to come together. Her fingers moved with the grace and flow of a seasoned professional as she watched herself. It was something beautiful to hear and see. Suddenly everything about that particular music made special sense to her. There was life in the music she didn't understand. She felt what Beethoven must have felt when he created this piece of music. She was now changed forever.

It was as if her hands and fingers had a mind of their own. She would watch herself playing this difficult and beautiful famous piece of music flawlessly and seemingly without effort. She decided to play this masterpiece every day for practice and her own enjoyment. At first she disliked this assignment and the professor that assigned it to her. She felt he assigned her a much more difficult assignment than anyone else and it wasn't fair to her. She first believed he did this to set her up for failure, something to which she was not accustomed. This could not have been further from the truth.

The instructor knew that eventually Anna would break the musical code Beethoven had composed and then she would understand so much more about music. He knew this was exactly what she needed at this time in her education. He secretly loved her passion and love of learning. She was unaware. She was right about one thing: it was the most difficult assignment he had ever issued. Later she understood and told him she was grateful.

Now that she had mastered it, she loved the piano. After the first time she played this piece for an audience, she was truly hooked. She noticed the music's effects on everyone listening. She enjoyed the limelight and performing in front of an audience. For Anna, it was a dream come-true.

Practicing repeatedly until she mastered a skill never bothered her again. The practicing was so worth the effort for her now that she had tasted this major success. She now knew that she had the talent she was previously uncertain that she possessed. This was something her teacher did know. This new knowledge increased her everyday determination to complete other tough challenges. At that time, she did not know how important her determination to succeed would be for her and her future family. Later, challenges of a different kind would threaten her and her entire family with certain death. Anna's skills and determination would be tested beyond any and all of her expectations. Almost immediately the piano practicing became more fun than work. She then began the tasks of mastering other difficult masterpieces. Time for romance was whittled down even more. Drama was her first love, now replaced by music. Another first love was soon to replace drama.

*****

Army qualification training was much more different than Max had imagined. Former lessons were replaced by new theories and strategies. He had previously been educated in the history of warfare with its past successes and lessons-learned. In the past, soldiers had to position everyone for battle by building and maintaining defensive positions. This was called digging in. After attacking and digging in, troops would wait for a counter attack. During World War I, with both sides dug in, it became known as trench warfare. It was pure hell for everyone involved including the commanding officers.

Communication between the Army and other branches of the military was poor to non-existent. This was the way it had always been until now. New tactics had to be developed and this was Max's new training program. The training was difficult for everyone to learn and execute properly. It was something new and not battle tested yet. Max found most of his Army training to be fun. He was being paid to camp outside with friends; drive all types of vehicles; and shoot guns of all types and sizes. He felt powerful being the man in charge some of the time. Lower ranking soldiers were required to salute him. He loved this honor and respect from subordinate soldiers. However, he felt he had not yet earned it. He was not battle tested.

It was early in his career and he had not fought in battle. However, he knew the future would validate him and possibly soon. He knew he had to be strong and take all the training seriously. He knew how important all of it was for him and his men. He valued the training more seriously than most of his fellow comrades. He would be in command and responsible for his men's lives.

There is something else all military men think about that is difficult to train or overcome. Max was no exception. It is the killing of another human and how to deal with all the consequences. His way of coping with this issue was simple. He refused to think of it as much as possible. It was his duty to the fatherland and he sincerely believed leading men into battle was one of his destinies. Killing other soldiers was just his duty and the less he thought of it the better. His way of thinking would allow him to focus on everything he needed to learn and not get distracted.

Anna enjoyed showing her talents without being a showoff. She knew her audience loved whatever she was performing and she fed off the joy. She was always asked to play something when there was a party or gathering especially if a piano was present. The shyness she once had as a child was no longer part of her. That shell was broken and she would never go back under it again. Entertaining and enjoying what every day had to offer was just too much fun. It was at one of these parties she met Max.

His charmed life had him believing it was not possible there was a bullet out there with his name on it. He knew it was not possible for him to be killed. His talent, training and luck would also not allow such a thing to befall him. This new specialized training stressed the cooperation between forces to create one unbeatable fighting unit. Previously, units within their own military did not intertwine that well while fighting. Organization and communication between tank forces and the infantry was continually updated and drilled. Critical training that very soon would make the difference between life and death for Max was stressed.

Restructuring the military enterprise went beyond the Army. Each branch of the military was still independent, but would now be more dependent on each other for assistance. Because of the increased complexity of this new joint forces concept, new training had to be developed and started with diligence and urgency. Cross training was now heavily introduced to the program.

The coordination and communication to the airplanes for assistance and aid to the infantry was constantly drilled. It was demanded that every student learn every aspect of this new strategy. He had to know what was expected from everyone as well as himself. It was not until later there became a special name for this new kind of warfare. Its name would soon send fear throughout the world. It was called Blitzkrieg.

All the soldiers knew that this new training was not a game. It was serious and required that all troops get trained rapidly. War was on the horizon. They all knew their lives and those of their fellow brothers depended on them learning and executing their assigned tasks as perfectly as possible. Hitler, in a short span of only six years, brought the fatherland up from a humiliating defeat and surrender to a very powerful and feared nation. Germany was now again a proud and self-reliant nation. Other nations feared Germany. It was not just fear but respect. That was very important to everyone in the country at the time, especially the soldiers.

Respect for Germany's military had been missing ever since the French made Germany surrender on May 7, 1919. It was called the treaty of Versailles and the French insisted on the terms of the surrender. This humiliated and angered almost all the German People. The economy steadily grew, as did the military. Both now had renewed strength and respect.

The life of a young lieutenant in the Army at this time made him full of pride and hope for a better future. To Max the future was the present and he was enjoying all of it. It was offering him a great life. The company of women was something he always seemed to have. They were what he considered less intelligent and easy to control. He never really had to put much effort into meeting or keeping them around. Soon after his promotion in rank and with the fancy officer's uniform his attractiveness soared even higher.

He was tall, blond and physically fit. He was self-confident, bordering on but not falling off into arrogance. Woman seemed to be falling at his boots all the time now. Even fathers wanted their daughters to meet him. They continually would bring their daughters over to meet him soon after they met him themselves. This would be a little embarrassing for most, but not Max. He liked it. He also knew this newfound fame would only be temporary. He had decided to enjoy it for now and take full advantage of all its pleasures and gifts.

As he did so many times before, he strolled around scanning the room at a party. In his impeccable dress uniform, so handsome and tall; he spotted her looking so beautiful. He suddenly stopped as if someone had taken hold of his arm. He unknowingly held his breath. He temporarily forgot what he was thinking. He stood there memorizing her. He wanted to burn her image into his brain. His first view of her was from her left side. She was wearing a long red dress as she smiled and talked to three people.

Max stood there staring at her. He noticed all the full shape of her body. She was stunning. He had to remind himself to concentrate on anything other than her breasts when he talked to her. He did not want to get caught by her looking there. He told himself to concentrate on her eyes. At this time he did not know her eyes would captivate him and that he wouldn't want to stray from them anyway. She was so beautiful and desirable. He was lost in the moment. He didn't want to move. He failed to notice that he was staring at her.

She looked to be in her early twenties with distinct taste. Her red dress flowed freely over her petite curves. Her style suggested an air of high society. The dress looked tailored for her perfect frame. She was talking and smiling when she turned his way and saw him. Her eyes caught his and there was electricity. Her face was that of an angel. At the same time, Anna noticed that he was tall and handsome. She not only caught him looking, but he knew she just caught him staring and he knew he would have to react and fast.

Without even blinking, he slowly walked toward her. He was a brash, brave young officer not fearful of anything, especially a woman. Even a beautiful woman such as this was not going to scare him away. She watched him making his way toward her never, losing eye contact.

Being approached by men happened almost every day to Anna. However, this time something was different. No one before caught staring would dare continue to stare, much less approach. She knew this young handsome man had courage and self-confidence; traits she admired in a man.

This situation started to stir up some new emotions in Anna. Her breathing became heavier. Her heart was beating faster and harder than usual. She could feel it beating through the thin fabric of her dress. She could feel the blood rushing to her face. She was getting flushed.

When he got very close to her he stopped. He was much closer than Anna would have been comfortable with ordinarily. She was looking up at him as he was looking down at her, very close; they were almost touching. But there was something nice and different this time. She knew he got that close for a reason and she smiled at him. It was to take in her scent. Realizing this made her heart seem to stop beating. She involuntarily held her breath. It was exciting and made the moment extraordinary.

Then with confidence he took in a deep breath, looked in her eyes and said, "Hello, my name is Max."

Anna was used to men stumbling over their words or giving her a stupid line to meet her. This time was different. He stared into her eyes and waited for Anna's reply when Max heard his name called out from behind him. He turned around and walked away toward the man who called his name, not bothering to look back. This was not what she was used to and it really caught her by surprise.

After what he did, Anna decided she was not going to give him another chance, she felt insulted. She would find a way to pay him back soon as possible. She was always kind and gracious. She had class. Although he had looked so handsome in his officer's uniform, the confidence he displayed to Anna bordered on arrogance. Anna decided when she saw him again that she would act indifferent toward him. She was going to snub him, and then be done with him. Even though these feelings were misguided, she decided the brash young officer needed to be put in his place. It would be a sweet revenge for being ignored that way. She convinced herself that he needed a little humility, delivered by her.

She enjoyed the occasional party and break from school. The interacting with new and regular friends was now beginning to make her feel somehow she had missed something. Many of her friends were already married with children. After her initial meeting with Max, Anna went to more and more military parties secretly looking for this impetuous young officer. When she would find him, she was going to have some fun. She had thought up several different plans.

Several weeks later she thought that perhaps fate had stepped in to tease her, and she would never see him again. She had changed her mind and no longer wanted to punish him. Now she wanted to meet and get to know him. She decided not to risk her second chance with him by doing something childish. Strangely, she felt if she did get another chance then it might be the last she would ever have with him, and she didn't like that feeling. There were more rumors of war coming soon and as an Army officer he would most likely be involved.

She felt something inside her that was different this time. For the first time in a long time, she was excited to see this man again. She had always wanted more in her life than just raising a family. That was why she went off to college. Now that her studies were nearly over she began to plan her future differently, and the young officer just might be part of that new life.

*****

It was unusually hot and dry for May and for some unexplained reason the top brass decided that the troops were to wear their winter fighting gear. Everyone except Max was complaining. Max had complete faith that the upper brass knew what they were doing. It was never his place to question what they ordered, ever. Besides, lately he was constantly daydreaming about something else.

Sitting beside Max was a new driver and Hans, Max's best friend. All three were bouncing around inside this military vehicle call a half-track. It had two regular tires in front and a track like tanks have in the rear. It was painted the Army color with a palm tree and the Nazi swastika painted on each side. It was built for war not comfort. All three were aware of this, but were still were enjoying the ride. The fastest speed it could reach was about forty miles an hour, and the driver had the gas pedal pressed to the floor and hardly used the brakes at all. About halfway to their destination, Hans poked Max in the ribs and brought him back to reality, "You are dreaming about her again aren't you?"

Max replied, "Yes I just can't get her out of my mind."

Hans let out a sigh and said, "I've never seen you like this before Max. It has always been leaving them after you're done with them or something like that."

They both chuckled. Hans was always messing up old sayings like that.

Max said, "No, it is different this time."

Hans smiled, "Sure it is. You have told me a thousand times how captivating she was, I know."

Max looked at Hans and said, "No it's not just that. It was how I acted that bothers me the most."

Hans laughed, "I thought you were daydreaming about that when you got the tank stuck."

Max said, "Not funny, that's something I'd rather forget."

Max and Hans almost did not notice just how rough the driver was making the ride except for the occasional times he purposely hit a big hole in the road. Every time all three would almost hit the roof with their heads and would just look at each other and laugh. The harder they hit something the louder they would laugh. No matter how much the driver tried to shake them up he couldn't stop their talking. Max and Hans did not want the driver to know that sometimes it was getting to them and hurting a little. It was male pride.

It was after Han's stuck-tank remark that captured the driver's attention and slowed him down. He wanted to hear more. Max and Hans decided to recount Max's getting the tank stuck story for their driver. It was just two months earlier when Max and Hans were ordered to go to a school on tanks. As officers, they were sent to many different schools for all kinds of different types of training. This one was no different. These classes were about the mechanics of driving tanks and crew discipline. Other aspects and details were reserved for a later training date. They were to learn what it was like to live with the crew and drive the tank.

Becoming part of the crew would teach valuable lessons not able to be learned by books.

When in battle, an officer in charge must be able to adapt to any and all unforeseeable situations. This kind of training Max simply enjoyed. There was always something different to do and learn. There was this one day when Max was allowed to be the driver and shooter of a tank when ordered. He was not the commander for the day, as he would have liked.

Until recently all tank training was done in fake mockups. These were jeeps with plywood bolted to them to look like tanks. Real tanks were in short supply and so was ammunition. These mock up tanks were used later as diversions. Appearing from the air as real ones made them valuable later. Their enemies would have the wrong information when these mockups were deployed. These decoys allowed the Germans to exploit misinformation. Many times their enemies would attack these mockups, expending their bombs on useless targets. Other times they did not attack because they believed there were more tanks present to return fire. For now though, Max had a real tank with live ammunition and his chance to shoot.

One month earlier the school was issued twelve new tanks. Crews were assembled with seasoned Sergeants in command. War was coming soon and these new tanks and crews would be the first to be deployed and fight. First of the line ammunition was also finely issued. This was a special day for all these soldiers. It was the first day to include a live fire exercise. Max was scheduled to drive the tank and fire one shot. One shot would be all he was allowed that day.

They were sent to a sparsely wooded area that was ideal for tanks. It was rolling hills with patches of forest. This kind of area for training with tanks was preferred. There were not many obstacles to interfere and cause accidents. At least that was what the planners believed. Max was assigned to the most experienced tank crew at the school. Max was the highest-ranking officer on the tank that day, even higher than the tank commander. However, he would not be in command of the tank, he was the one being trained. The commander of the tank at the time was a seasoned and excellent Sergeant quite capable of training anyone.

The Sergeant really disliked training upper-class officers. He knew one simple mistake with one of them could be disastrous to his career. He did not like being placed in that position. For safety on this particular day, Max was to follow the Sergeant's orders to the letter with no deviations. It was now field time. The classes were broken down into stages for easy learning. There was the driving of the tank. Everyone had to learn what each and every knob and lever meant. There were a lot of gauges, wheels and levers in tanks at that time. Max should have paid closer attention. In a battle, this kind of cross training knowledge has been known to save lives and win battles. Max was well aware of these facts.

Next were classes on being the tank commander. These he really liked. He enjoyed being the man in charge. Last but not least was gunnery training; the loading, aiming and firing of the big gun. They were taught how far away they could shoot and still hit their targets. Things like that, but mostly just the basics. The actually shooting of the big gun Max and Hans were really looking forward to doing. All this training had to be passed and completed in just a short two-week span all accumulating with this day.

Max was following the commander's orders in their tank perfectly as he slowly inched his way toward the forest line. He was told by the Sergeant to get about one tank length away from the tree line. The close forest would help them duck and hide from any airplanes in the area. Max already knew this tactic from some earlier training. Max headed closer to the trees following every order perfectly. He even repeated the Sergeants orders allowing the Sergeant to know he fully understood.

The Sergeant was impressed with Max. He showed the Sergeant he had the capacity to learn quickly. Max also gave the Sergeant and crew the respect they deserved. The Sergeant was not a man impressed easily, nor did higher-ranking men intimate him. He actually relaxed this day and let Max gun the engine and play with his baby as no one before. He ordered Max away from the forest line to begin maneuvers. He was to take full control and get the feel of the tank. He let Max run at full speed. Max was enjoying this and sometimes changed direction so fast it bounced the crew hard inside. The crew wasn't complaining this time. It was fun and not one of the usual boring training lessons they had to endure day after day.

The Sergeant was so comfortable with Max at the wheel. The tank was bouncing up and down and side to side with the contours of the land. As they were passing two trees in the open the Sergeant yelled something that Max did not understand. If it had been anyone else the Sergeant would have stayed well away from any and all trees. However, the Sergeant let his guard down for just a moment.

The Sergeant yelled his order louder. He ordered Max to stop immediately as they were way too close to those trees and going too fast for his comfort. Instead of pulling the brake handle he pulled the wrong handle, turning the tank. It turned on a dime but didn't stop. It kept going at full speed. The Sergeant yelled again for Max to pull the emergency stop lever. Max was trying hard but was confused. Now with the Sergeant yelling at him he was totally lost.

Then Max pulled all the levers hoping to get the right one. The tank did stop and one lever he also pulled was to manually fire the cannon. Boom! The gun went off. It was so loud momentarily Max could not hear. The next thing Max heard was the Sergeant yelling, "You jackass not that lever."

The tank had jerked forward and slid to a stop in between those two trees. The tank was wedged in tight. Hans was in another tank and the first to come close to Max. Everyone in Han's tank was laughing and everyone in Max's tank was laughing too; except Max and the Sergeant. Hans was quick, "Max you need to go back to gunnery school. You missed everyone by at least fifty meters."

The Sergeant in Hans's tank also had to get in on some of the fun. He took off his leather helmet and yelled at Max's Sergeant, "If you must signal us please don't shoot at us."

Everyone now was laughing. It was all good-natured humor aimed at Max and the Sergeant. They had to cut one of the trees down to get the tank out and that was the end of tank training for Max. Max wanted to help the Sergeant get out of the trouble he knew he would be in, so Max marched into the commanding general's office to take the blame. It wasn't necessary. The General knew all the details and explained to Max and the Sergeant that this was what training was all about. So impressed with Max the Sergeant decided he wanted to become Max's friend. Hans looked at Max and said; "I always thought they shouldn't have put those levers so close to each other."

Max smiled back and replied, "Yes let's just blame it on a design flaw!" They all laughed again like a couple of teenagers. All of a sudden, the driver slammed on the breaks. All three were astonished by what they saw.

It was the largest gathering of airplanes and military equipment they had ever seen at one place. They had come around the bend in the road expecting to see hills and an empty valley. What they saw were hundreds and hundreds of all types of planes. The planes in the open had some kind of camouflage covering them with many more hidden among the forest. There were all kinds of military vehicles and people running around everywhere. They looked at each other with the driver speaking first, "This is more than just another training exercise."

Max and Hans looked at each other with amazement. They both were ordered to this place not knowing what to expect. During earlier training they had passed by this very same place and it was empty. Now it was a secret and very impressive military base. It looked like the whole German Luftwaffe, supplies and all were there in force. Suddenly a horn from behind them blew, startling all three. The driver started to roll forward looking for the entrance.

Max was first to see the front gate. He pointed and the driver began his turn. They were early and Hans whispered to Max, "We need to look around and find out more before the meeting."

They checked in at the gate and were issued an escort. Standing on a small platform on the driver's side he directed the driver where to park. This escort informed them they were to stay in their assigned area and go nowhere else. The driver was to go no farther than five meters from the truck and any breach of these security measures was serious. This gathering of these forces was bigger than Max and Hans could have imagined at the time. It filled both of them with so much pride. It was a great display of German might and Hans blurted out for anyone to hear, "It is a great time in our lives to be a German!"

Max replied with, "There will be many more days like these I think."

They then ducked under a tent flap to enter their first assigned place. Just inside was a desk with two guards checking papers and assignments on everyone entering. Standing in line Hans whispered to Max, "We are the lowest ranking officers here except for the guards. How does that make you feel?"

"Shush," said Max. "No joking now, this is serious."

Inside this huge tent were maps and rows of tables and chairs. Everything set up and ready for obviously a very important meeting with special people. They dared not speak it but wondered if maybe their Fuehrer would make an appearance. After Max and Hans checked in at the desk, an enlisted soldier said to them, "Please let me assist you," as he lead them to their proper seats.

After everyone was seated, a general's aide addressed everyone and began announcing a special guest. Then he stood at attention and ordered everyone else to stand at attention. Max could not believe his eyes when the guest walked on the stage. Carrying his Reich Marshall wand and wearing his usual white dress uniform, and standing just a few meters away, was the one and only Field Marshall, Herman Goring. He was a tall and large man with extra weight around his waist. He commanded the attention and respect of everyone in attendance. He was one of the most powerful men in Germany, and the absolute leader of the Luftwaffe, only second to Adolf Hitler. The skies over Germany belonged to him and him alone; and soon he would have all the skies of the European continent.

He stood there in front of them and spoke words that Max memorized so he could tell everything to his mother. "The magnitude of what we are going to accomplish. The things that very soon all of you will accomplish will enable the Reich to last a thousand years. We are about to stun the world. We will have revenge on the tyrants that forced the treaty of Versailles on us. We will no longer stand by and watch our families starve while the rest of the world does nothing to help us. We are the masters of our own destiny. I am prepared to tell you men this. There is a plan and all the hard work you have put into your training will now reap our motherland her greatest reward yet. We will instill fear and respect the world has never seen before. You are the leaders that will make this happen. Follow your orders and conquer all our enemies and we will last a thousand years."

He then saluted with his arm stretched forward saying, "Hail Hitler."

Everyone raised his right arm in the salute repeated, "Hail Hitler."

He smiled, turned and exited the tent as quickly as he entered. Max and Hans left the tent all excited and proud. It was an inspirational speech and just being in his presence was accelerating. After the speech Max and Hans then proceeded to their assigned tent for their individual briefings. This was going to be a long and important day for everyone there. Max spotted the Colonel before Hans. He was their new commanding officer, Colonel Von Ryan. He was well known and respected amongst everyone, including the Fuehrer. It was well known how important he was to Adolph Hitler. He was a pure military genius. His intelligence concerning military matters was much higher than that of most men.

He once demonstrated to Hitler how with the right troops, timing, and tactics, certain countries could be conquered with minimal losses and in a very short time. This was a capability believed not possible by most in that period of history. He was a man way ahead of his time, and everyone who knew him was very much aware of this, especially all the other high ranking Army officers. The Colonel was making his rounds around the tent making sure to stop and shake everyone's hand. He seemed to know everyone's name and more. This man had really done his homework.

As the Colonel approached Max he wondered how much the Colonel knew about him. He was still feeling the pride from the general's speech. He was excited to meet his new commanding officer and also a little intimidated. At this point he wished he had done his homework and learned everything he could about his new commanding officer. He vowed to himself never to be in this awkward, unprepared position again. The Colonel approached Max, shook his hand firmly and said, "Lieutenant Max Shelling, it is nice to finally meet you."

Max stood a little taller and replied, "It's my honor, sir."

The Colonel then said, "I have been following you very closely for some time. I know about your family and have read several accounts involving your father. He was a great soldier."

"Thank you, sir." Max replied.

The Colonel went on, "I am very pleased you ended up in one of my units. You will be treated with the same respect I give to my wife and my three children unless I am disappointed. I believe my soldiers are also my family. We will fight together and some of us will even die together. However we will never disappoint each other, ever."

Max held out his chest a little and replied, "With all my heart, sir."

The Colonel took a step away then turned around as if he had forgotten to say something. With a little smile he said, "I also watched you during some of your training." He then winked at Max and added, "I am glad you are leading one of my infantry units and not in one of my tanks."

Both Hans and Max smiled at the comment as the Colonel turned toward another soldier waiting for the Colonel. Hans' turn was coming up. The Colonel began briefing everyone in the tent on the coming events. He was a direct, to the point, no-nonsense officer. Everyone briefed was not allowed to divulge any information they received. Operations were scheduled to begin in late August or early September. Now everyone knew they were going to war and when.

Max was mesmerized by the Colonel. His heart was beating so hard in his chest he found it difficult to concentrate. Looking to his left, he was relieved to see Hans taking notes. His friend would surely help him with anything he might have missed. The whole situation seemed almost unreal to Max. He asked himself if he was going to wake up soon. But not only was all this real, he would soon be in a real battle of life and death. Even with all these thoughts he was not scared at all. He knew he would be fine. He knew this was his destiny. He may now become a war hero, like his father, and make his mother proud of him too. At this time he had only a partial understanding how important the Colonel would be to him and his future family.

*****

She did not see him enter the room. She was playing the piano and singing along with everyone else at a small party. Someone had asked her to play something, anything. The party needed some added life and she was the right one to ask. She was smiling with everyone surrounding her and singing along. She was playing a drinking song that nearly everyone seemed to know and enjoy.

When he saw her, he froze, and took in all of her view again. As before, he was spellbound and wanted to memorize the scene. He seemed to have stopped breathing for a moment because he found her again. This time she was wearing a long lace white dress. As with her red dress, it fit her perfectly. He had to meet her and somehow win her over. In his spare time all he thought about was meeting her again and what he was going to do then.

He was a brave soldier. Whatever she could dish out he would have take it like a man. He had to take a chance and speak to her again. Taking in a deep breath and holding up his head, he slowly walked toward her. As he got closer their eyes met. Such beautiful eyes - full of intelligence and mystery. He would never get tired of looking into them, never.

He was seeing her in a new way. Never before had he looked at a woman like this.. True, she was beautiful but there was so much more to her. He felt vulnerable and could not help himself. He had to put himself out there if he was ever to have another chance with her. He knew it would be worth it if only she would give him one more opportunity. As Max approached her, he mustered all his strength just to hide his nervousness, and spoke first. But all he was able to do was smile and say, "Hello."

Anna stopped playing the song and everyone quit singing and looked at Max. It got eerily quiet. Everyone's attention was now focused on Max. This was a perfect setup for Anna. He stood there waiting for Anna's response like the strong-willed man he had become. She took a moment knowing she had complete control of the situation. She could make this cocky soldier regret forever snubbing her or she could do the classier move. She gave him a little smile and simply said, "You going to run off again?"

With obvious sincerity Max leaned on the piano and said, "I deserved that. I am sorry for the last time. Will you please forgive me?"

Anna smiled at Max and started playing the song again softer. Everyone relaxed and resumed singing.. Some giggled while trying to sing. None knew why she had stopped playing. It was now obvious she knew him and everything was fine. Max was now more impressed with her and at that moment fell in love with her. Something he realized later.

He was glad she had remembered him. She could have made such a horrible scene that he would have remembered forever, but she didn't. This woman was more special than he even daydreamed. He wanted to know everything about her. That whole night they talked and talked. He had lost his male pride and was totally relaxed around her. Several times he poked fun at himself, making her laugh. Making her laugh made him feel special. Her laugh was so sweet that just hearing it made him smile and laugh more.

Anna was intrigued by him too. She was almost immediately was glad she gave him another chance. She loved the way he talked. He refrained from talking about himself as much as possible. He was truly interested in getting to know her. He was different and she liked this. They laughed all night. He was becoming special to her. He was making her happy in a new way. She was having different feelings deep inside.

There was a spark between them, some sort of electricity. She felt a connection with this young man she had never felt before. She wanted to know more about him and all these new feelings. They agreed to meet the next day and then the day after. They did not want to be apart, even for just one day. They became inseparable. They wanted to do things they did alone and liked only now together. They were learning that it was more fun sharing the experience than being alone. They were now starting to live life to please someone else and enjoying each day so much more. This was a new and exhilarating aspect of life. They could not seem to get enough of each other. They were always looking for ways to make the other one laugh and be happy.

They never argued about anything except for one item. They disagreed about him having to go to war. She was scared and hated the idea. To her, war was neither honorable nor noble. To Max it was different. He wanted to prove himself in battle. She did not care about him having to prove himself to anyone. She knew he was a brave and honorable man. She knew he was a caring and a lovable person. He did not have to prove anything to her and she was scared she would lose him.

This subject Anna found unpleasant and upsetting even to think about, much less argue with Max. Her stomach would turn and she would lose her hunger whenever they discussed this. Max had told her repeatedly not to worry. He had not gone through this life to find her and to end up dying. He told her he knew he would live through this conflict. She was something he would hurry home to. Their love would keep him safe. He knew this for sure. He also knew he wanted her for his own and for all time.

He started discussing with her that he might not make the military a career after all. He might do his required years and then get out. He was smitten. This was the first time since joining that he even considered not making the military a lifelong commitment. His mother saw this change in Max. He hinted to Anna that Germany would punish Poland for their involvement in World War I and convinced her that it would not become another world war. With patriotism in his voice, he told her, "This will enable our homeland to reclaim the things lost in the previous war, including our national honor."

She could see the pride when he said things like this and always changed the subject. He also told her it would not last long. They would be together again as it should be, loving each other and playing with each other every day. One night in particular he told her, "I have fallen in love with the most intelligent and beautiful woman in Germany and all I want is more time with you."

She felt the same way. She knew this love was special and rare, not worth risking for anything. She knew this special connection that they had would never be duplicated should something terrible happen to him. Anna just could not wait to be married to Max. It was not just because of the upcoming war that everyone knew it was going to happen. It was mostly she knew he was the one she had been waiting for all her young life, her Romeo. She wanted their relationship to go further and deeper, something that only marriage could offer. She wanted him to herself. Whenever they would escape and be alone she would burn with a special desire for him. These were new and exciting feelings she had never experienced before. She was sure she was truly in love. It was intoxicating. She was drunk with desire for Max in every way.

She dreamed about how it would be when she would give herself fully to him. She wanted everything to be right and perfect between them. She knew she would not be able to say no to Max much longer. She desired him so much. Max never pressured her to do anything she was not comfortable with, and this made her want him even more. He was always so patient and caring. This strong desire for him that she had never felt before burned so hot within her, at times almost conquering her restraints. She truly believed she desired him more than he did her. But that was not true.

Max did things to her when they were alone that switched all her emotions on high. Then he would let her cool down and then start again driving her wild with renewed excitement. She knew when the time was right; making love with him would be something special. Something so special and memorable she would cherish the memories forever. He usually started with soft kisses. At the same time he would stoke her hair, gazing into those eyes.

She liked the feel of his strong hands on her body and especially on exposed flesh. They were strong and yet so gentle with her. He knew what he was doing. He liked building up her heat and passion. She became putty in his hands, melting with desire under the pressure and movements of his hands. His joy was in pleasing her. After he knew her heat and passions were almost too much for her to contain he would, without warning, suddenly stop. He would let go of her, light a cigarette, and exhale while smiling at her. He liked how this drove her crazy and pulled her closer to him. She loved it too. He was so much different from anyone else she knew.

She knew he desired her too. It was obvious every time they were alone. Something a man sometimes just cannot hide. Stopping never seemed to bother him like other men. The times he would stop for no apparent reason made her believe it was because of his respect for her. She knew he wanted her but she also knew he wanted everything to be right and proper. No matter how hard it was he would wait until she said yes and they were husband and wife. Then he would show her what it was like to be made love to by someone who truly loves you. He desired to prove to her that in bed he too would be her only true love, forever. These reasons and more were why Max asked Anna to be his wife and the sooner the better.

He had insight he did not share with Anna about Germany's plans concerning the approaching conflict. He knew he needed to marry her as soon as possible before September. Their time apart was fast approaching. When Max asked her to marry him it was not as romantic as he planned. It was planned for the next night after dinner in front of everyone including his mother. However, with the excitement of a young schoolchild, he just could not help himself. They had another beautiful day together holding each other and not wanting to say their farewell for the night. They were kissing their last goodnight kiss and he just blurted out before thinking, "Be my wife, please." It was as if he was kicked in the stomach and to hide the feeling he had to say it quickly.

She knew what he said was not how he wanted to say it either. He was nervous and obviously stumbled over his words. She knew he must have practiced several times and still he said it wrong. Sensing the possibility of Max being embarrassed, she knew exactly what to do. She lovingly kissed him and said, "Yes."

After laughing a few moments, they decided they would never forget this moment in time. She had not seen him so nervous since the piano meeting. She thought it was funny and charming. Beginning with first time they first got together, they became inseparable. The only time apart was when the Army so ordered. No one else was strong enough to come between them. Not even Max's mother, Elsa.

The time Max and Anna were now spending together was not to the liking of Max's mother. She wanted Max around *her* all the time. She was lonely when he was not around. She loved Max unconditionally. And although everyone expected Max to follow follow the footsteps of his father and become a flyer, Max knew after his first ride in an airplane that it just was not something he really wanted to do. He wanted to be in the military but not in an airplane flying. He wanted both feet firmly on the ground.

His mother was also happy with this choice. She believed he would be much safer on the ground. She also knew that every time he would take off in an airplane, she would be frightened the entire time he was gone. She did not want to go through these pains again. After Max's father died, his many friends would visit his mother regularly. They took a great interest in Max and his mother. Most were retired with current connections with active military leaders. These were lifetime connections, some bonded by combat. Some would become even closer to their comrades than with their real brothers.

These older men were a help to Max without him even him knowing they were helping. His mother knew and approved of every action that these men took. Whenever Max wanted to try something new there was always a letter or a meeting between old friends. These meetings and letters was one reason why Max made it as far in his career in such a short time. He accomplished most of his advancements with their help. These men opened doors and made life a lot easier for Max, and his mother was grateful.

One of these men was General Kleist. He was one of the leading generals with the responsibility of the defense of the motherland in World War I. He was decorated several times for leadership and bravery with valor. The last two years of World War I was mostly trench warfare and this was the General's expertise. This was a miserable way to fight, as the general knew so well.

What he enjoyed the most now in his life was Max's mother and writing his history. She was still a fine looking woman even after all her years. She was small, petite, blond hair mixed with some gray. When she first saw Max and Anna together it reminded her of the way she looked with her husband. It was not that Elsa really disliked Anna for any good reason. She just hated not seeing Max as much as before he met Anna and she was jealous.

She was also very much aware that there was a war coming soon. The time he was spending with Anna she considered her time. When war would break out she would have no control of Max's time at all. Anna was intruding on her precious time. There was also a possibility of Max not coming home and if that were to happen she would never forgive Anna for taking Max away from her.

Several Veterans introduced themselves to Max and his mother. Each assured her they would do everything in their power to help and protect Max. With Max's training and all her powerful friends helping, she knew Max would be able to do his part and come home safe. Max always suspected these friends were somehow helping him but he chose to ignore it. Whatever made his mother happy was good enough for him except now when it came to his Anna. It was going to be a grand wedding, Max's mother told all her friends. Max and Anna told her that she was in charge and could plan almost anything she wanted. This made her so happy.

Max and Anna were not spending much time with her and they believed this might help. To Elsa this would be so much fun, one of her dreams coming true. She was especially looking forward to the party afterwards. She would be able to dance again. It had been a long time since her husband died and she had not danced since. It would be right and proper for the first time and she liked to dance.

She had once feared that Anna and Max would run away and get married but not now. She was very pleased that they asked her to help and were not running away. Everyone knew time was running out for special weddings and certain events that needed a lot of planning. They told her they wanted to be married in less than a month, not giving Elsa much time to plan. She did not like that and tried to talk them into waiting. This did not work. She also knew better than to push Max and Anna too hard and risk that they might change their minds and elope.

She daydreamed about dancing with all the handsome men, including General Kleist. Over the years she grew fond of him and they became close. Since her husband died, she dedicated herself to her son and had few other interests. She pushed away any man attempting to get close, except the General. She knew he liked her a little more than she. He had made several romantic advances and she gently shot him down. This way they could remain good friends.

Now that Max was getting married she decided it was time to maybe change things. She knew she still looked good and caught men looking at her almost everywhere she went. She decided it was time to dance with several of her male friends and flirt for a change. She had not wanted to or seemed to be able to do this for years. The timing never seemed right until now. As she planned the wedding she decided it had to be a military event with all the men in their formal uniforms and the woman in beautiful dresses. It would be a beautiful sight. She decided to ask General Kleist to help her. His involvement would be a help and added fun.

****

August 1, 1939

The wedding

Everyone stood up as beautiful Anna entered the room. Her hair was up and perfect. Her dress was white with her favorite accessories and lots of lace. A veil covered her smiling face and was not enough to hide her beauty beneath. Her walk was slow and graceful. She moved as if she was not walking at all; a graceful slow gliding on the arm of her father, Otto. Max had not met Otto before this day. It did not matter. He could not remove his eyes from Anna once she entered. It was as if he was seeing her for the first time. He was stone cold, as if frozen in time.

Max and all his friends and acquaintances were now in his special wedding. His best friend, and now best man, Hans was there at his side. All the other men in uniform lined up on both sides of the aisle at attention. As Anna entered, the men drew their swords and held them high and crossed,, allowing Anna and her father to pass underneath. It was a beautiful sign of respect. Everyone in the room was smiling and happy.

Anna's parents were her only family members present. Anna's father walked Anna down the aisle appearing so proud. He was always so proud of his little Anna and this day was no different. He was wearing a nice dark suit and tie, obviously well worn, but cleaned and pressed. He was supposed to wear his old Army uniform. All the men, including Otto were asked by Max's mother specifically to wear their formal uniforms with all metals and decorations displayed. Otto refused.

Anna spoke with Elsa and told her he couldn't wear it because it did not fit him properly anymore. This did not go well with Elsa. She did not believe her and later was overheard remarking that 'not fitting' was an excuse and there was something else not right. She did not know what it was but she planned to find out soon. As he walked with Anna arm-in-arm, it felt so good to be holding each other again. Otto and Rianna,

Anna's mother, could not come and see her very much. They were very busy owning and operating a bookstore store in southern Germany close to the Austrian and Czechoslovakian border.

When Otto and Anna reached the front of the room, Max and Hans stood at attention so proud and handsome. Max was smiling so big with his chest held out as far as he could. It was a wonder he did not pop a few buttons.

In classic fun, Max earlier had bet one of his friends that Anna would trip at least once before getting to the front. Anna found this out later at the wedding party. She just laughed and held her head up and said to anyone listening, "Fooled him, didn't I? I did not trip even once."

Everyone loved this about her. She could take a joke and sometimes dish one out herself.

They said their vows and turned around. Everyone was standing, clapping, and shaking hands with each other. It was a wonderful sight for everyone. Elsa was very proud of herself. She made the event grand for her Max. Rianna was standing beside Otto holding his arm and softly crying. These were genuine tears of joy slowly drifting down her pretty cheeks. She was so happy for Max and Anna. Elsa was not crying, only smiling. She was happy everything went so well. It did not matter who Max was going to marry, Elsa would not have liked anyone. However, there was something Elsa also did not like about Anna's parents. She did not know what it was, but she would make a point to find out.

The party was even better than the wedding. They had a band playing dance music that was also all state approved. Someone asked Anna to play something and she almost said yes. She was already the center of attention and this was how she had dreamed her wedding would be. Anna danced and talked with everyone. She loved it so. One minute she spoke with one group and then another. It almost made her dizzy. She smiled and laughed so much her face hurt the next day. She was so happy.

During the party Elsa questioned Anna's parents about their pasts. They were polite but did not like her prying into their lives. They answered most of her questions with truthfully, others with outright lies. Her questions surprised both of them at the time and caught thm off-guard. Later they wished they had been more guarded because they had a deep dark secret they desperately wanted to remain hidden forever.

They did not want to upset Anna, especially on her wedding day, but they had to warn her. So when the three of them were alone, Otto and Rianna sat Anna down and warned Anna to beware of Elsa. She had been inquiring about them and for the first time informed her that there may be things in their past that were not good. Anna pressed them for more information, but to no avail. They were able to reassure her everything was fine, and not to worry, but to be careful nonetheless. They told her they would tell her more later. That was how they left Anna that night, happy but wondering.

General Kleist spent a lot of time that day and night with Elsa. They danced and laughed together almost the entire night. It was almost a perfect day for Elsa. Everyone there that day could tell he fancied her a lot. She also knew she could toy with him as she pleased and get him to do almost anything she wanted if she wished. This fact would turn out to be a lot of trouble for Anna and her parents several years later. Elsa enjoyed power and status within the community and within the Reich.

On instructions from Elsa, General Kleist started investigating Anna and her family the day after the wedding. It didn't take him long. He acquired a copy of Anna's birth certificate but could not obtain a copy of Otto and Riana's marriage certificate. This was very unusual except there was a fire in the storage warehouse and almost all the documents inside at the time were destroyed. There were extra copies somewhere else and if Elsa wanted, he would find them for her.

He knew there just wasn't something right, so before continuing, he warned Elsa that if he were to investigate further and find out something bad he might be required to report it. She did not care. She told him to continue.

*****

They both had waited anxiously for this night and it had finally arrived. Max so much wanted to have Anna in ways she had never been taken before. The way he wanted her almost hurt him. He had never wanted a woman as much as he wanted her. He wanted their first night together to be so special, something they would remember forever. He knew she was a virgin. The time was right and if he were not extremely careful he would hurt her. If he hurt her in any way he would feel it too. He would take his time, enjoy every movement and make sure she was moist and fully excited before he would ever attempt entering her. His heart was beating so hard with excitement he continually had to keep reminding himself to calm down.

He decided their first night would be at a plush and expensive hotel in downtown Berlin. With the city lights and plush surroundings, the setting would be perfect. She was excited and nervous at the same time. She knew he would be gentile and loving. She knew it was going to hurt her and yet did not know how much. It did not matter. She wanted him as she had wanted no man before.

She knew he would open her to new and enjoyable pleasures she had heard about and wanted to experience. She was so much in love and lust she did not care about any pain or discomfort. She knew everything would be fine and they would be as one forever after this night. This night would make a bond between them that she wanted so badly; the bond that only a husband and wife can share.

She was physically so small she did not know if he would even be able to enter her at all. She decided to help him whenever she could and not let him know he was hurting her if she could manage. She knew Max would not want to hurt her but also knew he had built up passions that might control him more than his desire to not hurt her.

She was pleasantly surprised by how slow and patient he was in the beginning. For some time they laid fully clothed on the bed simply holding and lightly caressing each other. He couldn't help gazing in her eyes whenever he could and spent extra time there. Anna knew she would have to somehow let him know she was ready too. Anna felt enough was enough; it was time to encourage him to continue. After a sensual, long, passionate kiss she suddenly pulled away and sat up next to him. He had a surprised look and feared he had done something wrong.

She slowly unbuttoned the front of her dress while smiling at him. He didn't need any more encouragement. He sat up, kissed her neck, cupped a breast with one hand and the other hand around her small waist and pulled her closer. It took no time at all and they both were naked and entwined. Feeling and seeing her naked body next to his only excited him more; her spirit possessed him. His movements that night were of a man knowing he was the luckiest person alive. What he did not know was she was thinking how lucky she was at the very same time. They were soon to be truly soul mates.

She was ready for him with the desire from waiting in anticipation for this night. She had never been this excited and wet before. She wasn't scared at all. He held himself above her with great care not to have his weight hurt her. He was so much stronger and powerful than her. He was about to enter her. This excited state Max was in did not escape Anna's attention and it only served to excite her even more. She was pleased he desired her so much.

It felt immensely pleasurable to Anna that she almost felt no pain at all. There was a little pain, but not much. But this was a pain was mixed with a new type of pleasure. She liked these new feelings and also knew Max was trying hard not to hurt her. When he was away up inside her, he looked into her eyes and liked what he saw. They both at the same time knew they had taken a big step in their relationship. They were sealing their love and devotion to each other with the act of lovemaking. She was now his and he was hers, forever.

They were totally spent and exhausted as they held each other for hours. He lay there, endlessly caressing her face and hair. She held him as tight as she could as if never letting go. If she did this special moment would be lost forever. She knew no matter how hard she held him she could not hurt him. He was so muscular and strong. Max did not know it that night but he released Anna from something she did not even know contained her; pent up passions. She had a beautiful night of lovemaking and now she wanted more and Max was going to give it to her. Naked, exhausted, and entwined, they fell asleep.

CHAPTER 3

A Soldier's Vow

Max's mother was a terrible racist and bigot. She believed everything the Department of Information said about people of Jewish descent without question. The propaganda spread terrible, slanderous accusations. Tactics included clever slippery-slope fallacies that resulted in shocking conclusions. Truth was used only to support lies; that Jews were filled with diseases. It was reported that they were plagued with syphilis and that simply being in their presence was enough to catch the malady. Many Jewish people were displayed publicly as inferior and mentally deranged. This fear helped the Nazis instill fear among other citizens. Jews were accused of being a cause of World War I. This, more than anything, infuriated Elsa.

Having lost her husband in that war was bad enough. Now that her son may be involved in another war caused by Jews was too much for Elsa. The press blamed the imminent problems on the Jewish people and she believed them. Elsa disdained Jews as the lowest form of human life and pure evil at that she was an active member of The Committee for Racial Purity. This committee was organized to find and expose what was known as 'hidden in plain sight' Jews. These people somehow had managed to hide their past. They would have all the proper papers and live among the 'pure ones'.

In a short period of one and a half years, Elsa managed to expose eleven such families. This included not just individual men and women but entire families including the children. She was crafty and smart in her ability to get documents proving the families had lied, and that there was Jewish blood somewhere in their family's history. She would turn them in almost without deliberation, and she was always sure to be somewhere close when the family was arrested. Their possessions and homes were confiscated on the spot. Elsa made certain that a small crowd would be present, by calling friends and acquaintances, to clap and to yell obscenities at the family as they were led away. She treasured the power and prestige she received from being on this committee. She seemed to get extra pleasure from cleansing Germany of as many Jews as she could discover. But Elsa also enjoyed an added reward.

Sometimes Elsa's reward was a portion of the valuables confiscated from families. She collected pictures of the family's trophies and displayed them on a dedicated wall inside her home. She was very proud of this wall. Whenever anyone would visit, she was sure to point out her trophy wall and explain its meaning. The wall itself was inside a home that she was rewarded to her for the tenth family she exposed to authorities. It was a lovely three-story brick that was excessively large for just her and Max. She even left the previous family's portrait hanging in the living room, instead of her special wall, hoping a visitor would ask about them. She would then proudly inform the visitor that it was she who discovered them and cleansed the neighborhood.

*****

August 12, 1939

Max and Anna's last night before deployment

From the time of their wedding until now seemed way too short. Anna anticipated more time. She was so disappointed when she received the news of his immediate deployment. Because of secrecy, the Army waited until the last moment to mobilize forces. This caught Anna by surprise. Max was not surprised, but had to keep this a secret, even from Anna. Several hours after receiving the notice, all she could do was lie in their bed sobbing. Holding her stomach while in the fetal position did not ease the gut wrenching pain. She was glad that no one could hear her, especially the love of her life who was out collecting supplies.

Max was ordered to leave by train in the morning. He knew approximately where he was going, but not how long it might be. No one knew. Even if Max knew, he would not tell her. She knew he was a professional soldier and never asked. She did not want to put him in an awkward position of either telling her or having him lie to her. He did, however, give her a little hint. He asked her to pack his gear with some extra warm clothes. It was late August and this could only mean that he would be heading east and would be away for at least several months.

There was tension on the Polish border being reported almost every day for months. The newspapers reported that Poland attacked a German patrol on German soil and thirty-nine out of forty soldiers were massacred. The lone survivor was able to make his way to a friendly radio station and report it before they caught up with him. They shot and killed him while he was on the air broadcasting what had happened. Pictures were taken and published the next day for everyone to see. Everyone knew the Fuehrer would not stand for this kind of aggression and were bracing for his response.

Adolph Hitler did not seem to the people, at that time, as a warmonger or really wanting to go to war with anyone. In fact, he had just signed a nonaggression treaty with Russia. He fooled them too.

By the time Max returned from collecting supplies Anna had showered and completed her makeup. This was a trick to hide her day of tears. He announced to Anna that this was her special night in the bedroom. He was going to make everything special for her. He was going to ravage every inch of her this night. Since their wedding night, every night seemed to be special between them. They were experimenting and enjoying everything about this new existence between them. He now knew just about everything she liked. There did not seem to be anything that Max would do that she did not like. She was now a woman possessed with emotions and desires she did not know existed inside her before. She reveled in every minute of foreplay. He was so tuned into her that she did not have to say anything to lead him. It was as if, at times, he was reading her mind. She loved it.

He was a man that paid such close attention to her that all it would take from Anna was a little moan or a little body movement to guide him. He knew what all her moans, sighs and breathing meant. Just a subtle shift of her body would tell him everything he needed to know. He seemed only to care about how she felt. This only aroused Anna more. She also enjoyed pleasing him, but it was obvious that pleasing her turned him on much more.

She noticed that whenever she was enjoying what he was doing, he would get more aroused. His erect penis curved upward, almost touching his stomach. She did not know whether Max's penis was considered large or small, but it did not matter. It was perfect for her. It slid in and out hitting the right spots inside her. It never hurt her again--after the first night--but it would swell up and feel so hard that sometimes that she was concerned.

She wondered if it was painful for him. He got her so stimulated and wet that when he finally entered her, there was a rush of added excitement. Heat and electricity spread through her as he penetrated deeper with each thrust. It all felt so tight that when he paused she could feel him pulsating. He would stop moving long enough to bring the passion down a level, only to bring them to a higher level. She surrendered to multiple orgasms that released all tension and left her quivering.

When she first started making love to Max, Anna felt she needed to pleasure him more than she was doing. She was inexperienced and unsure. She did not know that simply having her in this way was more than he had ever wished. When she attempted to reciprocate, he seemed to enjoy it, but his reactions were less intense. He seemed to gently divert her attempts. Once after her attempt to please him seemed to fail; she started to cry and asked if she was doing something wrong. It bothered him so much to see her cry that he swore to himself to never again be the cause of her pain or sorrow within his power. He smiled at her, stroked her hair lovingly and reassured her that there was no problem.

He just wanted to be different than he thought other men to be.

He lightly kissed her and quietly told her a story that happened several years before that inspired his way of thinking. One day he walked into a hotel lobby. There were three women talking and they did not hear him come up close enough for him to hear. One said, "My fantasy is to marry a young man, a virgin and have my way with him for his first time and teaching him what I like and do not like."

Another said, "I wish my husband would take more time and care more about my pleasure."

The third one replied, "My husband is so bad that I do not like it anymore. I did at first, but not now. Now I cannot wait until he is done and gets off me."

He told Anna that his plan was to be different from all the men he knew. He swore to himself that in the future he would be sure to please Anna first. He revealed to her that in doing so, he found out a little known and little talked about secret among women. It was so much more exciting for both to take everything slow and not rush. Take whatever time was necessary to allow the woman to enjoy everything. He discovered that there was strength and a certain power in making love this way. The discovery excited his senses so much he felt he needed to learn more. He even found himself asking more questions.

More pleasure for the man by pleasing the woman? How could this be true? He felt that it took the act of making love to a much higher and intense level, a level that enabled both to enjoy each other so much more. He also discovered with Anna an intimacy and a bond. There was a newfound trust with her. She was now his best friend and confidante. He was able to discover that by not being selfish in bed there were other benefits. The most important being, that for him, he would be able to keep her satisfied longer. This is why he had conditioned himself not to be selfish in bed. Just the thought of only caring about himself l could affect his performance and erection.

After that night of reassuring Anna, she knew there was nothing wrong with her and how truly remarkable Max was. She believed him and was able to relax and let Max take her any way he wished. She learned to relax and enjoy every moment, sending her into ecstasy. She had no fear of anything he wanted to do in the bedroom. He was her lover and protector. Alone, she sometimes thought about what Max had overheard the three other women saying. Every time she would smile a little and feel sorry for them. He was hers.

The lovemaking began soon after they had finished dinner, not even waiting until the dishes were cleaned. He snuggled next to her kissing her so softly as if she were so fragile she might break. His lips sometimes barely touched hers. He ever so softly kissed her eyes, slowly moving to her forehead and neck almost tickling her. It was so sensual and sweet. It was not long with this attention that she showed signs of increased excitement. He was turning her on again by finding the right buttons. Max slowed her down by running his hands through her hair and looking deep into her beautiful brown eyes. This time his smile was not as playful as usual. It had a serious look, one of extreme intensity. Both new this could be the last time. She knew Max would do everything in his power to come back to her. Nothing would stop him from returning to her. This she knew. However, the small thought that somehow he might not be able to was there.

As Anna calmed down, Max began again, allowing the intensity and pleasure to rapidly increase past previous levels. He liked beginning each time with her neck. Kissing her softly was erotic for both Anna and Max. He slowly and carefully increased the pressure of the kisses while advancing toward the base of her neck. Where he knew biting Anna's neck would always excite her more. She loved all of Max's special attention. She also knew and trusted him to only bite hard enough to feel good and not hurt. The trust was complete.

He continually ran his hands through her beautiful hair. He pulled it firmly several times that night. She moaned each time. In the past, he pulled her hair during orgasm to increase her pleasure. This night was no exception to everything he wanted to do to her, but he remained unpredictable. After biting her neck and stirring up more emotions in Anna, he went to her ears. He lightly blew and whispered something sweet in her ear. She could feel the air giving her shivers up and down her body. She scarcely heard him say, "I love you."

Several times in the past, he would softly whisper in her ear something funny or outrageous simply to see if she was listening. She always was and sometimes they would both break out in laughter temporarily breaking the moment. Not this time. He wanted her to remember this night every day until he returned. He did not know how long he would be gone.

As they lay together perfectly entwined as they always did, the feeling of comfort was evident. She was wearing a simple one-piece dress that buttoned all the way up her front. She picked this dress that night for a reason. She had a surprise for him. She knew he would simply love her idea. She wore nothing underneath that would inhibit the lovemaking. She wanted him to remember this night forever too. He slowly started unbuttoning her dress, one button at a time, letting her feel new, cool air. Then he noticed Anna's surprise gift for him. He looked Anna in her eyes and smiled.

He took his hands and slowly caressed each of her breasts. They were so white and firm. Her little pink nipples were already hard with anticipation. It felt so good the way he caressed them. He drew slow faint circles around each nipple with his fingertips. He wanted to build the pleasure and it was working. She so loved the way he fondled and caressed every inch of her. Her nipples were so sensitive that a mere summer night breeze could make them respond sometimes.

He blew softly on each nipple while tracing them with the light touch of his tongue. He never allowed them to go.

After a few minutes of lightly teasing each nipple he began kissing and sucking each one. At the same time with some of her breast in his mouth, he circled each nipple with just the tip of his tongue, driving Anna wild. Her body began arching from pleasure. All of his motions were slow and precise. There was no hurry in his actions. He continually went back to her neck and ears with the tip of his tongue knowing how much she loved this action. He took great care to leave no moisture from his tongue. She only felt a soft erotic touch along her skin.

After a much-needed soft sensual kiss, he asked her to roll over on her stomach. He wanted to pamper and enjoy her as much as possible that night. Then he rose and straddled her now naked body. He proceeded to massage her neck and shoulders. He felt the day's tension in her neck and shoulders start to fade away with the pleasure she was receiving. However, this massage was not for that purpose. It was an erotic massage meant to relax and excite her. Her waist was so small and pretty. Then he bent over her back and slowly blew cool air all over her back. This started to make Anna relax and she began to just squirm a little with delight.

He then took his well-groomed fingernails and raked her back just a little. It was not enough to hurt but just enough to feel good. Whenever Max would sit or lay on top of her, he made sure that his weight would not ever make her uncomfortable. He was so much bigger than she. She loved just laying naked with him. She felt love and protection radiating from him. He would even give his own life for hers if he ever had to, and she knew it.

He never spent too much time in one area or when using any certain technique. Just enough time for her to enjoy and make her wonder what he would do next. He gently rolled her on her back placing her arm above her head so he could run his fingers down the entire length of her arm. Even though she enjoyed this, she now wanted him on top of her and his penis deep inside her. Max was not going to do that yet. He had other plans. Across her arm and right straight again to her waiting hard nipple went his fingertips. At the same time, he gazed into her eyes and slowly kissed her again. Anna melted into his kiss.

Then he got slightly rougher with Anna. He pinched her nipples harder, keeping them aroused and making them ache for more attention. But he never pinched too hard. Then he pinched them gently with his teeth making Anna arch her back again with pleasure. She so wanted him now and he knew this too. He knew holding onto her hair as if he would never let her go and kissing her at the same time always made Anna press harder into his body.

It was obvious how much he was enjoying this too. His erection left no doubt. Anna had to look and see and was not displeased with what she saw. He had not even touched her between her legs yet and she was already wet and ready for him. This was her night to always remember. He slowly started kissing her skin on the way down. She knew where he was going next and could almost not wait. It was going to feel so good. He stopped at her belly button having his tongue dart in and out. Max new it did not necessarily feel good to her; it was a little signal between them. The signal about what he was about to do.

Knowing what was next increased her breathing. It got heavier and deeper as she kept her eyes closed. It seemed to intensify her pleasure. She only opened her eyes when Max went back to her face. She wanted to look at him too. They both had desire on their faces. He kissed and circled this whole area between her legs and softly blew hot air directly on her clit. He took great care not to touch that area yet. Oh how he knew what to do to her. Then slowly parting her hair to expose her better he lightly touched her clit with just the tip of his tongue. He started out with little circles and then changed to the whole tongue licking up and down. Then he flicked it lightly with his tongue alternating back and forth building up the intense feelings inside her until she knew she was going to explode.

Tonight he teased her, got her ever so close, and then stopped. It may be the last time for months and he was focused on this being the best night she would ever have. He already felt it was his best night and one that might help him in the coming months. After she almost came, he stopped to just hold her. She was quivering and shaking with delight. He knew she loved the closeness of what was happening between them, and so did he.

He was holding her so tightly that it made her a little frightened. He was doing this not for her safety. She knew it was something else. She knew it was fear of not returning to her. She had never seen fear of any kind from him before. A light tear ran down her cheek. She did not even try to wipe it off. She knew she could easily explain it away if he should see. It was now time for Max to take her. He slowly crawled on all fours hovering over her. Anna knew what was next and her breathing increased. This gave both of them a warm feeling inside. She was so ready. He had teased and played with her until she shook from the pleasure.

She knew he wanted them both to explode together this night. When this happened, her toes would curl up and seemed to burn a little. It did not hurt. Burn was the only way she had to describe it. She would lose feeling in her hands and fingers. Shake, shiver and feel him ejecting inside her. The feeling of him planting his seed was always special to her.

Then he reached down grabbed hold of his stiff manhood and rubbed it up and down across all her sensitive area being careful to not enter her. Just the head of his penis sliding back and forth across her entire sensitive area was driving her wild. This made her ache for him more. His hard penis slipping and sliding across her felt so good. Knowing excited he was made her feel empowered. He was nicely teasing her. She was not going to be able to take much more of this teasing.

Then he looked into her eyes and saw something he liked. He saw that she burned with desire and wanted him to stop teasing, to give it to her. Looking into her brown eyes, he slowly entered her and stopped when he was only halfway in. He stopped himself there and waited for her reaction. She grabbed his butt with both hands and arched her back and drove all of him into her hard.

Max liked this too. He was glad she did this. Max pushed and pulled himself in and out of Anna. Every stroke felt so good. Several times he changed the tempo and rhythm. He pushed very hard getting all the way in and then just held it there taking in all of the pleasures of the moment. Then he would suddenly jerk back until he nearly exited her. This was what Max called his reverse thrust, and it was another thing Max would do that Anna just adored. She innocently believed that Max was the only one that knew this technique.

Just before he would reverse thrust, she could feel his muscles tense and harden just before he would pull back and enter her slowly. Then, while still deep inside her, he stopped and just gazed into her eyes. He simply stayed there lying in her arms not moving. She could feel the fullness and hardness of Max's penis inside her. She could even feel him throbbing and ready to explode. Usually they would take breaks during lovemaking, but not tonight.

They changed positions many times that night flowing like a well-rehearsed dance. Then he had her get on her hands and knees facing away. Anna had told him she really liked this position so he made sure this night to both start and finish the same way. Max mounted her from behind like an animal. He pulled her hair and bit her neck just like lions. Oh, how much Anna loved him. That night it was important for both to climax together. It would mean so much later. Max knew Anna so well that with her moaning and her moving she was holding back a little while waiting for him.

That night he felt it building inside him. She was pushing back against him hard and fast as if she had lost control of herself. He liked this wild side to her. He grabbed her tiny waist with both hands and pushed her back and forth shoving his penis in and out as fast and hard as he could. Then she heard Max's deep low moans. She knew now he was lost in the moment.   Then he could not hold it any longer. He came with an almost violent thrust. He felt his sperm exit him and go deep into her. It felt so good to let go this way. She felt it at once. First, a throbbing then came a warm feeling between her legs. He groaned and kept squirting inside her. She loved the feeling of him throbbing and filling her up of her with his seed. Then Anna shook. He triggered something in her. Now that she knew she had pleased him, did not want to hold out any longer. She couldn't. It was ecstasy. Her toes curled and tingled as never before. She could not open her hands. She was frozen in bliss. For a brief moment she even seemed to pass out.

They collapsed together. He stroked her hair and kissed her softly while helping her regain her senses. They loved each other so much. Not even realizing, they both fell asleep.

This is how it was during their last night together before he was to leave and go to war.

*****

August 13, 1939

Morning

Anna was the first to awaken. She lay awake just looking at him while he was still asleep. Life just could not be better with Max. Just the thought of them being apart was bringing tears to her eyes. Max had told her this day would come. It had come too soon for her. He had also told her it was important that they cry after they were separated and not while they were still together. He wanted them to both remember their last time together as a time of celebration and togetherness rather than one clouded by tears. She knew it wasn't going to be easy holding everything inside her from him. However, she was going to try.

He smiled immediately after opening his eyes. She was so pretty, even first thing in the morning. He could only see her beauty and never anything else. He did not have to reach out very far for her. They fell asleep entwined and woke up in the same comfortable position.

They had previously discussed the letters they were going to write to each other. She promised to write every day. He had to tell her he knew he would not be able to do the same. Reassuring her, he said he would try, but that he would think of her every day. He would write her as much as he possibly could. He also told her something she already knew but liked hearing anyway - that the letters that she would send him would mean the world to him.

Almost everyone in Max's command was scheduled to leave by train together. When Max arrived at the station, Anna was on his arm. Both held their heads high and managed to avoid tears. He wore his perfectly pressed uniform. Anna knew just how to make it that way. She had asked Max what he wanted her to wear that day. Max's favorite dress was the red one he first saw her in. She liked this choice because she knew she would stand out from the crowd and leave Max with a nice image of her.

She did do one thing differently when she prepared his uniform this time, but this change was not against military regulations. She placed her favorite perfume on every one of his shirt collars and his coat. She knew Max would love this small gesture for a long time. She envisioned him lifting up his collars to smell her and smile. She knew he would be made fun of by his friends when they found out. He would just have to deal with the problem.

Max did receive a lot of ribbing. He also knew secretly that his friends that made fun of him were jealous. They must have secretly wished their wives had thought of perfume trick too. At the station it was busier than normal, nearly chaotic. With soldiers and supplies being loaded and everyone trying to say their goodbyes made it seem as if there was no organization. The steam coming out of the waiting train's engines added to the air of urgency. There was no spare room at the station for privacy. All the women and children were crying and kissing their men goodbye. As Anna took a moment and looked around at everyone without thinking, she just blurted out, "Oh my God, some will not return."

Max heard her and pulled her close. He smiled and said, "Some of them. But not me baby."

Every one of the soldiers believed it would be the other person and not him that would be wounded or killed. In the crowd were two fellow officers both Anna and Max spotted at the same time. It was his commanding officer, Colonel Von Ryan and Max's best friend Lt. Hans. The Colonel was saying goodbye to his wife and three very pretty young girls. The Colonel's eyes met Max's and each one smiled and nodded to each other. There was mutual respect between them. They were fellow comrades about to go to war.

Hans also spotted Max and Anna. Hans was alone secretly wishing he had a wife to say goodbye and to miss him too. Anna looked so beautiful that day. Everything she did to herself was perfection. The small amount of makeup she had applied was just enough. She really did not need any. She wore her hair as Max loved and not how she preferred. As difficult as it was for her that day, she wanted to do whatever Max wanted.

The moment they both dreaded was finally here. Beside his train and shrouded in steam from the engines, they held each other very tight not saying one word. Both knew whatever was said would bring tears. It was better this way. Even as the conductor blew the whistle and began moving the train, they did not want to let go of each other. They held each other until the last possible moment. Max pulled away from her, turned and grabbed Hans's outstretched hand. With one sweeping motion he jumped aboard the train. They never spoke the word 'goodbye.'

All the men had boarded the train and all the women and children were in the train station to watch it leave. All were looking and waving as the train slowly pulled away. Max and Anna were able to watch each other as the train pulled out of sight. Neither waved, they just watched each other as the train pulled out of sight.

Now, Anna could cry.

*****

Sept 15, 1939

Anna sat down at her kitchen table early to write as she had done ever since Max left. She wrote him every day telling him what she did and how she felt. His letters were the only things she hoped for each day. Wondering and worrying in times of war was proving horrible as she was now learning. Writing and receiving letters became a way for Anna to keep her mind from thinking the worst.

She knew it was about the time the mail carrier was due. She would have to hurry this day because the letter wasn't ready yet. She would usually write the letter the night before, so she was running a little late. She decided on a quick note. A short note was better than none. Besides she was not about to break her word and miss a day. She knew about Poland and knew Max was there. Every one of Max's letters said for her not to worry and that he was fine. It helped a little, but she worried constantly anyway.

As she was finishing her note to the love of her life, something seemed different. The words did not flow as they usually had. She was not feeling well. She had a bad feeling in the pit of her stomach. She hoped it was the morning sickness that had just begun and not anything else. She started the note by telling him she was well, and that the morning sickness was not as bad as it had been. Then she explained that she had little time and this was all she could write for now. She wrote 'I love you' and sealed the envelope with a kiss.

She was so delighted after she told him she thought she was pregnant. His lettered reply was a delight for her. He was happy that she might be with his child. He also said something dear to her: that he could not wait to play with his son or daughter. Fears that Anna had about being a good mother were dispelled when Max told her how good she would be. It somehow made a huge difference in her dealing with this new fear.

She knew Max would be a great father. Together they would enjoy watching and helping their child grow up and just enjoying the little things that children do. They really wanted to wait to start a family, but as fate seemed to have it, it was to begin now, not later.

Max said he did not care if it was a boy or a girl but Anna knew he secretly wanted a boy first. So she hesitated at first in telling him. She did not know how he would take the news. She also did not know how it would affect him given everything he was going through. She wanted to do nothing to hurt Max in any way. However, something told her she needed to tell him and right away. It was the right decision.

She was so happy that he was pleased. Not only did he seem pleased but ecstatic. This meant so much to her. Now they had one more thing to share together while he was away. Sitting at the table and not knowing why, she started to cry. She did not know if it was the emotions of being pregnant or something else. When she heard the mail being delivered, Anna snapped out of her daydreaming and rushed downstairs to the mail carrier.

She had not received a letter from Max in days. This worried her so much. He told her before he went away that he might miss a day or two. His reasons were that he might just be too exhausted. He may not be allowed to write and there just might not be enough time. He reassured her many times that he would be just fine. On one occasion, Max told her something so sweet. He said, "Your love will be enough to carry me safely through whatever I will have to face." Whenever he would say something like that, she would just tear up.

When she went downstairs, she handed her letter to the mail carrier and he handed her two letters and politely said thank you while leaving. There were two letters making her heart jump with joy for an instant. One letter was not from Max. It was from Max's best friend Hans. Whispering aloud to herself she said, "Why would he be writing me?"

Then the smile left her face and it just hit her. She had to sit down. It felt like someone had just kicked her in her stomach. Her heart was in her throat beating so hard it felt ready to explode. Her knees went weak and she began to shake. She just knew it was going to be terrible news. With shaking hands, she slowly and carefully opened the letter on the stairs.

Dear Anna, I do not know where to begin. As Max's best friend, this is very hard to say. Max was killed today. I am so sorry. Max insisted that if something were to happen to him I would be the one to tell you. He made me promise. He felt this terrible news would be better served by coming from me. I wish to begin by telling you that Max loved you so very much. So much that at times when he would speak of you he would for a second or two lose his breath. I can tell you he thought of you every day. He longed to be back with you so much. I even think it hurt him a little.

I knew Max long before he met you. After you two hit it off, he changed. I would like to say for the better. He was always so full of ambition and commitment to the Reich, the Army and the defense of our country. Everyone knew with his strong convictions that pushed him he would become a General some day. He might even win the war single-handedly.

After he met you he became a better person, a better man. He no longer cared mostly about himself and his career. He allowed himself to care more about someone else, you. Every day that we were together, he couldn't stop talking about you. How beautiful you are. How smart and caring you are. He confided in me once that he was not worthy of you. He believed you were in a higher class than he. You not only accepted him but also embraced him. Even with all his faults.

When he found out he was going to be a father, he walked as if he were ten feet tall all day and night. He held his chin and head so high up I know his neck had to hurt for days afterwards. You made Max care. He loved living life every day. He said many times if we do this or that right then we could all go home to our wives and children sooner. Many times he pushed everyone under his command so hard, believing it would help him return to you sooner. I heard him say many times he had to get home to his Anna.

This is why he was so driven. He could not wait to return to you. He cherished all the time you two spent together. It was all he seemed to talk about when we had spare time together. I do not say these things to hurt you or make you sad. You just need to know how much he missed and loved you. Max wrote a letter to you last night. He gave it to me to hold and sent should this happen. I am sending that letter with this one. Again, I am so sorry for our loss. He will be missed by all who knew him.

Your friend in grief,

Hans.

Anna collapsed on the stairs and hit her head hard. It hurt and started bleeding. She picked up the letters from the floor and staggered up. She put the letters on a table and sat down weeping. For what seemed like hours all she could do was cry with her head down on the table. Staring into space not really looking at anything was next. Sometimes she would pick up Max's letter, start to open it and then put it down. She broke into tears repeatedly. At one point she was on the floor in the fetal position holding her sides with her hands crying aloud, "Oh God no. Please do not let it be true."

Several times, she picked up the letter she had already read from Hans and tried reading it again while wiping tears off her face. She tried to get control of herself only to break down and start the cycle all over again. She was stalling. She somehow felt that if she did not open this letter from Max it would make the news somehow not have happened. It would have all been some bad misunderstanding or nightmare and she would wake up soon. However, she did know she would have to open it sometime. She stood up, walked over to the sink, took a deep breath and washed her face as best she could. Determined to finally do this, she walked back to the table, sat down and opened the letter.

My dearest and beloved Anna, if you are reading this then the news you are receiving is not good. I only hope this reaches you before any other way. I can only hope this will help you with the pain that I know you will be going through. In case this is your first realization of our bad news, I will begin this way. Please forgive me. I only wish to make all of this easier for you and tell you things I need to say.

We all write these letters in case the worst happens. We usually write it just before a battle or if we feel a special need. Sometimes we just want to. In our case, it was because I wanted to and I had a premonition. I need you to know just how much I love and cherish you. Do you remember shortly after we met the excitement we both felt? We finally found someone that so perfectly fits. That night we were on the ground holding each other looking up at the stars. It was a beautiful summer night. The stars were so bright and clear. We felt they were so close we could reach out and pluck one from the sky. As I was looking up it happened a shooting star streaking across the sky.

I asked you if you saw it. You did not. However, you asked me what it was and I told you. You then asked me if I had made a wish and I told you I had. You then wanted to know what my wish was and I would not tell you because I wanted it to come true. You did not say a word, just reached out, held my face with both your hands and softly kissed me. Startled, I looked into your eyes and said; "How did you know that was it?"

The time we had was so special. It just was not long enough. In fact knowing you a lifetime would not have been enough time for me. I so enjoyed you.

Please forgive me for leaving you. I did not wish to. It is not your fault either. The short time we had together was my lifetime. You gave me something to believe in other than myself. I needed to love you and be loved by you. I had the most intelligent and beautiful woman in this world. You were a gift to me.

Now that you are carrying our child I know you will be all right. I worried all the time about you. I knew if something like this were to happen to me, you would want to die too. We always felt the same about everything. We enjoyed everything together. I leave the name of our child up to you. I hope he or she looks mostly like you my angel. Please be sure to tell our child I would be there if I had a way. It was not up to me. It just was not meant to be.

I would be forever grateful if you would please tell our child something important to me. Our joy and happiness was so great, you coming into our lives blessed us. What was meant to be was you, and you make us proud. You are the product of our love. With you, our love will last forever. If there is anything to life after death, then by just the pure existence of our love, I will find a way to look after you both.

You now have a mission in life. You cannot hurt yourself because if you do you will also hurt our child and my legacy. Hurting either one of us, I know you just cannot do. Please, my loves, always try to be happy. Find happiness with our child and without me. Remember me but always take care of our little one and yourself. You now have a bigger responsibility to bear than I do. After you have read this letter, I will be at peace.

A little while ago, there was no one except you and me, my cherished one. However there now is another one you will have to protect and cherish without me. This person will know everything about me. I know you will make sure of this and about the love we shared. Knowing that our child will know of me is important to me, especially now, my dear. There is so much more I wish to say but no more time to do it. Goodbye my love. I am forever in your debt.

All my love,

Forever, Max.

The tears ran down her face without any sign of ever stopping. The pains she now felt were horrible. Her heart was totally broken. Her stomach would never be hungry again. She felt completely numb. Her knees were so weak she knew she could not stand up. She knew this pain would never go away. She even found herself at one point cursing at what she had inside her. She did want to die and be with him as Max had written. She knew she could not die now. She had to go on. He expected her to and she was not going to let him down.

*****

Elsa gets the bad news much later that same day

Elsa was sitting in her parlor reading when she heard someone knock at her door. When she answered the door there were two Army officers she did not know standing there. She was puzzled and scared at the same time. Before they even said a word, she got a chill all over. She could feel her heart in her throat. It was beating hard and fast. Her knees were weak. She knew something was wrong. When they asked her if she was Max's mother. She closed her eyes and put her hands in front of her face.

One of the soldiers did not waste any more time. He said, "I am sorry to tell you but your son was killed in action."

Elsa collapsed and everything went black. The next thing she remembered she was in her parlor being assisted by these two men. She had fainted and was carried to the room and placed on her couch. Elsa sat up and opened her eyes. She took a deep breath, looked at her two guests and said, "Get out."

As they were leaving they told Elsa a few more facts they felt were important. She sat there for some time shaking and thinking. She did not cry one tear, yet. She picked up the phone and called her close friend General Kleist. He came right over. What he found when he arrived was what appeared to be someone not in grief, but someone filled with anger. She was furious and full of rage. All she kept saying was it was the Jews' fault. They were going to pay. She would hunt down every one she could possibly find. She even told him, "You need to find me several suspects to investigate, now."

He replied, "I will help you with whatever you need. If this will help you I will have names tomorrow for you."

Then she told him, "They told me Anna has already been notified. She told them to come and inform me. They also told me she knew before they had arrived."

He was somewhat guarded with his response and said; "Maybe she just thought it might be easier for you this way."

Elsa answered in a sharp angry tone, "Well it wasn't. It was rude and I will never forgive her for this and the time she stole from me, never."

He tried to calm her down but it was no use. She was on a rampage. She was now replacing grieving with hatred and revenge. Someone was going to pay a price for Max dying. She was so upset with Anna she asked the general how the investigation was going.

He told her, "Not anything new to report." He did not want to tell her he had stopped investigating.

She took a breath holding up both hands and calmly said "Keep looking, I want to know everything about her and her parents."

The general reached out taking both her hands in his and softly said, "Are you sure you want to do this?"

She did not even reply. She pulled her hands away and glared an awful look at him. He knew not to even try to talk her out of it, at least not then. Anna was too depressed and in pain to be the one to tell Elsa. She knew Elsa would hate her even more now that he was gone. She would surely blame her for missing time that she wanted with him before he left. She had not told her she was with child. Max in a letter had told her to wait; there would be plenty of time. He was wrong.

CHAPTER 4

Von Ryan

Otto, Rianna, Eli, and the Secret

Anna's parents grew up together having the same teachers and classmates year after year. Otto developed a strong crush on Rianna as soon as he started noticing girls. As their relationship developed, Otto followed Rianna's lead on most activities. She loved his attention and companionship but only thought of Otto as a good friend.

They were the best of friends having fun together all the time until she began to blossom as a pretty girl. She began noticing other boys and they began noticing her. She thrived on this additional attention so much that Otto was many times forgotten and left out. When Rianna was asked about her relationship with Otto, she would tell people that he was her best buddy. She wasn't aware of his deep affection. He loved her.

Otto had another good friend, across town, with whom he enjoyed hanging out. His name was Eli. Otto idolized Eli from the first time they met. Eli was everything Otto wasn't. Eli was tall with curly dark hair, handsome, and outgoing. Eli was slightly older than Otto by just over a year. They did typical boy stuff, including getting into trouble. There are certain things boys do that may create an unbreakable lifetime bond, and at the same time give a glimpse as to how they will mature as adults.

In their early teens, Eli convinced Otto to swipe some tobacco from his father. They went off and smoked it as they had seen their fathers do. They did not like it. They both coughed and almost threw up their food, but they had tried it together as best friends. They knew if they were caught they both would be punished and this added to their excitement. As usual when they did something wrong, they were caught.

A relative of one of the boys smelled the smoke on them and informed each of their parents. Although what they had done was not that bad, both of them belonged to strict families with parents who wanted their children to be become exceptional young men. The boys stole and now would lie about what they had done. This kind of behavior was not tolerated by either set of parents.

Confronted by his father, Otto looked right in his father's eyes and lied. He feared his father. His father was strong and could be intimidating. What Otto did not know was that he already knew the truth and wanted Otto to confess. Neither knew that this was going to be one long afternoon. Otto's father sat with Otto at the kitchen table and questioned him repeatedly. Otto continued denying the allegations, lying, as he had never done before. Having been caught doing something wrong so many times before, both boys had rehearsed a very believable story in case they were caught. Otto was sticking to his story regardless of what his father said or threatened. He was hoping his father would believe him or give up.

Otto and his father sat at the kitchen table for hours. His mother tried helping by taking several turns at questioning Otto; a different approach that also didn't work. Otto was more stubborn and determined to not give in and confess, as they had never witnessed before. His father was determined to break his son. It soon became a contest of wills. Otto's father became furious.

The interrogation was so intense at times that Otto's father had to take smoke breaks to calm down. Otto's mother was calmer as usual. Without letting Otto or her husband know at the time, she admired her son. She saw something beyond the lies and petty theft on which his father was so focused. She saw an honorable trait emerging from her young son. Someday this trait might serve him well. Somehow she knew there was honor involved. Her little boy was becoming a man.

With a smile and a light hug, Otto's mother soothed her husband. Trying in her own way to defuse the situation, she reminded him how ironic it was that he was trying to get his young son to admit to smoking tobacco as he was taking a smoke break. At that moment they managed a little giggle. He told her there was something else happening and he was determined to find out. It was important to get Otto to confess, but it was more important to find out why he was being so dammed stubborn. Otto's father contemplated a beating but somehow knew it would not work this time. He had stopped the corporal punishment a few years back, knowing little Otto preferred that to lectures.

The reason Otto was more stubborn this time was that he would have to tell on Eli, and he was resolute that this was not going to happen. He knew Eli would lose his respect and friendship if he broke down. So it continued, hour after hour, with neither relenting.

Otto's father suddenly realized why he was being so stubborn. Several times lowering his voice and approaching in a different way, he asked Otto why he was being so stubborn. Every time he asked this question, Otto would not say a single word or give a single hint. Otto would only close his mouth and stare at his father or look at the table with his head down. The hours of interrogation were a punishment in itself.

Otto's father had already discussed everything with Eli's father earlier and knew all the answers. Who stole the tobacco? Whose idea it was, and where they smoked. Frustrated and tired, Otto's father invited Eli and his parents to their home.

Eli and his father came over, and with everyone in the kitchen, re-told what they both had done. Not the made-up story, but the truth - except whose idea it was that started everything. Otto decided it was now ok to give in and confess. Eli obviously had broken down and told everything so there was no longer any need to lie. Otto's father told the boys to go outside while they decided the punishment.

Outside, Otto asked Eli, "How long did you hold out?"

Eli replied, "Not at all. I knew he knew. So I just told him everything."

Otto looking surprised, "You mean I went through all those hours for nothing?"

Eli replied, "Well, maybe not nothing."

"What do you mean?"

Eli smiled. "I have never seen your dad so exhausted. I think a little while longer he would have given up."

They both laughed. It did not matter to Otto. Eli was his idol. The time he endured was worth it. This event would later become important in many ways; bonding them together even stronger while uncovering good traits and deep flaws. The good traits would serve Otto well while the flaws would be horrible for everyone. They could not even remember later if they were punished or not; it didn't matter.

Otto had kept Rianna a secret from Eli as long as possible. He knew Eli would want her and he also knew that when they met, Otto would not be able to stop Eli from pursuing Rianna. This would also mean the end of their special friendship. Otto kept this secret for almost two years, until Eli finally met her. As Otto suspected, Eli was immediately attracted to her.

Eli was already quite a ladies' man. He was tall, muscular and had bright green eyes. Eli's father was German and Jewish. His mother was Austrian and beautiful. Eli looked more like his mother without any traits associated with someone being Jewish. He was self-assured and brash with women. He was confident with many girls. This came easy for him. While most of the boys his age struggled with knowing the opposite sex, Eli did not. He often wondered what all the fuss about being scared of women. He had no problem walking right up and talking to them.

Nothing slowed Eli down once he met Rianna. Not even his best friend's alliance. He knew Otto idolized him and he would always be there for him. He would be mad for a while, but he would also get over it. It was a whirlwind romance, and after only four months of seeing each other, Eli and Rianna were married.

As expected, Otto was heartbroken but decided not to let this affect the rest of his life, as he secretly hoped it would not last long. He figured Eli would stray, as he always had, and just maybe he would be around to pick up the pieces. Otto knew he would love Rianna forever. She was his first love.

Shortly after the marriage, World War I broke out and they both enlisted in the Army. They were going to fight for their country. Eli wanted to return a hero while Otto just did what was expected for his family and country. Otto was sent north and Eli went south.

Soon after his training, Otto decided to write to Rianna because he missed her. He also had to admit to himself that he missed Eli too. Letter writing between Rianna and Otto was fine with Eli because he wanted Otto to forgive him. Eli was not jealous. He trusted Rianna explicitly. Whenever Eli had free time, he frequented bordellos. Somehow, even with the war around him, he could always find a woman who wanted him. Eli did not care if someday his actions would hurt Rianna. It was nice when he could get home and have her waiting on him. He liked her warm loving body at night. However, he felt he was no longer in love with her. The only person Eli really loved was Eli.

Otto had forgiven them both in his way. Forgiving Rianna was easy. He could not stay mad at her. As for Eli, Otto stayed mad as long as he could and then gave in. Eli was his idol and his best friend. With everything they had done together, including the hours and hours of interrogation, he just couldn't give up on that special friendship. Not even for a girl such as Rianna.

With both Eli and Otto writing to her, she devised a plan and arranged a clandestine meeting. She knew if she could just get them together one time, then everything would be better for each of them. They both took leave at the same time and Rianna arranged for Otto to arrive at their place almost at the same time. Immediately when they saw each other, everything bad was forgiven and all three hugged just as she wished.

She had done it; the three of them were together again and from this time on, they maneuvered to have all their time off to be together. One of these times, Otto paid for a picture portrait of all three of them together. This picture would have disastrous consequences later. They were so happy and proud being together again as evident in the picture. They were as tight as friends as they were as teenagers. No matter what was to happen, they would be there for one another if needed. Rianna loved them both. She once wrote to both about a story she had just read called The Three Musketeers. It so reminded her of the three of them that she decided that was what they would now call their family.

At the conclusion of the war, Eli came home to Rianna and after only one night of lovemaking, he abruptly left her for another woman. She had no idea this was coming and didn't have the time to tell him something very important. Eli agonized over leaving her knowing this would again break the bond between him and Otto. It didn't matter. He had made up his mind.

It was a woman and the glitz of the times that lead Eli away. The roaring twenties in America were also the roaring twenties in Germany. Nightclubs featured themes involving all kinds of American culture. There was even a place called The American Gangster Club. It had posters on their walls of Al Capone, Machine Gun Kelly, and others.

Berlin was an open and fun place to live. There was nudity in the theater and clubs only soon to be outlawed by a man named Adolph Hitler. Eli was drawn to this lifestyle not caring what it did to anyone, including Rianna. She was shocked, devastated, heartbroken, and pregnant. Eli was not aware of her being pregnant. They had tried the whole time together without success. He did not even suspect that it was possible.

Otto, on hearing the news of Eli's departure, rushed to Rianna's side. He was there for days, through all her crying and anger. There were many mood swings. He was patient through them all. After a few days, she got up the courage to tell him about her condition. Otto offered to find Eli and tell him. She was not sure that that was the right thing to do. She was very mixed up and confused. She did not want him to return if he did not want to be with her. She did not know what to do.

That is when Otto shocked her. He told her that he loved her. He was still in love with her and always would be in love with her. He asked her to escape with him. They would move far away to where his parents lived. They lived in the southern part of Germany where the beautiful Austrian mountains were visible. They would move there and tell everyone they were husband and wife with child. They would not even tell his parents the truth. It would be their secret forever.

The only thing that mattered to him was she. She would be his and he would always have the family he had dreamed. He would love this child as his own. He was glad he had saved much of the money he earned in the Army. He wanted to be with her and the money would help so much in their new beginning. They left the next day, never regretting that decision.

CHAPTER 5

Nine Days Left

April 24, 1945

Six years later, and only nine days left until the unofficial surrender

Shortly after Poland was securely in German hands, the Colonel came home making a point to visit Anna. He wanted to explain as much as possible. He knew she would have a lot of unanswered questions and if she needed his help, he would try. He thought she might remember him from the train station and realize that he was responsible for Max's death.

He followed her into another room with his hat smartly tucked under his arm, which signaled to her that he would not be able to provide certain details. His stern eye contact indicated, however, that he would tell her what he could. He described the scene in Poland and the mission to secure a bridge so that tanks could cross. He had ordered Max's unit to approach and secure the bridge. There was fighting all around the bridge as the Pole's were doing their best to slow down the advance.

"We knew they would, if possible, blow up this bridge and more than likely attempt this when some of our troops would be on the bridge. It was very important to get to this bridge secure on both sides quickly. I ordered Max to quickly seize the bridge and secure it with hast. Speed was essential. There was no time for extra planning."

Anna quietly sat and listened to everything the Colonel said, knowing he would not lie to her. She heard him say that he was the one who gave Max the orders. He told her that Max was in front of his men advancing on foot toward the bridge when, only a few meters away, a sniper shot him in the chest. He went down immediately. His fellow comrades went to his aid. There was nothing they could do to help him. He had died almost immediately. His unit killed the sniper and was able to secure the bridge. He concluded, "Max was a brave soldier. He led his men from the front. I hope you will be as proud of him as we are."

Anna was polite and teary-eyed as she stood up and thanked him. She had begun to show her pregnancy and the Colonel conveyed his delight. As he was leaving, he made a point to emphasize that if she needed anything at all, to call him. She had questions, but decided to ask him later.

Anna felt that the Colonel had done well. He was right in giving Anna some time to reflect on what she had been told. She later accepted his decisions and forgave him. This was one of her best decisions. After her grieving subsided, her world only existed for whom she later named, little Max. Taking care of the little gift growing inside became of most importance. She delivered what her husband had secretly desired. She had carried him knowing that he would never meet his father but that a piece of him would always be with her. He became everything to her, at times believing she did not deserve this little man.

While she was pregnant and from the first day of birth, Anna told little Max how special his father was and fulfilled her promise. She knew he was too young to understand, but felt compelled to tell him anyway. It was important. He looked just like his father except for two cute little dimples that appeared every time he smiled; that endearing feature he received from Anna's mother, Rianna. He was a well-behaved and adorable child. Shy around strangers, always hiding behind his mother's legs. He never let her get very far away. Anna loved this and they just adored each other.

Anna usually wore her hair in a ponytail or bun so not to attract a male admirer. The love of her life was her adorable little son. She did not want anyone else in her life at this time and maybe never. The two of them together was all she truly needed. Years before, Anna was very wary and scared that the state would take him away from her to give him to another family. They would raise him as they wished and she would never see him again. It was a mandate of the master race doctrine of Germany. She did not want to re-marry or even get involved with another man. This attitude put their lives together in jeopardy. She would rather die than give him up.

As good fortune would have it, Colonel Von Ryan took extra interest in Anna. He felt burdened by Anna's predicaments. He wanted Anna as a nanny, housekeeper, and companion for his wife and three children. The children were all girls. One was less than a year old, one was three and the oldest was six. He also had a feeling that his wife and Anna would become friends. His being away from home so often was hard on his wife and the girls. This just might be a perfect situation for his family.

This was of great help to Anna and little Max in several ways. The small widow's pension was not enough for Anna to give little Max as much as she wished. Also, she just was not interested in meeting other men, believing the special relationship she once knew between her and Max would never ever be duplicated. It just wasn't possible while still feeling the pain in her heart. Anna and little Max did everything together. They both especially enjoyed bedtime. Every night she quietly talked with him often reading him something to help him sleep. Other times she would read bedtime stories with the Von Ryan children present, including them whenever possible. However, she preferred this special time with little Max alone.

One particular story little Max liked, was about people and fairies ice-skating together around a pond. They would all fall down, not the fairies of course. As everyone knows, they have wings and cannot fall. As the children fell down, the small fairies would laugh and make fun of them. This enchanted little Max every time and he would laugh.

It was a medium sized blue book with lots of white spaces. After the first time she read it to him, he always wanted to carry it with him, everywhere. She tried to make sure he always fell asleep with a smile on his face. He looked just as big Max had always envisioned an angel would. Little Max woke up excited one morning after she first read the story to him and told her something she would never forget. "You know mommy, I can skate when I am asleep." She wished she could have shared this moment with his father.

It seemed as if everyday something surprising was coming from little Max's mind. Some were inspired by Anna's bedtime stories and some were inspired by the other children. Whatever it was, Anna loved it all. He was developing a kind and fun personality every day. As the live-in servant of an Army Colonel, potential suitors were scared away, which further pleased Anna. The only suitors having the courage would have to be high-ranking officers and most of them were married.

Whenever she would go out shopping or just walking around with little Max, she could overhear people talking about her and the relationship with the Colonel's family. He was an important man. His status gave Anna clout and influence. It meant better food, best seats for outside pleasures such as movies, a play, the opera, and restaurants. This situation just could not have been better for her. Even the occasional visits home by the Colonel were enlightening, so much so that she began listening and recording his stories. She understood the importance of listening and remaining silent.

Rumors of rape, torture, and almost unspeakable things were written in German newspapers only if it suited their purpose. When it benefited the Reich, the papers embellished the stories, repeating them over and over. The newspapers never wrote about the wrong deeds performed by Germans. No matter how much the government tried to suppress rumors, they were still quietly passed on. Any talk that was not pro-Reich had to be told very carefully. Exposure for such talk could mean torture, disappearance, or even death.

Rumors concerning Jews were only told to someone trustworthy. No matter how hard the government attempted to suppress such talk, information was shared. A question that never got answered was what became of the deported Jews? People were frequently arrested for saying something that the state deemed inappropriate and would disappear. All atrocities were kept quiet. It was not a free press.

Anna continually stayed in touch with her parents. They were her confidants and her only friends except the Von Ryan family. Mrs. Von

Ryan became very close and personal with Anna. She trusted her. Mrs. Von Ryan knew whatever she told Anna would never be repeated. Anna had no one to tell. This is what Mrs. Von Ryan believed. She did not consider the one exception – Anna's parents.

Anna realized whenever she spoke or wrote to her parents, she had to be careful. If she was overheard sharing classified information, then she was committing a crime punishable by death. Someone was always watching and listening. Anna never said much about her family to anyone. Everyone knew about her parents little bookstore, where they lived, and that was about all. When asked about other members of her family, Anna would just say she really did not like them, and left it that way. Everyone would get the hint and not ask anything else.

When the Colonel was away, the two women would talk about almost everything. Mrs. Von Ryan was fascinated by the stories Anna would tell her about her college years. Anna was fascinated by Mrs. Von Ryan's interest. The songs Anna could play by heart on the piano amazed her and the children. There wasn't any printed music that Anna could not play effortlessly. Soon after Anna came to live with them, Mrs. Von Ryan insisted her husband purchase a piano for entertaining. One was quickly acquired from a deported Jewish family. She practiced and performed a piece almost every day. They all became one larger family.

The Colonel made sure Anna would entertain his friends whenever he came home; an added benefit befitting his rank. She was always the hit of his parties. She was charming, eloquent, and pretty. The Colonel's wife tried to set Anna up with one of his friends once. She was polite, but made it clear that she was not interested. She never made that mistake again.

Anna and the Mrs. talked for hours and hours never tiring of their conversations. She eventually confided to Anna what the Colonel had told her in secret during all his visits. She did not know Anna had already heard them. Anna always looked surprised when she was told. She did not want her way of snooping to be eliminated.

Colonel Von Ryan was a very ambitious German officer. He was dedicated to the defense of the Fuehrer and the fatherland. Many high-level meetings were in the presence of the Fuehrer. There was a level of honor concerning the standing positions when Hitler was present. On his left side would be his most honored and on the right the lesser important. Colonel Von Ryan's place was on Hitler's left.

During one such famous meeting, the Fuehrer and others, including the Colonel, were hurt and almost killed. The meeting was at a place called the Lion's Den at Rustenburg on July 20, 1944. A bomb planted there by a high-ranking inner circle officer named Colonel Count Von Stauffenberg missed killing Hitler and set off a countrywide search for the conspirators.

Colonel Von Ryan's injuries included a broken arm, broken collarbone, damaged spleen and temporary hearing loss. He was allowed an immediate medical leave to go home to recuperate. He was cleared of any involvement with the conspirators, thus giving him extra power and influence in subsequent days.

In the beginning, little Max was scared and intimidated by the tall, mean looking man that would suddenly appear out of nowhere with spit polished boots and then disappear just as fast. The Colonel tried everything to get little Max to warm up but nothing seemed to work. Little Max always hid behind his mothers' legs avoiding direct contact. It was cute but a little frustrating for the Colonel.

Unbeknownst to little Max, the Colonel had a soft spot for him. It was simple. He had always wanted a little boy. He loved his daughters, but it was nice having a boy in the house. Though he could have easily removed him from Anna and made him his own, he was glad that he made a different choice, so far.

His wife had become her old self again now that Anna and little Max were living with them. She was full of energy, not always tired when he came home. This benefit increased the Colonel's desire to come home more. This relationship was exactly what everyone needed. He was proud of himself for making another correct important decision. The only decision he wished he could alter was the one that involved Max.

Even with her getting older and delivering three children, Mrs. Von Ryan desired to have the Colonel take her in his arms and make love to her whenever he visited. No longer was she too tired for him.

When he arrived all she wanted to do was care for him. Her full attention was focused on him.

Only after he had time to reacquaint himself with his daughters would Colonel Von Ryan then turn his attention toward his wife. He would signal to her he was ready by a wink, take her by the hand, and lead her to the bedroom. After weeks and sometimes months in the field, he was ready for sex. He needed the soft touch and feel of a woman. The woman he loved and the mother of his three beautiful children was whom he desired. He devoured her like an animal on almost every visit.

The lusting for her, she also enjoyed. She knew it was not simply his need for sex. He needed her. He removed her clothes quickly and tossed her on the bed like a doll. He took her as he did the first time they made love; fast, furious and with passion. This was a message telling her how much she was needed and wanted. Being needed and desired by the man she fell in love with after all the years was a beautiful thing she cherished. As with all past visits, she knew later that night or early the next morning he would be much gentler. She liked it both ways. Something he was aware of too.

Having Anna there to help and be a friend meant Mrs. Von Ryan could devote herself to him and his needs when he came home. The Colonel, being a typical man, told no one he appreciated these changes. He always brought the children little gifts when he came home, including little Max. After several such visits, things changed. If the visit was more than just a few days, little Max would start to warm up to the Colonel. He showed everyone he was developing a little bravery, eventually sitting on his lap without Anna present. He began trying to talk to the Colonel and attempted to show the Colonel different things.

Anna was aware that potential problems with the other children might arise with this added attention, so she carefully monitored the time. She could easily tell a soft spot for little Max had developed. Anna felt part of the family. She knew her place without being told and always kept the children away from the parents' door when it was obvious they needed time alone. So it became to the Colonel and his wife, not wanting to remember what it was like before Anna and little Max came into their lives.

*****

Eli was in southern Germany, April 5, 1939. It no longer mattered that a man had served the motherland in the war to end all wars. It no longer mattered that you distinguished yourself in battle. If you were tainted you were in trouble. It did not matter that Hitler himself was exposed with Jewish blood relatives. This fact was covered up and buried. Eli was one of many struggling to make a living in Germany as a Jew.

The Kristallnacht or "the night of broken glass" was on November 7, 1938 and helped seal the fate of everyone of Jewish descent inside Germany and across most of Europe. The Nazis arrested thousands of Jews that night, wrecking over 7,500 shops and 119 synagogues. They confiscated five million marks from the Jews they were persecuting. For the broken glass alone, the victims were fined. It was as if the government threw something through your shop window and subsequently fined you for the broken glass.

New laws against Jews were published almost daily. They were not allowed to go to beauty or barber shops. They were not allowed to go to theaters. Some in the beginning were allowed to work and then later were denied work permits.

Eli knew this was the end of his life as he had known it and decided it was time to run. He was also again in trouble. The further away he could get the better. He decided to just slip away one day hopefully undetected. He took what little money he had saved and with just the clothes on his back set out to find two old and dear friends. He had discovered where they were living together. He hoped it was far enough away from all the madness. If not, he would travel further away with their help.

Eli was not sure if Rianna and Otto would help him. He destroyed their trust not once but twice. He heard they were together and felt this was good for him. He could return and see them both at the same time increasing his chances to be forgiven. They surely would not turn him away. Besides, Otto was now with the woman he wanted all along and in a twisted way he felt he could exploit this fact. He believed that even if they could not or would not help him, they would surely at the least find someone who would help.

The day he left Berlin was a Friday where he was not expected at work until Monday morning. He still had a current work permit soon to expire and knew he probably would not get more time. He did not want to be seen carrying a suitcase so he did not take one. Except for a few extra clothes he hid on him and the little bit of money he had he simply closed the door and walked away. He had previously seen two mutual friends that told him where they lived and worked. He filed this information away in his mind knowing he might need it someday. He was careful in hiding his trail and didn't ask anyone for directions.

He arrived in their town without any problems and located the apartment building in which Rianna and Otto lived. It was a brown and red brick three-story building with a door opening in at the street and mailboxes inside on the right side wall with names on them. Eli searched the names until he saw what he was looking for. Their names were on the last box. It was on the top floor. There were two apartments on the first floor and a staircase leading upstairs in the back. After climbing to the second level, Eli looked down the hall noticing only two apartments on that floor also. Slowly and quietly, he climbed to the third floor. Rianna and Otto's apartment was on the left with another apartment directly across the hall.

Eli anxiously but lightly knocked on their door. No one answered so he knocked a little louder. As he did, a neighbor slightly opened her door. She was short, slightly heavy and older. She softly asked Eli, "Are you looking for the Heinz?"

Eli cleared his throat and replied, "Yes I am. I am an old friend. Do you know where they are?"

Looking suspicious she answered, "Well yes. They are still at work. Do you know where that is?"

Eli gave her his special smile and answered, "No."

She liked his smile, as most women did, as she opened her door a little more to give Eli a better look, "They own the little bookstore at the end of this street. You go out the door make a right and you cannot miss it."

Eli tipped his hat smoothly. "Thanks I will go see them now and I hope we will meet again."

She closed the door smiling. It had been a long time since a man had talked to her that way and she liked the feeling again. He was handsome and charming; she would be on the lookout for him again. He wished she had not seen him. However, there was nothing to worry about and he was proud of how he handled the situation.

Eli stopped at the bookstore's front doors and took a deep breath as he opened the door and stepped inside. A little bell tied to the top of the door announced his arrival. Rianna was on a small ladder and looked directly at him. She recognized him immediately.

*****

As Anna listened to the horrible story she learned something valuable at Colonel Von Ryan's house. On this particular visit, Anna was to overhear horrible things that would become important to her later. Confidential conversations between the Colonel and his wife in their bedroom were not as confidential as they believed. Anna learned to listen at a vent that joined their rooms. She had to put her ear close to the vent to be able to hear. Doing so, she could even hear soft-spoken words.

She overheard the Colonel telling his wife on this visit about a particular modest town called Venders. The fighting was fierce all around the little Russian town. It was on Germany's eastern front. The fighting was up close and personal with hand-to-hand combat at times. The Russian fighters were determined to stop the German advance at this small and seemingly unimportant town. It was more important than they realized since it was at the intersection of two important roads.

The timing for the Russians was somewhat fortunate since supplies and re-enforcements were several days behind the Colonel's advancing unit. After two days of fierce fighting, there was a stalemate. The Germans were determined to capture this Russian town and the Russians wanted desperately to stop them at all costs. Both sides were losing too many soldiers in this seemingly unimportant battle.

Anna listened to as much as she could every visit. She paid attention to all the details and wrote down everything to send to her parents. She knew these things might, in the future, be very important to her family; and she was right. She knew whatever the Colonel said would be up to date and true. So much different than rumors she heard. All of these things were fascinating to her.

The newspapers told stories with just enough truth in it to make the stories believable. Therefore, readers would not know what was true and what was not true. They were always saying that they were winning the war even in the end when it was almost evident to the contrary.

It was enriching for Anna to know the truth. The only ones she repeated any of this information to were her parents. She knew she should not do this, but she could not help herself. Anything overheard that might help her family she would send to them, no matter the risks. She never considered this might make her a spy by definition. As smart as she was, she still overlooked this possibility.

When his troops entered the town there seemed to be no one left, only destroyed buildings. After searching for about an hour, they discovered some women and children hiding. All the men and teenage boys were gone. He gave expressed orders not to harm the captives. The Colonel felt sorry for them and was reminded of his family.

During light integrations, he learned Stalin had issued orders for everyone to burn down the little town and leave. Stalin, a few weeks earlier, had ordered all young boys and men shipped away to fight further east. After the Russian troops exited the town, the women and children decided to refuse Stalin's orders and wait for their men and boys to return. They felt they did not have a choice.

The Germans had captured the town. However, they were too far ahead of reinforcements and supplies and felt that they were not in a defendable position so they retreated to outside the town that night, leaving behind the women and children. Two days later when supplies arrived they advanced back into the town, slowly making their way and especially looking for the women and children. In the middle of town, two days before, was an undamaged small church. The constant bombardments of artillery and bombs had destroyed everything around the church.

Colonel Von Ryan told his wife he was leading his forces into the town and looked in the area where this church once stood. In spite of no fighting since they were last there, it had burned down. Getting up closer to the area, he saw it first. Across the street tied to the building outside were the women. All were naked, shot, and some disemboweled. They were probably forced to watch the church burn.

After getting within a few meters of the church they could smell freshly burnt bodies. After a closer inspection, the church had been full of the children. Someone had chained the front door and burned the church down with them inside. The women were raped and killed after the church burned. They looked like they were in a lot of pain when they died. His voice cracked with emotion several times during the story. He needed to tell someone and it had to be her. He said, "The Russians did this to send a message. It was a warning from Stalin. Obey my orders or else. We knew the Russians would say we did this terrible thing. Therefore we decided it would not be reported."

If this story was printed or repeated, it would surely frighten all women and children. While listening, Anna imagined it was her watching the church burn with little Max trapped. A tear went down her cheek as she listened. Oh, she thought, if the Russians make it to here, what will I do? I will have to develop a plan just in case. I have to warn my parents. She did not know at the time just how important these two actions would be.

*****

He saw her the same time she saw him. She smiled first. Eli breathed a little easier. Climbing down the ladder she held out her arms and embraced him. Eli knew at that moment how much of a fool he had been. He should have never done what he did to her. Much less, allow someone else to have her. She felt so good in his arms. She was still beautiful and such a good woman. There was not anyone else in the world like her. Even after all he had done wrong to her she was happy to see him again. Briefly, he began thinking that just maybe, she still loved him.

He now hoped Otto had forgiven him too. He heard Otto and Anna were happy together and if anyone was lucky to have her he was glad it was Otto. She did not even ask him why he had arrived unannounced. She was truly happy to see him. She knew because of his heritage and their bonding he might show up at their doorstep someday and need help. She pulled away from Eli and said, "Otto will be back soon. He just went to get us some lunch, please sit down. You must wait until Otto gets here to tell me everything. Otherwise, you will have to tell it all over again. Instead I will tell you about us."

Looking around as if he were nervous he said, "That would be great, but I think we need to go somewhere out of sight."

Rianna took Eli's hand and nodded. "You are right, follow me."

They went in the back room, sat down close to each other, never letting go of each other's hands. Eli inhaled through his nose, filling his senses with her perfume. It was stimulating. Even after all these years, she still stirred Eli's emotions.

Without missing her chance, she squeezed his hand and blurted out, "Otto and I have a daughter." She smiled larger while adding, "She was named after me except we dropped the first two letters. She is our Anna. She is away at school at The University of Music and Theater in Leipzig. She is doing so well, and prettier than I ever was. We have this little store and a nice little apartment. From the top of our building you can see the mountains of Austria." She said everything so fast Eli was having a hard time keeping up.

Then the bell on the door sounded, breaking the conversation. Smiles went away from them as they listened. Rianna held her finger up to her lips signaling to be quiet. She cracked the door and saw Otto. Rianna was quick to get out the door and greet Otto with, "Guess who from our past has come to visit us. I will give you a hint. All for one and--"

Otto smiled and replied, "And one for all."

Rianna looked deep into Otto's eyes waiting for his reaction. They had talked about their reactions if they should ever see him again. They both had decided it turned out the best for them and no matter what, they still loved him. Even with all his bad traits. She still wasn't sure how he was going to react so she patiently waited.

Stunned and smiling, he asked, "Eli is here?"

"He looks about the same too."

They headed back while holding each other's hands. Otto smiled and offered Eli a big hug. Eli was extremely relieved by Otto's response. Otto looked at Eli's eyes and said, "We will close up shop, take this food home, and celebrate. We have a lot of catching up."

Eli began to say something when both stopped him and said at the same time, "Later."

Otto and Rianna smiled at each other and gave each other a small kiss on the lips. This was a fun ritual they had between them. Whenever they would say the same thing at the same time, they had to give each other a kiss. Not knowing when or how this tradition started didn't matter. It was something they both loved to do.

Otto asked Eli, "Do you know where we live?"

"Yes I went there first. A neighbor across the hall told me where you were."

Otto replied, "Good, you go now and we will follow in about ten minutes." Otto knew there was some serious problem that brought him there and they all needed to be careful from now on. He added, as Eli was about to exit the door, "You need to be careful and limit how much you are seen."

Eli smiled with his usual confidence and said, "I will wait for you at your door upstairs. Do not worry, I am charmed."

Otto shook his head a little and looked at Rianna. She was happy and smiling. Just after Eli was out the door, Otto looked at Rianna and said, "I think we know why he is here and it is fine with me to help him, if it is fine with you?"

Rianna put her arms around him and said, "I love you so much."

Eli placed his hat on his head, tipped mostly across his face to hide as much as possible. It was a cold and drizzly day and that made many of his actions less conspicuous. The few that were outside did not pay any attention to him. He searched for anything unusual as he walked stopping several times to check the reflection in shop windows. Once he dropped a coin on the ground, allowing him to glance behind him as he picked it up. He learned these tricks while in the Army. He wasn't scared, just cautious. He was aware that one simple mistake might cost all three their lives.

As he approached Otto and Riana's building, he looked around. It appeared safe, and he quickly ducked inside. He watched the outside from the darkened hallway just in case. He breathed a small sigh of relief and quietly headed upstairs. He waited downstairs in the shadows for Otto and Rianna to show up. Time seemed to slow down, allowing him to ponder. He had told them that he would wait by their door. After thinking about it, he decided maybe that was not such a good idea. If that neighbor was to see him hanging around their door that might be a bad thing, so he changed his plan.

Otto and Rianna briskly walked home. Occasionally one of them looked around just in case. They were bundled up in their usual hats and coats keeping themselves warm and dry. They always walked together hand in hand or her on his arm as he preferred. He always felt special holding her. They meant the world to each other.

They entered their building and checked behind them, same as Eli. After determining, everything was fine they checked their mailbox and headed toward the stairs. Eli suddenly stepped out of the shadows slightly startling them. All three chuckled, breaking the tension. Rianna whispered to Eli, "We need to be quiet, we have nosey neighbors. The one you already met is the worst. We will go ahead of you and if she does not open her door, you rush inside. If she opens her door, you stay out of view and wait. We will talk to her until she closes her door."

They slowly made their way up the stairs. All their hearts were beating hard with excitement. It was so quiet they believed someone surely could hear their hearts beating. Quietly, Otto slid the key in the door and slowly opened it, ushering Rianna and Eli inside. After a glance to make sure everything was safe, he quietly shut the door. Otto held his finger to his lips signaling everyone to remain quiet as he walked across the room and turned on their radio saying, "It is ok to talk now."

Eli was first to start the conversation. "You two look nice together. We all have aged a bit but you two look swell."

"Thanks Eli, we are really enjoying our lives now," Otto said.

Rianna returned with three sandwiches as fast as she could, not wanting to miss anything.

Eli devoured his sandwich fast, not realizing he didn't thank Rianna. Rianna smiled at Eli and asked, "Been a while since you have eaten Eli?"

Eli wiped his mouth. "I am so sorry. Yes it has and I was starving. When I left all I took was a little money and these clothes. If I had planned it better, I would have at least brought some food. Whenever I hurry, I seem to make mistakes."

Rianna sat down and looking directly at Eli said, "I'll bet there was a woman involved."

Eli took a deep breath, smiled at both and replied, "You know me so well. I will tell you two the whole story later. Boy is it a good one too. Someday I will write it all down as a book."

Otto spoke up, "Before you tell us, I need to ask you several questions."

Otto had Eli's complete attention and replied, "Sure thing, but remember you might not like the answers. However, I promise you I will tell you everything."

Otto got right to the point, "Are you wanted by the police or Gestapo?"

Eli said, "Yes, I think so."

"Do they know you were headed here?"

"Absolutely not," Eli quipped.

"Do you think there is any trail that could be followed that would lead them here? Letters or notes you left behind? Something you may have said about us to anyone?"

"Nothing I can think of."

Rianna interrupted, "We have a daughter and one of the reasons we came here was to protect her. We will help you any way we can without endangering her."

Eli, with a cocky smile, replied, "Of course not, we are family."

"I am glad we got that out of the way." Otto said as he sat down anticipating a new and exciting story, "Now tell us everything."

Eli took a sip of water, sled his hands together as if rolling something between them and said, "As you both know, I love women. One of you, sometime long ago said it would probably be the death of me and most likely it will." Pointing a finger upward he added, "Just not yet."

Otto and Rianna sat back making themselves more comfortable and listened. Eli looked sad, "After we separated I went away with her." Eli did not want to say her name. Both knew he was talking about the other woman. "We traveled all over our country. She had plenty of money and we did anything and everything we wanted. She bought us a beautiful little house just on the outskirts of Berlin. There were bars everywhere with American themes. One such place called Gangsters. They had posters of Al Capone and Machine Gun Kelly. We frequented all of those nightclubs several times every week. We saw every play and movie possible. Several stage acts were topless. It was so much fun every night."

Realizing Eli's water was empty, Rianna asked, "Need more water?"

Eli smiled and replied, "Yes, thank you."

Waiting for Rianna to return, he said something that upset Otto. "Then there are the new laws concerning us Jews."

Otto quickly stood up and said, "Don't say us Jews. Rianna and I are not and you must never say anything like that again. You must not, ever."

Eli held up one hand knowing he stepped out of line. He lowered his voice and said, "I know what you mean. She was married to me and that makes her tainted too. After today I will never mention it again."

There was an awkward silence. No one seemed to know what to say next. Otto was still mad and Rianna was a little shocked.

Then at the same time Otto and Rianna said, "Go on." Otto smiled as he approached Rianna and softly kissed her. It was just the right thing at that moment, breaking the awkward silence. Turning away from her, Otto looked at Eli and said, "If I were to forget to kiss her she would be mad and this I would not like."

"You know it," Rianna added.

All three laughed. Eli knew it was time to continue, "Everything just seemed perfect. We were having the time of our lives. She was perfect. I was able to tell her anything and everything, so I thought. However, I got a little bored again and it happened. Someone else caught my eye."

Rianna first looked at Otto and then at Eli and said, "This surprised you Eli?"

"I sometimes just do not understand myself. I found this perfect woman and I mess it up again. I just get bored and move on to someone else. I think up until then everything just came too easily to me. It is different now."

Otto and Rianna looked at each other with disbelief at Eli's last words.

"Until then, what do you mean?" asked Otto.

"I had fantastic fake papers. I had her money to play with as I wished. I was well known and admired by many. I didn't have to work. This was everything I had hoped and dreamed." Eli lowered his head and wiped a tear from his eye and then added, "She told me to get out. She told me to leave Berlin and never come back. That was her town. She told me if she ever even saw me again she would turn me in, fake papers and all."

Rianna, with her voice shaking a little asked, "Did you ever tell her about us?"

Eli said, "I am sure I did in the beginning of the relationship. Not much I'm sure, I did not want to tell her what I did to you both. She has difficulty remembering details and gets details mixed up a lot. I am sure I never mentioned where you two are so don't worry about her. We will be fine. I am sure."

Otto asked Eli, "How long ago did this happen."

"About, a year ago," Eli replied.

"The Gestapo and police are smarter than some give credit and we must not underestimate them. Please go on Eli," Otto insisted.

Eli sipped a little water to help his parched lips. "I left Berlin that day and went to Düsseldorf. I knew several friends living there and knew they would let me stay with them for a while. I was afraid to get work with my fake papers in case she had changed her mind and already turned me in. I just didn't have any other choices. I chanced it and found work. Factories are working around the clock turning out materials. Mostly war materials, and as long as you have proper papers, you can find work."

Rianna leaned forward and asked Eli, "Then what happened?"

Eli liked her attention and smiling at her said, "I messed up again. Everything was going fine. I worked in the Mercedes factory manufacturing airplane parts. The pay was good. I was still staying with friends and saving most of my money. It had been almost a year and I was in good enough shape to move out and thank them properly for everything they did for me. My papers were up to date and good. She obviously had not reported me earlier."

Otto got up and turned the radio down. He also put his finger in front of his lips and whispered, "I heard something at the door."

He cracked the door open and peeked out. The hallway was empty. He closed the door and looking at them said, "I must be getting a little skittish. I know I heard something. We must always be very careful, no mistakes. We will always have the radio on when we are here, understand?"

Otto turned the radio back up, sat down and lit his pipe as Eli continued. "I told my friends that I would treat them to a show or a ballet and then supper at any place they wished. After the show and dinner, I would take them to the Gangster nightclub to finish off the night. This was going to be a night they would never forget. I needed to get out and have some fun too. I should have chosen a different city. I knew Berlin and wanted to show off, that was my big mistake."

"We watched the opera at The Berlin Opera House and it was magnificent. It was a joint effort with Adolph Karajan and The University of Music and Theater in Leipzig. The music was a rendition of Wolfgang Mozart's 40th. Although his 40th had only four string instruments, the school brought in an entire orchestra and added their own mix." Eli took a sip and returned to his story. "It was wonderful. It made me forget for a moment that we were a country at war, although the theater was full of men in their uniforms. I have to tell you, I was brash and daring. My papers passed inspections several times without any problems. I had total confidence with them. They were that good. It even listed my occupation as an actor. Several times when questioned, I saw their curiosity. I even had one ask for my autograph. I had to become well versed in what was playing so I could lie when questioned. I liked the attention."

Rianna leaned forward with excitement and interrupted, "We know someone at that school. Sorry, please tell us more."

Eli took another sip from his drink. "There was this piano player that really caught my eye. She was in the darkened orchestra area. I just could not get my eyes off her. She was wearing this long black dress with her hair up, she was stunningly beautiful."

Rianna leaned forward again and asked, "If they were in a darkened area, how was it that you could see her?"

"We didn't have the best seats. We were up high in the balcony and off to the left allowing a perfect view of the orchestra and I brought opera glasses."

Otto looked at Rianna and with a big smile asked Eli to continue. "Go on, we are fascinated."

Eli was delighted they were paying close attention and continued, "The music was better than I could have imagined. I have heard this piece before without the extra instruments but the way they blended the old with the new was exciting."

Almost being rude, Rianna blurted out, "More about the piano player."

Smiling at Riana's excitement, Otto interrupted, "Forgive her, there is more to this story than you know. Please go on."

Returning to his story he said, "She seemed to glide through the music. She never looked at the conductor more than once or twice the entire night. It was obvious she memorized everything and was enjoying everything. She looked up and smiled at me. It had to be too dark to see me but I felt her. My heart stopped for a second. It was at this point I realized I no longer was watching or listening to the opera. She fascinated me. There was just something different about her. I got a weird feeling inside me."

Rianna raised an eyebrow and said, "Some connection other than physical?"

Eli quickly replied, "Yes and I had to meet her. After it was over, I tried to get backstage. I was stopped before I could even get close to her. Maybe someday I will get another chance."

Smiling, Otto said to Eli, "I believe someday you will meet her."

After getting up and passing by Eli to the kitchen, Rianna put her hand on Eli's shoulder and added, "I know you will."

CHAPTER 6

Disillusioned

The Colonel's visits become fewer and fewer as the war continued. Vacations were not allowed for him. The demands by the Fuehrer were too important. The Fuehrer demanded almost all of the Colonel's time and it had almost been a year since his last visit home. By that time Anna and little Max had become family. Mrs. Von Ryan so much enjoyed their company and they did just about everything together, especially what both ladies loved; shopping. Sometimes Anna offered to watch all the children to allow Mrs. Von Ryan personal time, but she was never gone for long. She preferred to stay at home with Anna and the children.

Little Max's bedtime stories were never missed. Anna became very good at making up stories, including scary ones, for the older girls. To them, Anna was another mother never raising her voice in anger to any of the children. She helped tuck the children in every night accompanied by Mrs. Von Ryan, except when the master was home. The adult time was enjoyed so much by both women as they became close friends.

The addition of Anna and little Max eased the missing of the head of the house and father. This particular visit turned out to be the most enlightening of all his visits. He told his wife in confidence a true story about what everyone simply called the Jewish situation. He was very upset with something he witnessed. He needed to confide this to someone, his wife.

The Colonel had only this one-day to visit his family before this emergency meeting with the Fuehrer. He was not informed as to why, only and when and where he was to report. He was distracted by what he had seen and was also worried about this meeting. This extended war was hurting their relationship and he was missing the years seeing his children growing up. Time he would never get back. This war was not what he expected and he was getting very tired. He was also tired of the children just getting to know him again and then leave, time after time. This was like so many of the other visits, arriving late in the day and leaving early the next without much time for his children. Even the children were aware that one day he might never return. There were many people trying to kill him.

That evening all the children were sent to bed early. The Colonel was sad. He needed to tell his wife something that was bothering him badly. As Anna heard their voices coming from the vent she crawled silently on the floor and put an ear to the vent and began listening.

*****

Eli sat up excitedly and said, "We went to eat after the opera."

Rianna winked at Otto. "I will bet that woman was there wasn't she?"

Eli lowered his head saying, "Yes. I just didn't think about her or realize all the terrible consequences if I ran into her. I saw her at the same time she saw me. She never took her eyes off me as she walked over. She said only one thing. "I told you never to come here again, this is my town. I am reporting you tomorrow morning and everything I know about you. You have until the morning as a head start. Then she just walked away. She was cold and precise. I knew she meant every word. I just stood there frozen as I watched her walk away."

Otto gently asked, "Then you just left and headed here?"

"Yes," replied Eli.

Looking intently at Eli, Otto asked him, "What do you plan to do now?"

"I don't know. I was hoping you two would help me. I have no one else to turn to." He gave Rianna his sad look.

As a slide remark Otto muttered, "Burned a few bridges huh?"

Eli, acting as if he did not hear him said, "I figured that if you couldn't help me you would know someone who could. If I am caught, I will either be deported to a work camp or shot. You know work camps are not work camps don't you?

Rianna closed her eyes and said softly, "No one ever returns when deported. They leave but never return."

Eli, still looking sad, turned to Otto and asked, "Are you going to help me?"

Otto leaned forward in his chair. "We have already discussed it and we will do whatever we can for you." Speaking to Rianna he added, "I would rather you tell most of our story dear." She smiled back at Otto as he wondered if she was going to tell Eli that Anna was his daughter.

Rianna stood up. "Let me get us all more drinks and I will get started. I will now tell you our story." Rianna winked at Otto and added, "It is going to be most, but not all."

Otto smiled, he knew. She decided for now not to tell Eli. Otto always thought of her as his daughter. He was so proud of her always, pulling out a picture when asked how she was doing. The picture had become tattered and faded by him handling it so much. She was his daughter. He knew Eli should be told someday, not just now. Otto got up to stretch his legs. He placed both his hands on her shoulders and gently squeezed, signaling to her that he was pleased.

"Shortly after you left," she looked at Eli with a disapproving look, making him squirm in his seat. He reacted quickly with that smile she never could resist. "I was hurt bad. I cried for days. Otto was there for me every day. I even thought about ending the misery with suicide, it would have been easier. Otto listened to me. He held me. I needed him. He got me food, cooked, and insisted I eat. He was so sweet. I do not think I would be here today if it were not for him. No, I am sure I would not be here today were it not for him."

Eli was affected by what she had said. With genuine sorrow he looked at Rianna, and then Otto. "Then I am doubly glad he was there for you. Again, to both of you, I'm sorry."

She walked over to Otto and placed herself into his arms. Then, resting her head on his chest, she slowly turned toward Eli and said, "I am sorry Eli. I just love this man so much."

Eli was a little jealous of Otto, now feeling Otto was the lucky one. However, he had a good life so far. He had been so lucky and special having these two lifelong best friends. They had forgiven him again and now risked their lives and future for his safety. For now, he only thought of himself and what he might have to do to survive. Later he would find a way to repay them.

Rianna smiled with pride, as she was getting ready to speak of Anna. "Otto and I have a daughter named Anna."

Otto had to interrupt. "You know it is getting late. We will have a lot of time for catching up later. This is a two-bedroom apartment. We will make you comfortable in the other room."

Rianna lowered her voice to a whisper. "You make yourself happy here. You must be so quiet; the downstairs neighbors can hear footsteps. They know when we are here and when we are not."

Otto stood up and stretched. "We will discuss all things and what we will need to do tomorrow." Then with a twinkle in his eye and sarcasm in his voice, he said, "Remember which room is yours Eli." It felt good to laugh again as all three did with Otto's remark. Eli headed to his room as Otto and Rianna went hand-in-hand into their room for the night.

In the morning over coffee and with the radio on for safety, Rianna continued with their story. "Otto and I started a nice little business selling mostly pots and pans. Sometimes we would take our wares into the country and trade for food. We would return with the food to eat and sell. We preserved jams and jellies for resale. This is what we did week after week, not making a lot of money, but it was a living and we so much enjoyed our trips to the country. It wasn't like work, it was fun. We learned all about preserving and canning food. We would hold them until winter and mark up the price, selling them for a good profit. We needed to make more in the winter as everyone else."

"That was very smart," said Eli.

Rianna took a breath and smiled her sweet smile at Eli. "We thought so too. City folks, for some reason, never seemed to properly prepare for winter."

Otto crossed his legs. Exhaling smoke from his pipe, he added, "Everyone loved her jams and jellies. A few years ago, we got an opportunity to own this little bookstore. It was getting harder and harder for us to make our country excursions, so we decided to try this instead. We still made time to go to the country to trade some and see friends, but not as much as before."

Rianna was quick to add, "We stay out of politics and mind our own business."

Eli lowered his voice as if someone else might overhear him. "When the persecutions became worse, I became an angry person."

She replied, "We are very aware of what is happening. On many trips to the countryside families would have suddenly moved away. Some would stay until we arrived and sell us as much as possible. We would buy whatever we wanted and resell it in our bookstore on the side. We were known for being fair with everyone. We are aware of all the laws, including the ones forbidding Jews and gentiles from mixing. We saw a picture in the paper of a female gentile that was caught mixing with a male Jew. Both were tied up and paraded in public with signs hanging from their necks. The female sign read, "I sleep with nasty and dirty Jews." On the male Jew's sign it read, "I bring women home and give them diseases."

Otto added, "We heard most attempted to make their way to Switzerland. Most were going to live with family and friends in other places they believed were safer. We talked about trying to escape to Switzerland with Anna."

Rianna squeezed Eli's shoulder as she was saying, "If we were to take Anna and not manage to make it over the border, well that would be the end of all of us. She does not know of our past, Eli, and I do not want her to ever know."

With his other hand he softly touched her hand reassuringly. . "No, of course not, no one will ever hear of it from me."

It was time to reopen the store so Otto placed his pipe in an ashtray, and stood up, stretching. "Today while we are gone you must not walk around. You must not make any noise at all. People downstairs can hear us walking around. One of us will come back about noon."

Rianna stood up next to Otto getting ready to leave too. "Tomorrow we will get a cat and let the neighbors know. Then you can move around a little. The neighbors will think it is just the cat."

Otto shook Eli's hand and said, "Do not worry, we will think of everything." Otto and Rianna put on their hat and gloves together, with her helping him and him helping her. He lightly tucked her soft bangs under her cap as he gently placed her ears under the hat to keep them warm. She gingerly tied a scarf around his neck and tucked the ends inside his coat. She chuckled, thinking to herself, "If it were Eli, I would tighten it a lot harder."

Eli almost laughed as he watched them dress each other. Otto opened the door for her as he always did and they left. They waited to discuss the problems and solutions until entering their store. He turned and asked her, "Why did you decide not to tell him about Anna?"

Taking off her gloves, she replied, "You are her father and always will be. I just do not think we should tell him yet. He is brash and may do something stupid, like go to see her. He wouldn't keep it a secret; he would have to tell her or someone."

Otto placed his coat next to hers on a rack next to the door. "Yes, I see him doing that and I personally think I do not ever want him to know. I know it is somehow wrong to keep it from him but…." He took a breath and changed the subject, "I think I have a little better plan for where he will stay. He could stay here in the back room. It won't matter if he makes noise during the day, until someone comes in. He could slip in and out through the back door and alleyway if needed. It is dark and hidden from view, perfect, I think."

"It will drive him crazy staying in one place for too long. He will have to get out some, and if we could limit his exposure with him entering and leaving; well, you're right darling, this is a good plan." Rianna placed her small cold hands on his back around his waist and pulled him closer. She stood on her toes and softly placed her lips on his ear and whispered, "If he is caught do you think he would inform on us?"

Otto shivered with her breath in his ear. It felt good. He returned the favor and whispered softly in her ear, "It is possible for anyone to break under torture. In any case we are in too deep already not to help." They then hugged each other tightly.

*****

Eli slipped on a pair of socks and slowly walked across his room. He walked ever so slow as to not make any noise. He told himself, "I must do something to remember where any and all noisemakers are. He started placing convenient objects over every place that started creaking. He decided to leave them there until he knew them all by heart. He knew he should have taken their advice to stay put, but there were things they said that kept spinning in his head.

Getting close to the doorway, there were two spots he had to cover. Eli ripped a small piece of paper in half and placed them over each spot. As he entered the living room he slowly stepped on a spot that started to creak so he froze and reached for a small picture on a shelf. It was a picture of Anna. Eli smiled at the picture. She was very pretty. As he was getting ready to place the picture on the floor he stopped and stared at it. She looked familiar.

He started pondering. "She is attending The University of Music and Theater in Leipzig and is a piano player." He looked at the picture again and smiled; suddenly realizing she was their daughter. "That was what she meant by, there is more to it than you know." He carefully placed the picture back on the shelf, and then found something else for the spot.

Eli decided not to tell them he figured out the puzzle. There will be long days in hiding with plenty of time for small talk. "Maybe they might know how to get me to Austria or Czechoslovakia." He had heard many Jews escaped and lived a better life in both places. He felt it would be better to go there than hide like a frightened little child, and he decided he would ask them when they returned. One of them would come back around noon. He liked the thought of stretching out and moving around without worrying. He wished it to be Rianna. He wanted some alone time with her as soon as possible.

It was Rianna who came back at noon and as she entered, she immediately went to the radio and turned it on. Eli was lying on their couch with his socked feet hanging over the edge and smiling. "I was hoping you would be the one home for lunch."

"Why is that?"

He stuttered with his reply, "I... I... I have missed you."

Rianna placed her coat on their coat rack and smiled to herself. She knew where he was going with this and wanted him to struggle a little. Then she was going to shut him down. She had anticipated this encounter and was ready.

Eli stood up and with outstretched arms said, "You are still so beautiful and I was a fool for leaving you."

Rianna turned away from him as he approached and confidently said, "Yes you were, and thank you for the compliment. Otto and I could not be any happier. You must get any other notions out of your mind immediately."

"I am sorry. I just cannot seem to help myself."

"What else have you been thinking about today?"

"I think I will only stay one or two months. I am sure no one can trace me here, but I shouldn't stay here too long either. I ran into two mutual friends about six months ago, the Klaus'. That's how I found you. Someone else might think as I have."

"We saw them about a year ago. They came over for dinner. We were wondering how you found us."

Eli added, "Like I just said. One, maybe two months at the most. If she has not turned me in, I will be able to use my present papers. You know, she might have been bluffing. I will wait and check them out before I leave."

Rianna sat down in Otto's chair across from him, crossing her pretty legs. Eli tried not to look too long, but he liked how they looked. She didn't sleep well the night before and was tired. "Whatever you decide, we will help you." She inhaled a deep breath then exhaled and with a sigh, stood up heading back to the door to leave. "I must go back to the shop now. Otto and I will talk. I will tell him everything you have said. We have a lot more to talk about tonight."

"Not everything I hope?" replied Ely.

Rianna gave him a disagreeable look as she went to the radio and turned the knob off. Without saying another word she put on her hat, coat, and gloves and rushed out the door.

Eli pondered for a moment, "No noise. No moving around. I will not be able to do this for long. Time to lie down and read."

After Otto helped her off with her coat, he asked her seriously, "Did he flirt with you?"

"Of course, you would not expect anything less of Eli would you?"

They both laughed as Otto placed his warm fingers inside her cold palm to help warm her. "You have always made me so proud to be with you. You let him down easy didn't you?"

Rianna smiled, responding, "He will recover."

"He also told you how beautiful you still are, didn't he?"

She placed his head between her hands and said, "Yes and you are only saying that because you want some affection tonight." They both laughed again while locking the door and briskly headed home arm-in-arm. They could not wait to tell Eli the rest of their story.

*****

Anna put her ear to the vent and started listening intently. Somehow, she knew this was going to be very important for her in the future. The Colonel believed that no matter what he told his wife it would be confidential, and there was no way anyone else could hear. He trusted her with his life. She was the only one he had ever completely trusted. This event only recently happened during his train ride. He was ordered back to Berlin for a round of meetings with Hitler and other important military leaders. The weather was awful, cold rain mixed with snow. The expected forecast was worse; heavy cloud cover and snow to continue for the next several days, so traveling by airplane was out. However, this time he could not wait for the weather to improve. He had to take this train.

His train had to stop and take on water at a remote refueling station. A place for everyone to stretch out, the station consisted of an old warehouse with broken windows and a loading dock large enough for all to stand and relax. There was a water tower and all the typical railroad signs everywhere. While the Colonel's train was stopped, another train heading from Germany toward Poland approached and stopped on parallel tracks. There were dozens and dozens of boxed cattle cars filled with men, women and children, all Jews. He told her he could smell the train even before it stopped.

It was disgusting, smelling of urine, vomit and death. These people were packed in so tight without any spare room to move or sit. Stretched out of every window were people with their bare hands reaching out trying to capture a little snow.

At first when the train pulled up everyone was eerie quiet. The only sound heard was the train as it screeched to a stop and the steam hissed out the sides. No one spoke. They just stared with such sorrow in their darkened eyes. It was evident they were going through an unbelievable experience. There was pain and suffering in the sad eyes.

"Our solders kept eating and drinking in front of these starving people not caring. Suddenly someone started taunting; I don't know who started it. Then someone threw a piece of food at them like at the zoo. It was obvious the food thrown was not meant to be caught; another way of teasing them. They never had a chance. They kept reaching as far outside as they could manage in the futile attempt to catch anything. The men laughed every time someone almost caught some. The scene was horrible. Then the men started yelling obscenities. That's when I should have stopped them." He looked at everything happening, almost not believing it was real. The terrible actions of his fellow soldiers disgusted him. This was not how he had envisioned war or its consequences. This was barbaric, reminding him of what the Russians did in Venders.

He was the highest-ranking officer on the platform and almost ordered the soldiers to be silent. He decided not to intervene, only to watch and learn. He told her, "This is now bothering me. I should have stopped them, it was cruel." He had heard rumors of where the Jews were going and how they were treated. He was beginning to believe these rumors. Some of his confidence and undivided loyalties concerning the war were now being questioned.

Mrs. Von Ryan then told him, "Last week one of neighbors, the Burins, were arrested and taken away; the entire family. They were exposed by the committee on racial purity for having a Jewish ancestor."

"If they were on the same train, I pity them." He continued telling her, "I attempted to view an area called Bergen-Belsen. I heard and didn't believe that this relocation camp was actually a death camp. Unannounced and without orders I was turned away. The Gestapo was in control of the outer area and without special permission, no one is allowed to enter, not even me." He had never been denied access anywhere before. Surprised, he simply left. What he witnessed made him ashamed. These were not the kind of actions he approved of, and if Germany lost again, these atrocities might be their legacy, shaming all Germans. Everyone, including himself, would then be held accountable.

Anna was so quiet, listening to everything. At the end he said something that surprised her. "I don't know what I will do now if I discover Jews in hiding. I am torn apart with emotions. I know my duties and what's expected. However, I'm just not so damn sure of myself anymore."

His wife smiled, and replied, "I know you will find the right thing to do if it should ever happen. I trust you," as she turned the light out and kissed him goodnight.

Anna sat back against the wall exhausted and pale, not believing what she heard. She knew the neighbors too. It was a family of four with two adorable children, a boy six and a girl three. She liked all of them and now knew she would never see them again. She had to tell her parents this immediately.

*****

Soon as Otto and Rianna entered their apartment, Otto went right over to the radio and turned it on. He commented again to Eli, "We must always do that first. Are you going stir crazy yet?"

"Not yet, but give me some time and I will."

Rianna went to the kitchen as Otto sat down, took off his shoes and lit up his pipe. Otto smiled as he looked over his shoulder at Rianna. "Now where were we with our story dear?"

Rianna smiled back at him. "I think we need to tell him who the piano girl was, don't you dear?"

Otto took a big drag on the pipe, exhaled and with a big proud smile said, "That beautiful little girl is our daughter Anna."

Eli faked nearly fainting with surprise, "You have to be kidding. She is just to pretty to be yours Otto."

All three chuckled. Rianna under her breath said, "If you only knew."

Otto leaned forward in his chair. "She is the light of our lives. She is in her last year of studies. She plays the piano as you have seen. She acts in their drama productions and loves it. We have all her letters and if you behave yourself we will let you read some."

Eli sat up on the couch and enthusiastically said, "Oh yea!"

Sensing the excitement in Eli's voice Otto replied, "Remember that is our daughter we are talking about!"

Eli lowered his voice saying, "Boy I am glad I didn't meet her after the ballet. I know me, and I would have made a pass at her; that would have been something for us to laugh about huh?"

Otto quickly said, "No, I do not think I would have been laughing at all." He then sat back in his chair, took another puff on his pipe, leaned forward in his chair and said, "It was because of our past that we moved here. We knew we needed to move away. We decided it was best to get away from Berlin. Too many people knew our past. We now have all the proper papers and so does Anna. If our history together is somehow discovered, well…I do not want to think of the possibilities."

At that moment, Rianna gave Otto a look. A serious, sad expression that suggested that if ever separated from Otto, she would die. Otto saw this and, replied, sadly, "It seems that anyone deported is never seen again."

Rianna sat back down next to Eli, slipping her soft hand inside his boney hand, saying, "We knew we had to go far away. We told whoever we thought should know that Otto's mother was ill and we had to go to help her. To some we just disappeared like so many others. Otto's mother passed away several months ago."

"I am sorry," said Eli.

Otto then added, "We used to love our country too and like you, we do not anymore. We fear loose talk like everyone else. We watch what we say all the time. We even watch to see who is listening. You never know who may hear. It is like living in a fish bowl with everyone watching and waiting to turn someone into the police or Gestapo."

"I feel the same way," said Eli.

"We do not talk about politics with anyone, ever." Otto was quick to say. "We only care about each other and Anna. Rianna tells me you will only stay here for one or two months. Is this what you have decided?"

"Yes, unless something happens to change my mind."

"We have been checked out several times and are accepted. We don't think we will have any problem hiding you," said Rianna.

"We have a plan for you to stay here." Then Otto proceeded to tell Eli their plans for him staying at the store.

*****

The back door and alley could not have been any better for everyone. He was never seen entering or leaving. Getting out every now and then was scary. Yet Eli found the danger refreshing. It broke the everyday monotony of hiding. Sometimes he would take chances by moving from shadow to shadow, walking around the town late at night for no apparent reason except the thrill.

There was a curfew in place so he had to be very careful not to be spotted during those hours. The only people permitted to be out were the police, so getting out and exploring was dangerous and fun at the same time. He liked the excitement.

Sometimes he would visit and stay at the apartment for a day or two, then return to his life of hiding.

Several times a week Army soldiers visiting or stationed close by would come in the shop. As instructed by Otto, Eli would just freeze where he was when he heard the bells. He had to stay still until it was all clear and safe. They never knew when the police or Gestapo would come in and want to inspect every room. Therefore, when the bells would ring there was fear. The tension was something they learned to deal with.

Three times in the last month two Gestapo agents came inside, looked around and bought something. They never seemed to suspect that just a few feet away was Eli. Eli always found this a little amusing, but only after they had left. If they had decided to inspect, all of them would have been caught. In spite of all the danger and risks Otto and Rianna still helped their best friend. As Eli said before, "Two months will be all I can take, I think."

It was now time for Eli to move on. Otto learned that there was a place for Eli not very far away in Czechoslovakia. He found out where Eli could go, and arranged a good contact. Otto discovered there was a priest at this church that had been helping Jews. Some were his previous customers. It meant that Eli would have to be in a war again. It also meant he would be respected rather than simply someone in hiding, waiting for the axe to fall.

The fear of being discovered everyday was driving him crazy. Every time the phone rang, he jumped. The bell at the store was also unnerving. This sound might mean they were coming to arrest him.

There was constant fear. He never saw any fear in Otto and Rianna. They were always amazingly calm, even when the Gestapo entered. He never asked them if they were ever scared. He was a little ashamed and it would have been worse if they were to tell him they were not.

At the same time, two factions within Czechoslovakia were fighting each other, the Serbs and Croatians. The Serbs were accepting Jews willing to fight on their side. No one knew that in less than a year, both sides would set apart most of their differences and band together to fight the invading Germans. Eli had to walk to where he was going. Otto drew a map to help.

It was a simple and easy map to follow. All Eli had to do was stay close to the road and out of site. Leave early in the morning and with luck he would be at the church and within five miles of the border by nightfall. The plan was for Eli to spend the night in or around the church and wait to meet the priest. If he could not find the priest, there was plan B. Plan B was for Eli to follow the railroad tracks until he spotted the border checkpoint. He was then to circle around following the tracks for about one mile. It was well known that this checkpoint was not well guarded and quite easy to evade. After crossing the border, he would be on his own. Otto could not get any more information without raising suspicion.

As Eli packed a small suitcase, he picked up Anna's picture and placed it under some clothes to take with him. He thought about what he was doing, and then he took it out and put it back. With genuine tears in his eyes Eli said, "Thank you so much. I will never be able to thank you enough. I will always be in your debt. I will somehow pay you back for everything you have done for me."

It was now in the upper seventies during the day and mild at night; a good time to travel by foot. Eli took out his papers and held them up in the air and with a deep breath said, "It is time to see if they still work. If I am challenged I will remain calm. I will act like it's no big deal, don't worry."

"You will be fine," said Otto. "You have always had a charmed life and there's no reason to believe that has changed."

"I hope you're right. In any case it was so nice being with you both again."

Otto and Rianna at the same time said, "Us too." Rianna then approached Otto softly placing her arms around him and they kissed.

Eli smiled saying, "That just makes me sick. Just kidding, it is cute. Don't ever stop."

They responded together again, "We won't," then sealed it with a short kiss this time, as if they knew the future.

Eli drew a deep breath as he picked up his suitcase. He took a little longer, hugging Rianna. She felt so good in his arms. He was going to miss her. She smelled so sweet. He absorbed these thoughts and one more. "He was the lucky one, but she was mine for a time."

It was early morning just after daybreak when sneaking away would be easier. It was a good plan and Otto and Rianna were going to miss him. He stood at the door taking in an extra moment to memorize the scene. They were standing together in each other's arms. With one hand on the doorknob, he blew them a kiss with his other hand. He opened the door, peeked out and one more time flashed them a big smile. Then he headed for Czechoslovakia and a new life. At least that was what they thought.

Soon as he left Otto turned toward her and said, "I am glad you decided not to tell him. He would have gone to see her and endangered all of us."

*****

One month later on June 4, 1939, Rianna was so excited to have a new letter from Anna that she pushed the letter in front of Otto's face as soon as he entered. Not looking at the envelope, he turned and as he was hanging up his coat, asked her, "Have you opened it yet?"

"Of course not, we always read them together. It seems so long since we have heard from her."

Otto began reading it out loud:

Dear Momma and Papa,

Everything is fine. I am sorry it has been a while since I have written. I have been very busy. These four years have just gone by so fast. I still love it here.

Our school has been following Adolph Hitler's instructions as he ordered and he is allowing our school to remain open, thank goodness. We must perform a certain amount of times for our troops, but we all like doing that anyway. My school has offered me a minor teaching position after graduation. It does not pay much. I think I will accept it anyway, I can't complain. Drama and music is such a low priority now. I guess I am lucky to be able to stay and have a job here.

I met an old friend of yours the other day, a private in the Army. He seemed a little old to be just a private. He told me he had rejoined to help the fatherland and the Army couldn't win without him. His name was Eli. He was funny.

He was a patient at Berlin Memorial Hospital where we performed. His arm was hurt and in a sling because of some training accident. He said he was fine and simply convalescing. He said he saw me at a ballet two years ago and told you when he visited. That is when he found out I was your daughter. He stayed a little after the show to talk to me. It was real nice to meet someone you two have known all these years. I was able to tell him all about Max. In fact, when I started I could not stop talking.

Max asked me to marry him and I said yes. We are letting his mother plan the wedding and she has set the date for August first. I so hope to see you then. You just have to get away for me. Even though Max and I have just met, I know he is the one. I can't wait for you two to meet him.

As I have told you before, he is so tall and handsome. The feelings I am having, I have never had before. I know I have fallen in what everyone calls love. When I look at us together, it reminds me so much of you. We are so happy. I miss being with him, even if it is just for one day. Is that how it is for you?

I am a little afraid for him. He is not afraid at all. He is so brave. He is going to make the Army his career and with the way things are headed… I have this fear I may lose him. He repeatedly has told me not to worry. I try to put on a brave face, but I am still scared.

I have to go now. I have several important things to tell you later. Please write soon. I so enjoy hearing from you too.

Love,

Anna

Otto placed her letter on his chest. "Our little girl is getting married."

Rianna snatched the letter off his chest and said, "Well, we now know Eli is still alive. He must have headed there as soon as he left."

Otto said, "I thought he was really going to Czechoslovakia. He fooled me again."

As Rianna inspected the letter again she said, "She sounds so happy. I think this young lieutenant is going to be good for her."

Otto puffed his chest out with pride said, "Of course we will attend the wedding. It would be too suspicious for us not to be there. We will have to be careful, stay for a short time only and go nowhere else."

Rianna walked over and lovingly placed herself in Otto's lap. "I know it may be a little dangerous." She smiled at him knowing that would be all that was needed, and said, "You are right; we have to go and see our little Anna get married. We will be fine."

Otto winked and, hugged her a little and said, "I agree."

With a puzzled look she re-examined the letter and asked Otto, "Eli somehow went back in the Army?"

Otto smiled and replied, "Not likely, he must have come up with hospital papers, put his arm in a sling and walked in the hospital. Knowing him, he probably put tomato stains on the bandage for effect, and to get sympathy from some nice-looking nurse. I will give him credit, he has always had guts. Sometimes I think no matter what happens to him he believes he is charmed."

Rianna jumped off his lap and went to the drawer as she excitedly searched for paper and pencil. "We must sit down and write her right now."

Otto and Rianna went to the wedding and that was when and where they met Elsa. It was also the beginning of Elsa's quest against Anna. Anna was very intelligent and strong-willed. She needed these traits and more to survive.

*****

Otto and Rianna were relaxing in their living room. Rianna was on the couch under some quilted blankets to stay warm while knitting. Otto was sitting comfortably in his favorite chair with a newspaper in his lap. He was in his pajamas and the corncob pipe that Eli had given him was lit in an ashtray.

"Winter lasted so long. I am glad Spring has finally arrived," said Rianna.

"This has been a long one," replied Otto. Then, barely audible, were three soft taps at their door. Both Otto and Rianna stopped what they were doing and listened. They heard it again; a faint tap, tap and one more tap. Someone was outside. It was about eleven o'clock at night - way past the mandatory curfew.

Otto whispered to her, "Rianna dear, did you hear that?"

"Yes." Rianna whispered back.

Rianna put down her knitting as Otto stood up and slowly walked over to the door. He put his ear to the door and listened. He turned around, looked at Rianna, and shrugged his shoulders as if to say he did not know what to do next. She waved her hands in the motion to open the door. He quietly cracked open the door open and there stood Eli, leaning against the wall, pale and wounded. Quietly Otto put his arms around Eli and helped him inside.

He was a mess with mud and blood all over his Czechoslovakian soldier's uniform. Rianna rushed over with blankets as Otto helped Eli to their couch. Both looking down at him Otto looked seriously at Rianna and went right to work, saying, "The dirt and mud has to be cleaned first. Then we will redress his wounds."

It had been years since he had to use his Army medical training. Rianna quickly adjusted the blankets over his legs to help warm and comfort him as Otto worked. Eli was shivering violently. Otto's voice was steady and firm. "You warm up his hands and feet."

Rianna smiled at Otto and in a loving, soft tone said, "Yes dear."

Even after all their years together Otto still sometimes surprised her. At first glance it appeared that Eli was shot twice; once in his hip and the other in his arm. The hip wound was the worst. Otto tipped him on his side noticing no exit wound. The bullet was still inside, having shattered part of his pelvic bone. In spite of all the pain, he somehow found the strength to walk and climb the stairs.

After further inspection, he realized the other wound was not from a bullet, it was a puncture wound made by a knife or dagger. It was obvious he had been in hand-to-hand combat. Sometime while Otto and Rianna were working on him, Eli settled down and the shivering from earlier disappeared as he fell into a deep sleep. He was breathing very low and shallow, as though barely alive. Rianna placed her ear close to his mouth to be sure. She felt his light breath and heard a light snore.

After looking up, she whispered, "This is good."

As Otto finished, Rianna quickly placed two more blankets over him. As they looked down at Eli as he lay wounded and helpless, Otto said, "One of us will have to be awake and watch him all night. We will have to make sure he does not make any more noise."

Rianna placed a hand on Eli's shoulder. "I don't think we should move him to the other room. He needs to stay right where he is for now."

"We will do four-hour shifts. Do you want to go first or second?" Otto said as he yawned.

Knowing how tired Otto was, Rianna replied, "I couldn't go to sleep now if I wanted to. You sleep first dear."

"Ok, if you insist. If you feel you are going to fall asleep before the four hours is up, then wake me."

"I hope he was not seen getting here. You better check the hallway for blood and mud before you lay down dear."

"Good thinking."

Otto was proud of Rianna for keeping her wits. He quietly opened their door inspecting everything. Carefully he went down the steps inspecting every inch of the steps and wall. Eli had not left any bad signs inside. He did not dare open the outer door at this time of night. It was too risky. He would have to check outside areas very early in the morning.

But this was a bad decision. He should not have waited.

There was a bloody handprint on the bricks outside.

*****

On the same day, Anna was at the Von Ryan's home. It was only three days before Mika and Mina's arrival. It was also close to little Max's fifth birthday. The entire Von Ryan family was planning a big surprise party. The Colonel had requested and received special leave for that time. He was still a shy child except when around Anna and the other children. Teaching little Max was easy. She rarely had to tell him twice about anything. He was very smart for his age. He remembered almost everything he saw and heard. Anna was proud of him. Every day with him was a delight. Each night, she could hardly wait to wake up and spend the next day with him.

His grandmother Elsa liked spending time with little Max too. However, Anna did not like the way her mother-in-law hated people of Jewish descent. She wished to protect Max as much as possible from her, so she limited her son's exposure. Instead of telling Elsa the truth, Anna just decided to limit the amount of time Max spent with her.

Elsa knew Anna was restricting her time with Max. This was another reason Elsa hated her. She had not forgiven Anna for stealing her son's time from her and what happened immediately following his death. Anna had complete control of little Max which infuriated Elsa even more. Anna and Max were protected from Elsa while they lived in their privileged home.

On the Colonel's last visit, she had heard him privately tell his wife the war was being lost. He told her more than likely it would not last until March. He was wrong. It was April and was still going on. The newspapers never said such things. They always said they were winning. She knew better and feared the Russians. She knew this knowledge might be critical to their survival. She began developing a backup plan should the Russians capture Berlin. The bombing raids were steadily increasing and sometimes happened in their part of town. They had a safe place to hide when the alarms sounded. It was a well-stocked basement with soundproofing.

She took great care in telling her parents all the information she learned, especially after she received a disturbing letter from her parents back in 1939. The letter informed her that if she were to see Eli again, not to stay around him and certainly not to trust him. They were old friends but he was dangerous. She knew there was more that her parents just wouldn't tell her. There had been hints on her wedding day that seemed like warnings about a deep, dark family secret.

Just what was all this about?

CHAPTER 7

Turn of Events

Eli awoke the next day, April 25, 1945, without knowing there were only seven days left until the end of the war. When he woke, he could barely move. He was so sore that moving even a little hurt. The warmth under the blankets was comforting and he stayed as still as he dared. It seemed very long since he was this warm. He had been cold every day for as long as he could remember and it felt good to be home again. He looked up and saw Rianna asleep in a chair next to him. She was his pretty little angel.

The bleeding had stopped and he looked better than just a few hours before. Otto had left for work without waking her. Eli and Rianna were sound asleep and he knew they would be fine that way. She had tried to stay up all night, but couldn't help falling asleep.

Eli decided to wake her up by asking, "How long have I been here?" As she woke, she smiled and stretched out her arms yawning. Looking at her in admiration and smelling her perfume was intoxicating. It was the same brand as when he left years before. He did not know if it was his wounds or Rianna that was making his head spin, but he was suddenly lightheaded.

Rianna stood up and replied, "You just got here last night. Otto must be at the store."

Eli grimaced with pain as he shifted his weight. He wanted to get more comfortable. Then he asked her, "How bad is my hip?"

"You are going to have to deal with a lot of pain if the bullet…" She stopped herself then decided to add, "You are going to have to see a doctor and have it removed soon. As long you don't get an infection I think you will recover fine. Otto and I were wondering. Were you running away when you were shot?"

Eli giggled and replied, "I knew Otto was going to have some joke about that for sure. However, let me make this perfectly clear. We were ordered to retreat and we all did; as fast as we could run. I was hit and my leg just gave way. A German Soldier then tried to stab me in the chest with his bayonet. I turned and he missed my chest and hit my arm. I didn't feel it till later until I had a moment to relax. Then the pain from both hurt badly. A comrade of mine shot the Soldier, picked me up over his shoulder and ran. He also helped me get here. He dropped me off at the edge of town. I walked the rest of the way. I didn't want to expose you as much as possible. I didn't tell him anything except where to take me. I certainly did not want him to know where I would be in case he was caught. I swear this is the truth." Changing the subject he quickly asked her, "Did your daughter tell you I saw and talked to her?"

"She sure did. When we read it, we thought you were crazy. However maybe crazy is what has kept you alive this long?"

"Let me tell you Rianna, she was lovely. She captivated all the men, and I do mean all. I can see why you two are so proud of her. It is not just her looks. It is everything about her."

"We know," said Rianna.

Eli almost interrupted her as he continued. "She is so talented too. There is just something so nice about her. She bounces around with so much energy and joy. I got tired just watching her."

"She gets that from me."

"Yes, I can see that. Especially her beauty," As he said that he watched her for a positive response.

Rianna left the comment alone and simply said, "Please go on."

"When I left you, I heard that her school was going to The Memorial Hospital of Berlin to perform for the patients. I don't know why I just had to try to see her one more time. I didn't think I would ever get another chance."

"So you put a sling on and faked an injury?"

Eli smiled and said, "Otto told you, he knows me so well. He was right. I knew if I looked like a wounded Soldier especially a lowly private, I would be able to blend in. I would never be challenged as long as I kept what some call a low profile. I made up a hospital pass. That was easy. Their security is almost nonexistent. Everyone wants out of the hospital not in." Then he laughed a little until he hurt.

Rianna smiled at him and said, "You will never change."

Eli liked her smile. He smiled back at her and said, "We even got a chance to talk a little. She is smitten you know?"

"Yes we knew. They got married. He was the son of a World War I ace pilot who died at the end of the other war. His mother is quite well known."

Eli looked puzzled and asked, "You just said he *was*?"

Rianna sat down and with an expression of sadness said, "Ann's husband was killed right after they were married."

Eli lowered his voice with respect and said, "I am sorry. When she talked about him she would just light up. It reminded me of when you used to talk about me."

"Thank you" she replied.

"I swear I did not tell her anything about us. Except we were old friends and I visited you two here."

"Good, please go on."

"I told her how proud you were of her."

"Thank you Eli but she knows that."

"What is she up to now?

Rianna covered him up with another blanket saying, "We need to wait for Otto to come home. He will want to be in this conversation." She paused a moment then cautiously asked, "Do you think you were seen coming here?"

117

"No, I do not think so. I was slow and very careful."

Rianna decided to change the subject and asked him, "If you want to read some of Anna's letters I have them right over here."

Suddenly they heard Otto whistling a tune from outside the door. This was a prearranged signal telling her he was coming up and everything was all right so far. He did not want to startle them by just opening the door as he usually did.

Otto entered their apartment and took off his hat and gloves, but keeping his coat on, as he said, "I can't stay long, I put a sign on the door." He looked worried and added, "This is unusual for us to do."

Eli shifted his weight and asked Otto, "Is there more that you need to tell me?"

Otto came closer to both of them and quietly said, "Yes and it is not good. Extra Army Soldiers have arrived. There are police and Gestapo everywhere. You or your friends must have been seen."

Eli said, "I do not think so. It was dark and we were very careful. I think and hope it is something different."

"Ok, I am all ears, but be quick," said Otto.

"I have been fighting with the Czechs against our own countrymen for some time now. They didn't care that I am Jewish. They only cared about what I knew and that I was willing to fight."

Rianna snapped at Eli. "You must hurry the story up. Time is short."

He was in a lot of pain and had to speak softly, taking breaks. "Germany has lost the war. If it lasts even more than a week or two it would surprise me. My battalion is only ten miles southwest from here. I am part of that unit scouting. German forces will not be able to stop them for long. They plan to take this part of Germany soon. Russians troops are getting closer and closer to Berlin from the east every day. The other allied powers, the Americans and British, are closing in on Berlin from the west. Berlin will be surrounded very soon and then it will all be over. The Army buildup around here is just a response to all this. The Gestapo is here to arrest collaborators. It has nothing to do with me."

Otto and Rianna were quiet and spellbound as they listened.

Eli, talking quickly, said, "Hitler launched a desperate offensive a few months ago. He attacked the allies in the west through the Arden forest, a very unpredictable place. Caught by surprise, many of the Allies' men were killed. The battle could have gone either way. One way was for Hitler's Army to break through the allied lines and create chaos. At the very least they would try to delay the end of this war and an unenviable total defeat. The allied forces would allow us a more dignified surrender and not the unconditional surrender they were demanding. The Russians would not like it, but would have to abide by it too. They want our total humiliation and destruction. You should fear the Russians, I do. It almost worked. The allies fought smart and brave. They found the weakness in Hitler's plan. This weakness was gasoline. They did not have enough to finish the campaign. They were relying on capturing allied reserves. Some German Soldiers were caught stealing gasoline during the campaign, which allowed the Allies to discover the weakness. The allies simply blew up their own reserves of gasoline, forcing the tanks and infantry to stop. Don't you see? We made it. We are alive and the war is so close to being over."

Rianna looked at Otto with new fear and said, "If what he said is true then I am scared Otto. The added troops will surely find him. What will happen if the Czechs attack and take our town? Will it be like Ann's letter?"

Otto went over and put his arms around her as she started to cry.

Looking bewildered Eli said, "What's going on? "Didn't you hear what I was saying? The war is almost over. It does not matter about my unit coming here. The end is here."

Otto without releasing his hold on Rianna looked over her shoulder and said to Eli, "We received a letter a long time ago from Anna. She told us a story she had heard about Russian cruelties. It was a terrible massacre on civilians. This could end up the same way."

Eli said, "Do not worry; if my unit does make it here I will be able to help, and they are nothing like Russians. All of us will be fine."

Otto looked at Rianna and with a re-assuring smile and said, "See, everything will be fine. You will see. I want you to burn all of Anna's letters. Wrap up anything that says Eli was here. It will go with him. I am sorry Eli. We are going to have to move you away from here right after dark."

Rianna broke the hold Otto had on her. She wiped a tear from her eye and asked him, "Where?"

Otto sternly said, "I really do not know, somewhere closer to his unit away from here. It is just too dangerous for him to stay here."

Eli nodded his head in agreement. "I understand. I'll be ready."

Rianna looked worried at Otto. "I don't think he can walk."

"Then I will just have to carry him as far as I can. It can't be helped, Rianna." Usually he would add something like dear or honey. Not this time, he was formal and direct which startled her. Noticing this she began to shake with fear again.

Eli said, "It will all work out Rianna, do not worry. Otto knows what he is doing."

Otto put on his hat and coat, looking at Eli sadly as he opened the door. There was a sick feeling in his stomach as he gave Rianna a worried glance; and quietly shut the door behind him. He was in a hurry and heading to open their store and missed it again. When he came home at noon he missed seeing it again. The bloody handprint on the outside door of their building was very visible now in the daylight.

With her small shaking hands, she hurriedly handed him Anna's letters. Well worn and crinkled by reading them over and over she said, "As you read the letters I will burn them immediately. I hate this, but Otto is right."

Eli, looking curiously at one of the envelopes, asked, "The envelope and stationary is from a Colonel Von Ryan, in Berlin." Eli's eyes widened as he read it again. "I think he was the architect of the battle we just talked about."

"Anna works and lives with his family. Oh, we almost forgot to tell you; we now have a grandson." Handing him some more letters, and placing some in the pot to burn, she was talking as fast as she could manage. "She was pregnant with little Max. That is what he is called. He was named after his father."

"I knew she would get married after we talked."

Rianna lowered her voice and sadly said, "He was killed at the beginning of this terrible war and never had a chance to meet him. Anna was able to tell him he would be a father before he died. I think the only thing that held dear Anna together was being pregnant. He is everything to her. She is a wonderful mother. I have a picture. Want to see?"

Eli was reading and not really paying attention, but responded when she stopped and looked at him saying, "Of course."

Rianna stopped talking. She was concentrating on getting the picture out of her purse when a tear formed in her eye. "Ah there it is," She handed him the picture. "We have not been able to go and see him much. Soon, if what you and Anna have said is true, we will make the necessary time happen. I want more time with him. He is so cute and smart."

Surprised, Eli stopped reading. "What has Anna said?"

"She writes us with information she learns from living with the Colonel. He allows her to use his stationery. That way it gets priority and secrecy. She doubts that the letters would ever be opened and checked.

She wrote us about the same battle. "It's here somewhere."

Rianna place a few more letters in the fire and then headed for the kitchen. "I will fix a warm meal and pack as much food as I can for you." She wiped a tear away. Her voice cracked as she was nervous and scared.

Eli quickly read several of Anna's letters, putting them aside for Rianna to burn. "Hurry up. We must burn them all now. Otto will be here soon and we need to be ready."

As she was in the kitchen with her back turned he hid one letter and envelope in his boot. Rianna wiped her face with a towel, turned toward him and asked, "Are you finished?"

Eli finished the last one and after handing it to her said, "Thanks."

Just as she placed the last letter in the fire, they heard police sirens in the distance and looked at each other knowingly. The sirens were getting louder and louder and heading their way.

The cars stopped in front of their building. Almost immediately they heard the noise of feet running up stairs and men yelling. There was banging on doors and screaming. Standing frozen in fear, Rianna couldn't move. With her heart beating fast, she heard what she dreaded. Someone banged hard on her door and yelled, "Open up, schnell, schnell!"

The door burst open and several armed Soldiers pointed their rifles at them, yelling to get down. One Soldier grabbed Rianna by the arm and threw her to the floor. Eli, obviously wounded, just laid there with his arms raised as a Soldier shoved a rifle barrel in his stomach. They quickly searched the other room and discovered Eli's bloody uniform.

The last man that entered appeared to be a Gestapo agent in a usual black trench coat and hat. He smiled at Eli and looked at Rianna on the floor. He was obviously pleased with this capture. "Take them away. The Soldier will go to the S.S. camp to be interrogated and she will go with me."

Otto was in the shop when he heard the sirens. As he listened to the up and down shrill of the sirens coming closer and closer, a sick feeling came over him. He closed his eyes and wished they were not coming for them. Otto went outside as so many other people had done. The cars approached and stopped outside their apartment building as he feared. He stood there numb as he softly said, "Oh my God, no."

Soldiers rushed very quickly out of their vehicles and with their rifles and pistols drawn rushed into their building. Otto slowly started walking toward them as he thought "I have to get to my Rianna. She will be so scared."

As Otto approached the building, Eli was being carried out by two large guards on a stretcher. Rianna followed, being held up by two Soldiers with the Gestapo agent directly behind her. Otto looked at Rianna and she looked back at him. She was pale with fear. Before she could stop him, he stretched out his arms as though offering her a hug and said loud enough so everyone would hear him, "My beloved, I'm here."

The Gestapo agent with a surprised looked on his face waved a guard away allowing Otto to approach and hug her and then said, "Take him too."

Eli was loaded inside the back of a covered truck while Otto and Rianna were shoved inside the Gestapo agent's black car.

Having previously discussed the possibility of being caught and what their responses might have to be, Eli told them he would die first before giving them up. If caught while together they were to forget about him and do whatever was best for each. He told them not to worry about him because he would be killed no matter what they said. These were brave words coming from someone who was not in danger at that time. It was also was not really his personality either. Otto would soon remember as a teenager how he acted when caught.

The Gestapo agent was about fifty. His hat covered his bald head. He wore thick, black rimmed glasses and was about six feet tall with a few extra pounds around his waist. He didn't look menacing, more like a jolly old uncle. His looks were deceiving; he was very intelligent and very dangerous.

In a soft friendly tone he said, "My name is Fritz. We will be talking for the next few days. If you tell me everything, the truth that is, then I will do everything I can to help you both. This doesn't have to be that bad. Do you understand?"

Otto squeezed her hand and asked, "Yes, may I talk to my wife?"

"Yes, but no whispering."

"Thank you." He turned looking at her face and now holding both hands tightly said, "I love you." Until then both were afraid to say anything. Rianna let go with one of her hands and ran her trembling hand down Otto's face as if to trace the outline.

Otto was worried that she was not able to burn the letters in time and Rianna wanted to tell Otto she had burned them all. Neither one wanted to say Anna's name or give the agent any idea to investigate later. The both said at the same time. "Everything is fine." They smiled at each other, leaned forward and kissed.

The agent watched with no emotion not knowing what had transpired. He was hoping to get them somewhat relaxed to get more information. In the past this technique usually worked. They both just sat there looking at each other. All that they cared about, except each other, was safe. They believed they could now handle whatever was to happen. They were wrong.

When asked about their family they had previously decided to tell the authorities they had a daughter that was killed in a bombing raid. There was no one else in their family still alive and time might help their story. For now, they just held each other gazing at each other's eyes as they did the first time they knew they were in love. Tears were in their eyes and one at a time began to fall. At least for now they were together. How much longer, they did not know.

Otto could have run away when he saw them at the building. One side of her wished he had and the other side was so glad he was there comforting her. She knew it just was not in him to run away from her. She should have been mad at him but, she just couldn't be because she loved him so much.

Otto had different dilemmas. He knew they were risking their lives to help Eli. He was the man of the house and could have stopped it many years ago. He could have refused to help years ago. This was also not part of his personality. He had to help his best friend in need. He may have never ever told Rianna no. Hurting her in any way hurt him more. He hoped now more than ever that she would understand and not hate him. He had not fully protected his family and this was his fault. He could not stand up to what may happen next thinking she hated him.

As civilians, Otto and Rianna were in Gestapo custody. Eli, possessing a Czech uniform and wounds, required him to be the property of the S.S. for interrogation. A cover story wasn't discussed due to the lack of time, so now his thoughts raced for some plan, any plan that might help; some believable story to come out of this alive. The end was so near he could almost taste it.

On the stretcher without any padding the bed of the truck was hard and cold. Every time the truck bounced, pain would shoot through his entire body. It was agonizing, pain without end in sight. Trying not to moan increased his suffering. The guards, aware of Eli's predicament, were enjoying his pain; smiling and laughing every time the truck hit something hard. Acknowledging the pain would only make things worse. Both his wounds started bleeding again. Feeling the warmer blood trickling down his leg, Eli thought if this ride continued like this much longer, he would certainly die.

Deciding to pee wasn't a hard decision. It would be warm and they would have to clean it up. It was warm and felt good for the moment, later not so nice. Maybe it would be best to bleed to death here and end this pain. "They may just fix me up and then shoot me anyway. Worse yet, they might torture me," Eli thought.

He had seen some of the past torture techniques firsthand and it was gruesome. People were hung by piano wire with the look on the corpses of such horror and pain. He did not want to go through anything similar. His mind started racing. He needed a plan and soon. He might be the one. The last Soldier killed by the last bullet. The war is lost so why was I captured now? What were they going to do to me, will I survive? What information can I give them so I will make it through the next few weeks? Maybe I can get them to decide to use me somehow.

Eli grimaced with pain as they hit another bump. Plans were now beginning to take shape in his mind. "I could offer to work secretly against the Czechs. They will get whatever information I now have out of me without torture. I will tell them whatever they want to know. This trip is killing me anyway."

Suddenly the truck hit another big bump forcing Eli to cry out. He couldn't hold back anymore. It hurt so much he wanted to cry. As he heard the two Soldiers laughing again; it was time to speak. He surprised them with his German. "If this keeps happening I am going to die. Your commanding officer will be very mad at you. I have information he will want and I am bleeding badly. It's your ass and I do not care about you either."

One of the Soldiers calmly said, "Brassy little bastard isn't he?"

The other replied, "He has nothing to lose now. Should we look?"

They decided one would look while the other pointed their weapon at him with his finger on the trigger in case it was a trick. One guard carefully pulled back the blanket. It was soaked in fresh blood. The guard banged on the back of the truck cab and yelled for the driver to stop. The driver slammed on the brakes abruptly stopping the truck. Thinking something was happening he jumped from the cab, drew his pistol and carefully walked to the back of the truck. As he pulled back the canvas with his luger he said, "What is it?"

"Put the gun down. We have to bandage him better. You must slow down. We need to deliver him alive if possible."

As the driver headed back to the cab, he replaced his pistol in his holster and said loud enough for everyone including Eli to hear, "Fix him today so we can shoot him tomorrow." He slowly pulled away avoiding potholes and bumps.

Eli had made his decision not wanting to die. He was going to do whatever it took to live. He knew he had to think of something new and important. Something so important that time would become his ally not enemy. Investigating takes time. It had to be something making him worth more alive than dead. If the plan was good enough he might even be able to bargain for privileges.

As he shifted his weight he felt the pinching of Anna's envelope in his boot. He felt bad for Otto and Rianna because it was his fault. If he had not come back into their lives, they would not be in this position now. If they had not helped him several years ago he would not have come back now. He also would have died the other day without their help. They bandaged him. They warmed him up. They fed him. They risked their lives. He knew they would die soon. They were caught helping an enemy Soldier; a terrible crime. What a shame if they were the last victims of this terrible war. What could they offer the authorities to delay their end, nothing!

The worst thing for them wasn't dying. It was being separated. They would not survive being apart. They only have one heart, each one believing the other one has that heart. They will stop eating and caring about anything if not together. Even the thought of Anna and little Max would not be enough to help either one survive. There would be no reason to torture them. They have nothing to offer. The brakes on the truck squealed as they slowed down to a stop.

"Now I guess it is my turn," Eli whispered to himself. The two Soldiers opened the back tailgate and stepped out. They saluted an officer and started talking. They held their voices low so Eli could not hear. Carefully sliding Eli out of the truck they carried him over to a large tent. Inside were rows of neatly tucked-in Army cots. He was carefully placed stretcher and all, on one of these cots.

As the medical doctor came inside the Soldiers all stepped aside. Without saying a word the doctor cut away the arm bandage and lifted away his hip bandage. It was warm in the tent. A potbellied stove burning hot was in the corner about 10 meters away.

The doctor's white coat, fresh with bloodstains, hung over Eli. He was a major and about sixty with silver hair. He went about his work as a real professional always doing his best to help. Eli watched him, and secretly hoped they had something in common, asked the doctor, "How long have you been a doctor?"

One of the Soldiers lowered his rifle and sharply said, "Shut up."

The doctor stopped working, stood up straight and stared at the Soldier. Taking in a deep breath he said calmly, "You have done your mission well. You may now wait outside while I finish treating this man."

Both Soldiers snapped to attention and stiff-armed the salute saying, "Hail Hitler."

The doctor responded the same way in return, but with a little less enthusiasm as the Soldiers left the tent. He smiled at Eli. "Yes, a very long time. I don't know what you did and I do not care. I will do my best to treat your wounds and heal you."

Not giving up Eli added, "Thanks. I was in World War l also."

The doctor cracked another smile and said, "Ok, and for what side?"

Eli looked seriously at the doctor's eyes, "The losing side - same as you."

Just as the doctor began to speak again, an S.S. Captain came into the tent followed by the two Soldiers the doctor dismissed. The Captain looked angry. "You will only treat his wounds. You will only ask him health questions. These guards will be with him at all times. Do you understand, Major?"

The doctor looked the S.S. Captain in the eyes and said, "Yes sir. I am through with him. He is all yours sir."

The doctor wiped off his hands with a towel, turned and looked at Eli with an expression of pity. The doctor turned around without saying a word and walked out.

The S.S. Captain slowly walked over to Eli's cot with hatred in his eyes. "Let us just review, shall we? You were caught on our territory. You are wounded and out of uniform. You are a spy. Does that about sum it up?"

"No sir."

The Captain replied, "I do not have a lot of time to waste, so I advise you to get to the point and no lies."

*****

To Otto and Rianna the ride seemed to go in slow motion. Their stomachs turned as thoughts of not knowing what was next went through their brains, but they were still together holding each other. As their eyes began filling with tears they occasionally dripped out and down their faces. Otto was trying to be strong for her and she was being strong for him. Rianna knew he was the bravest man in the world. She knew he needed her now. She knew he needed to feel like her brave protector that he had always been.

She did not want him to know many times before she may have been the stronger one. She wanted him to be proud of himself and believe there was nothing he could have done that would have changed this outcome. If she broke down now, he would feel he let her down and failed to protect her. Most anyone seeing the police at their building would have turned and run. She secretly wished he had not been so brave. At least he would be safe. She knew he could not face life knowing he ran away from her when she needed him the most. She took in a deep breath to help her say something without crying. There might not be another chance. "I would not have changed anything with you."

Even though he closed his eyes trying to hold back his tears, it was exactly what he needed to hear. Several tears escaped. Otto was coming to some peace with what was happening. He now will go on to this other life knowing she did not hate him. Somehow together they would watch over Anna and little Max.

The car suddenly stopped. The ride was over as they reached the police station. Politely escorted inside and ordered to sit down, Otto let Rianna sit as he stood still holding her hands. It was a small neat office, one desk, cabinets and papers neatly stacked. A typewriter with family pictures at the edges of the desk was all the décor in the room except a small photograph of Adolf Hitler with his arm raised at a podium on a wall.

The agent sadly said, "You were caught hiding an enemy Soldier. You gave him food, comfort and aid. This is what you are guilty of, and you both will be executed unless there are reasons you want to tell me that might change your destiny."

Otto and Rianna's hearts sank deeply. They knew the possible consequences, but it was different than they had imagined when they heard the words. They squeezed their small hands tightly as Otto's knees went weak. They were exhausted. The agent took a pitcher of water, poured some in a glass, and drank some in front of them and then acting as if he had not noticed them said, "Oh, I am so sorry. You both must be thirsty."

Otto took the glass of water and with shaking hands gave it to her. She held the glass and his hands with her hands and sipped. With parched lips and a whisper she managed, "Now you have some, my darling."

He was not affected by what he was witnessing. He didn't care. All he cared about was information, anything that might be useful for him. Otto and Rianna didn't have a makeup story. Neither one wanted to say anything wrong so they sat there silently.

The agent seemingly tried to help them by asking, "Do either of you two have anything to say in your defense?" The agent was now getting a little frustrated. He wanted to properly finish all required investigation matter and paperwork soon and get home. He was not getting anywhere with this interrogation and wanted to know their connection with the Soldier.

Otto asked, "Is there anything we can say or do to change things?"

"Probably not. But tell me anything that might help and I will see."

The truth wouldn't help. It was just as bad helping Eli hide even if he was not an enemy Soldier. Telling him that Eli was an old friend or Rianna's wouldn't help, only possibly expose Anna and little Max. As they both looked at each other they said, "No."

Smiling at each other they kissed a long kiss of love. It would be their last kiss. As they were lost in the kiss they both heard the rubber stamp hit the desk and the agent handed a piece of paper to a guard saying, "You know what to do."

They rose, and with one guard on each arm, were roughly escorted outside. They were driven away, together.

*****

April 24, 1945

Only eight days until the end of the war

Eli thought about it for a brief moment as he moaned and said, "Boy I hurt. I know what the Russians and Czechs are planning. My unit is poised about ten miles from town on the east. Several of us were sent to scout out the defenses and learn as much as possible and report back. We were to scout around unseen. We were discovered and attacked; that is how I ended up where you caught me. They are planning to attack very soon. It could be as soon as a day or two."

The Captain asked, "What is their strength?"

Eli watched him as he said, "Two thousand men, with artillery and armor."

The Captain leaned forward placed his foot directly in Eli's hip wound and pushed down hard.

Eli yelled in pain, "Damn it! Stop."

The Captain took his foot off Eli allowing him a second to catch his breath. "If you lie to me one more time and or do not have anything better than this you will regret it. You have one minute."

Without saying another word the Captain turned around and walked out of the tent. Eli was in pain and the injuries started bleeding again. Eli laid there just hoping the pain would subside. He knew he better be more careful with his future responses. This Captain is smart. It was a brief minute as the Captain returned and looked at Eli's hip. He lit a cigarette, blew some smoke in Eli's face and said, "It does not look good for you Soldier. Do you have anything you wish to add?"

Eli lowered his head. His bluff had not fooled the Captain, and Eli just said, "No."

The Captain turned around and said to the guards, "He is a spy. Take him out and shoot him. I will do the paperwork."

As he started out of the tent, Eli felt Anna's letter pinch him again, and Eli yelled, "Yes I do. This is really important."

The S.S. Captain stopped, turned around and said to Eli, "You have one chance, make it count."

"There is a Colonel that the Fuehrer has in his confidence with a spy living in his house."

Eli thought "Now I have done it. Otto and Rianna are probably dead anyway so it won't matter to them. I will give them Anna. She means nothing to me except freedom. This will take time to check out. They will have no choice but to see if it is true and give me enough time. He did not even think about little Max. To him she was a pawn, someone not as important as him. She was just another girl caught up in this crazy war so why should her life be worth more than his? It was the only thing he could think of to offer them that might do what he wanted.

The S.S. Captain, a little intrigued, said, "If you are lying I will personally find the right way to make you regret what you have said. Let us begin with the Colonel's name."

Eli in a strong and assertive voice said, "His name is Colonel Von Ryan."

The Captain and guards showed shock on their faces. He was in command of this very battalion. The Captain pulled out his pistol, cocked it and then placed the cold steel of the barrel on Eli's head. Pushing hard he pinned Eli's head against the cot. No one in the tent dared to breathe. There was only silence. Everyone expected the next sound to be the bang of the weapon. Eli closed his eyes and for the first time ever tried to pray. The Captain pulled the gun away and stepped on Eli's hip again. "Prove it right now or die."

Eli in pain screamed, "We were burning her letters when you caught us. There is one I put in my boot."

The Captain took his foot off Eli, holstered his Luger while reaching inside Eli's boot. Carefully pulling out the envelope he noticed it was the Colonel's stationery. He slowly took out the letter, unfolded it, and began reading. Eli thought he had hidden the letter describing the battle, he was wrong. The Captain read it and said, "There is nothing incriminating. Nothing to suggest you are telling the truth."

"Doesn't it have some military information?"

"No."

"Don't you see the address? You can go back to the apartment and retrieve more. There has to be something left. You will want to check out what I am saying. There is a spy in the Colonel's home costing you lives." He was screaming this at the same time winching in pain.

The Captain refolded the letter, placed it carefully in its envelope and in a soft tone asked Eli, "What do you want for this information?"

Eli was well aware that he might be tortured for this information. Instead the Captain asked what he wanted. This was a glimmer of hope in spite of his condition. Fearful his wounds might kill him soon, it was time to bargain. "I have given this a lot of thought and I want something I know you can give."

"Go on."

"All I want is to be allowed to go to a prisoner of war camp without anyone knowing what I have done and proper medical treatment."

"If I want I could make that happen." Then the Captain turned around and ordered a guard to go get the doctor. As the doctor entered the tent, he immediately went over to Eli and started treating his wounds again. The Captain took the doctor to the side and told him to keep him alive at all cost. "We have to go and check something. You have your orders, do you understand?"

"Yes sir," said the doctor, "Perfectly."

The S.S. Captain left the tent leaving his two guards to watch over Eli. Eli took a breath and relaxed as the doctor worked on him. After the doctor left he looked upward and said something no one could hear, "I am sorry. I had to do it. I had too." He quickly fell asleep.

The S.S. Captain took three men with him and went back to Rianna and Otto's apartment. It was in shambles Clothes, books, and items cluttered the floor. The beds were flipped over. The pot with burned items was still next to the couch just as his prisoner had stated. After poking inside the pot he saw that all was destroyed. There was nothing collaborating Eli's story.

His men carefully searched as the Captain stepped on a framed picture breaking the glass. He removed the picture. It was the picture of Anna. He studied it carefully and then to one of his men said, "This is probably her, if his story is true. She is very pretty."

One of the guards found Otto and Rianna's papers and handed them to the Captain. As he studied the pictures, he remarked to his guards. "They look familiar."

One of his men replied, "They own the little book store at the end of the street."

"We will go there next." They took out several boxes and placed them in their truck and headed down the street to the store. The door was partly open with a small amount of money in a cash drawer. The Captain grabbed the cash and scooped up the change placing all in his coat pocket. They searched the entire store including the back room. There were many possible hiding places so they knocked books off shelves and pulled down shelves in their search.

In a desk drawer in the back room the Captain found Otto's old military papers with his citations and medals for bravery in combat. Otto was modest about his Army days, even with Rianna. All these credentials were in perfect order wrapped up neatly as though not touched in years. He placed all the documents in a box. Then he discovered their photograph. It was the three of them smiling and standing together as the three musketeers with both men in their uniforms.

"They must have been old friends from long ago." The Captain said aloud. Then he placed the photo in the box. "We will take all these things as they may be useful. Leave the door open for the looters. It is what they deserve. They won't be back."

When they returned to camp the Captain carried the box straight to his tent. It was ten feet by ten feet with two desks, four chairs, and his sleeping cot. The smaller desk was for his much-needed aid and assistant, a Sergeant.

He saluted as soon as the Captain entered and said, "You look tired. May I fix you something, sir?"

"No thanks. Please see to the unloading and storage of the items we brought back. I will send for you later. You are dismissed."

"Yes sir," was his reply as he clicked his heels together and smartly turned around.

The Captain needed a few minutes to think and study the items. He had custody of an enemy Soldier with valuable information of a different kind and who was now his problem. His prisoner was not just a simple soldier captured in battle. He needed to find out everything he could and fast. After restudying all of the documents and pictures, he called in the Sergeant. He was a wry Sergeant in his middle fifties who was recently allowed to re-enter the Army because of his past experience. The S.S. Captain had personally scouted hundreds of personnel files looking for just the right aid until finding this man. They were a perfect match from the beginning. The candidate had all of the proper discipline and disposition the Captain needed.

The Sergeant entered the tent, stood at attention with a military salute, and patiently waited for a response from the Captain. The Captain smiled, lowered his voice, saluted and said, "At ease. I need your help on this one Sergeant."

The Sergeant quickly replied, "Whatever you need Captain."

"This is a real difficult one for me. I am just not sure what the manuals and memos say said about something like this."

The Sergeant knew this would take a while and offered to retrieve something to eat and drink. The Captain inhaled deeply, sat back in his chair replying "Coffee, a whole pot. We are going to need it."

The Sergeant left and the Captain heard him issuing these orders. "We need a large pot of coffee. We are not to be disturbed after delivery. I want a guard on duty outside our tent and no one is to be allowed to interrupt or listen, understood?"

The Captain liked how the Sergeant knew just what to do all the time. He took care of all the details and this allowed the Captain to command so much easier. A guard returned with the coffee and immediately left. The Captain took a sip and said, "The prisoner is a Czech Soldier. He is also an ex-German Soldier."

He handed the Sergeant the photograph with Eli, Otto and Rianna. "This alone makes him my prisoner. However, he has told me an amazing story that may change everything. He says there is a spy in the house of one of our high-ranking commanders. That might make him a Gestapo prisoner and take away our control." As he handed the picture of Anna to the Sergeant he said, "This is probably the spy and likely the daughter of the other two. I do not want to start an investigation on one of commanders and friend from just his word. My honor and duty dictates… well I am just not sure."

The Sergeant looked at the Captain. "You said a friend, sir?"

Leaning closer to the Sergeant he softly said, "Colonel Von Ryan."

The Sergeant looked pale when he heard the name. He knew him too.

"Do I investigate on my own or make an immediate call to the Gestapo? I feel I have to do something to help our Colonel and not just turn this over and walk away. I do not know exactly what to do and I hate this indecision. What I am going to need from you are copies of the regulations dictating what I am ordered to do and what alternatives I may have?"

The Sergeant stood up, saluted and said, "I will have your answers right away, sir."

The Captain saluted back. "Thank you very much, Sergeant."

It took the Sergeant about one hour to find all of the information. He was not smiling when he re-entered the Captain's tent. Standing formally at attention, the Sergeant held the papers under his arm as he saluted.

The Captain returned the salute asking, "What do you have for me, Sergeant?"

"Not good Captain. He would be all ours to do as we wish except…" The Captain paused, "Except there is a conflict. There must be an investigation of one of my superiors and it can't be conducted by me, correct?"

"Yes sir. He is supposed to be turned over to the Gestapo immediately."

The Captain took a deep breath and said, "We will do as regulations dictates."

"There is more, sir. According to regulations, we are to isolate him. He is to have no contact with anyone until a Gestapo agent arrives. The Sergeant leaned forward and whispered, "If I may say something off the record, sir."

"Yes of course, Sergeant."

The Sergeant looked around and still whispering said, "We could shoot him while he was escaping, sir."

The Captain smiled. "With a broken hip, Sergeant, and we need more information too."

"I did not say he would get very far, sir. We could shoot him again in the hip if you like," and with a smug look added, "We could say he grabbed a gun and we had to kill him."

The Captain thought for a couple of seconds and replied, "If the other guards had not heard him I think maybe I would. I owe that to Colonel Von Ryan. Too many heard what he said and if there really is a spy we need to stop her now."

"Want me to make the call, sir."

Reluctantly to respond, the Captain restacked the papers. "I think it had better be me. You need to go secure the prisoner per regulations."

The Sergeant turned around and left in a hurry.

The Sergeant entered Eli's tent still looking mad. Eli looked at him and knew something was wrong. Stopping beside Eli's cot he slowly unbuckled his holster placing his hand on the pistol, and pulled it out, never taking his eyes off of Eli's. With Eli's eyes wide open in sudden fear, everything went to slow motion. The Sergeant pointed the pistol in between his eyes just far enough away so Eli could see the hole at the end of the barrel. He knew the Sergeant was going to pull the trigger and there was nothing he could do. This was the last thing he would ever see. The Sergeant suddenly pushed the pistol back down in the holster and snapping it shut, turned around and snapped orders to the guards as he left.

Eli let out his breath as he escaped death again. He now knew he was going to have more time. The Sergeant would have killed him if allowed. He bought his precious time with Anna and little Max's lives. He lay down and relaxed. The guards were ordered to take up their stations outside the tent. He was not going anywhere. Every time they heard any noise all they had to do was peek inside. They were ordered to stand outside in the cold while the prisoner was warm inside. It didn't seem fair. However, they did not want to be in his boots either.

The Sergeant reentered the Captain's tent after formalities and said, "I have to tell you Captain. I wanted to shoot the bastard and take my chances. I had my hand on my pistol. It would have been so easy."

"I am glad you didn't."

"There is something else bothering me, sir. I cannot stand traitors. He is disgusting. I even think he is a Jew and that his friends probably are too."

The Captain picked up the picture of the three of them. With sudden enlightenment, he said, "Sergeant, I think you have something there. That is why he turned against his own countrymen. They planted this Jewish woman inside our commander's house to spy on him." Without hesitating he picked up the phone and asked for Gestapo headquarters. The same agent that had just interrogated Otto and Rianna answered the phone and took notes as the Captain was talking. His only reply was, "I will be there at 0600 sharp."

The agent quickly ordered a guard to chase down and stop the truck that Otto and Rianna were inside. He did not know if there would be enough time.

After the call the Captain looked at the Sergeant and said, "He will be here at 0600. We will let him handle this matter. I do not know how I can help the Colonel, but I will somehow find a way."

"Sir may I speak freely again."

"Yes, go ahead."

"One of my past commanders is a General Kleist. We became special friends. He has since retired and I trust him completely. I heard he is living in Berlin and I could call or go to him and give him information that would help us. He would know how to handle this problem."

"Let's wait until after we talk to the agent in the morning. I will know what to do by then."

The Sergeant stood at attention and saluted, "Permission to be dismissed, sir."

"Permission granted," The Captain said as he returned the salute.

Giving extra thought as to what was just said made sense. This retired General just might be the person to help. He doused the light and still in full uniform lied down on his cot to think things through. He was exhausted and went to sleep almost immediately.

Eli did not sleep much that night due to pain and guilt. There was no turning back now. He looked down at his hip, the bandage was soaked again. He had done the unthinkable. Now he would have to live knowing what he did. Riana and Otto were the best friends anyone could ask for and she at one time had been his loving wife. And he still loved her. He now thought that if only they had been blessed with children things might have been different. He would have never left her. It was her fault.

His thoughts were relentless: *She had moved on and since made Otto the center of her life. They were even blessed with the addition of a daughter. Why not him? Why did Otto and Riana have to tell me about Anna? If they had not told me, I would have never turned them in. It was destiny that I turn her in and it's their fault. Anyone in my place would do the same thing. I must continue and tell them whatever will help me. I deserve it.*

CHAPTER 8

Five Days Left

At exactly 0600 the next day; April 25, 1945, the Captain, unaware there were only seven days left, exited his car with the crunch of cold ground under his boots. The forecast for the day was cold rain with snow mixed. The Captain had other important things that needed his attention other than Eli. He was anxiously preparing a new battle plan. Something must be done to take the initiative away from his enemies. They were soon to be attacked just as his prisoner had stated, and he certainly did not need added trouble from superior officers or the Gestapo right now. However, he also wanted to find a way to help his commander - somehow.

He knew someone higher up in rank had once indirectly saved his life. His name was the very same Colonel Von Ryan who had personally gone to Adolf Hitler and risked everything by pleading to change a battle plan that Hitler himself devised. This courage was almost unheard of as he tried to convince Hitler that his plan was flawed and slaughter would ensue. There was also no contingency plan, something all proper plans must have. His bravery and knowledge was enough to have Hitler alter the original plans and the inevitable tragedy was averted. The Captain might now have his chance to repay the Colonel.

Escorted directly to the Captain's tent, the agent put up his right arm and said, "Heil Hitler."

He patiently waited for the return salute. The Captain slowly stood up and respectfully returned the gesture. He took off his hat and coat before sitting down, "I do not think I totally understood everything you said on the phone. Would you please brief me before I see the prisoner?"

"Certainly, and as you already know he was captured yesterday with two others. Would you like some coffee?"

"Yes please."

In a louder voice the Captain yelled, "Sergeant, can you come in here please?"

The Sergeant replied, "Yes sir." as he entered the tent.

"We need coffee right away please."

"Yes sir," as he slipped out.

The Captain lit a cigarette sat back in his chair and stalled. He was sizing up the agent until the Sergeant came back with the coffee. As the Sergeant placed the hot coffee on his desk, the Captain smiled and dismissed him.

"Please go on Captain," said the agent.

The Captain took another drag, remembered where he was and replied, "We went back to where they were captured and brought back documents and photographs. What the prisoner has said is very interesting and troubling."

The agent leaned forward taking a sip of coffee and replied. "Go on."

"He is wounded, likely from a skirmish just east of here and he had a Czech uniform. However, I do not believe he is a Czech. I believe he is German Jew." He put out his cigarette and handed the agent the photograph. "This photograph is of him in a German uniform when he was younger. Also in the picture are the two captured with him. They were much younger, but it is them. He has told us there is a spy in the home of one of my commanders. She is his housekeeper. I have a picture of her, I think."

The agent took the picture of Anna and said, "Interesting."

141

"I think they all are Jews," said the Captain.

"Other than his life what else does he want? I am sure he wants something for this information."

The Captain replied, "Just to be sent to a prisoner of war camp. Proper medical treatment and no one to know he was a snitch."

The agent smiled and said, "We will have to see. Not unreasonable requests. Looking at Anna's picture he said slyly, "I want to be the one to interrogate her."

The Captain gave the agent a disapproval look as he said, "That's all I have."

The agent stood up shook his hand and replied, "I will now go and see the prisoner. I don't need you there, I am sure you have more important things to do right now. I will keep you informed as much as possible if you wish."

The Captain wanted to say yes but did not want to appear too interested. Therefore, he replied with, "If you want to keep me updated that would be fine."

"Very well thank you Captain." The agent put on his hat and coat to leave.

When Eli heard the car pull up at 0600, he knew exactly what it meant. It had to be the Gestapo. They had been in the Captain's tent for what seemed to Eli a very long time; allowing Eli to repeatedly go over in his mind what he had said. He knew Anna's fate was now sealed. Now he had to tell everything he knew or they would torture him for the information and grant no privileges. Then in that case, he would be killed. No, he had a chance this way and he would just have to forget about everyone else including the little boy.

The agent entered the tent with two guards and stared at Eli. After a moment he walked over and lifted the blanket to examine the restraints and Eli's wounds. In a low tone he ordered one of the Soldiers guarding Eli, "I want you to go and get the doctor. Looking at the other guard he said, "I want you to remove his restraints and stay. You may relax over there where you can watch and not hear." In a pleasant and reassuring tone, he asked Eli, "At this moment do you need anything else?"

"Yes" replied Eli. "I need a new clean cot and a bed pan. I have messed this one up and I need to relieve myself again."

The agent was a professional interrogator. He was going to be careful not miss anything. Eli had no idea how good the agent was at his job. After Eli was refreshed, someone brought warm food for everyone. While Eli was relaxed and eating, the agent began his questioning by asking, "What is your real name? Not the one on your dog tags."

Eli looked at him and thought about lying. The agent had a look that told Eli he had better not. Eli did not want to tell him he had Jewish relatives even though he knew he had to tell him. He reluctantly said, "My name is Eli Swartz." He stopped with that comment and looked at the agent intensely waiting to see his reaction. The agent showed no outward expression at all simply kept taking notes and not bothering to look up. Eli briefly thought, "I might be ok after all."

The agent asked Eli, "Did you know the two that you were captured with?"

Eli replied with, "Yes. What has happed to them?"

The agent showed no emotion when he told Eli, "They have been released. They told us you came into their place last night and held them at gunpoint. They did not have a choice. They said you told him if he told anyone you would kill her and vice versa. We believed them and let them go. Is that what happened?"

Eli dropped his spoon and just stared at the agent. Eli was stunned; they are still alive and free. He suddenly remembered what he told them earlier. That was a good story. Why did I not think of that?"

The agent told him this lie to see his reaction and it worked perfectly. A reaction Eli could not fake. Eli was not aware that it was a ploy. The agent had other surprises. "We will go on now. Why were you fighting for the Czechs?"

All the wind seemed to have been kicked out of Eli. He was numbed by what he just heard. It was totally unexpected. There was not enough time to make up another story. He was trapped by the agent's cunning. He had to reply with the truth, "I am Jewish. I can't work and live here anymore. Germany is no longer my country."

"I understand." said the agent.

The agent decided it was time to tell him how it was going to be and step up the interrogation. This is the point in almost all interrogations that a prisoner might test his captors and try lying. The agent did not want to be chasing lies and wasting time. He knew that he could promise whatever he wanted and not fulfill any of them if he wished. Prisoners almost always trusted their captors. They were wrong. Lowering his voice to a whisper and getting closer to Eli he said, "I have been informed what you have asked for, and I am willing to grant them all to you. There are a few conditions. You will always tell me the whole truth. You will not leave anything out or lie in anyway. You will tell me all the details, even ones you consider minor. If you tell me just one single lie and I will find out, then the deal is off and I will have my pleasure with you as I wish. Do you understand?"

Eli swallowed and said, "Yes sir, I do."

"Good," said the agent as he opened up his briefcase and took out a yellow folder. From the folder he removed a standard form and quickly filled in some lines with his pen and placed it in front of Eli. "This is a standard declaration form. I filled in what you asked for and we agree to your terms, as long as you do as I have told you. It's all up to you, here it is in writing."

Eli smiled, and with some relief and asked him, "Ok, what do we do now,"

"Just sign on the bottom. Then you tell me everything. That is all there is to it."

Eli accepted the pen and unsteady shaking hands made his mark on the document. The agent then placed the paper back inside the folder and back inside his briefcase as if this procedure was official. The agent was clever. Eli now trusted the agent.

Eli shifted his weight making himself more comfortable and started from the very beginning. He was fearful that leaving out anything would void the deal. He also wanted to develop a working relationship with this agent. He might receive extra time and favors helping him survive these terrible circumstances.

He started with his childhood including his connection and friendship with Otto. He told him of his marriage to Rianna. It was easy. All Eli did was tell the absolute truth and included all details. Eli was so wrapped up in tell his story he didn't notice the agent underlined his notes concerning the marriage. Although Eli was obviously telling everything truthfully there was something missing and possibly important. A little detail Eli missed or was not aware. This agent had amazing instincts and insights always digging down deep until he had all the facts.

Eli reached the part where Rianna was burning the letters when the agent stopped him. This was the part he was most interested in and wanted Eli to slow down. He ordered the guard to bring more food and ordered a break. He knew little special favors could reap huge rewards and this prisoner was about to supply him with some. If what he heard was true then this case would be great for his career. He wanted desperately to expose another high-ranking officer of wrongdoings. He had done this following the assassination attempt and enjoyed the accolades. A Colonel with a Jewish spy living in his house would be the golden ring for him. He might finally receive that promotion he had been promised so often. He will make sure everything is iron tight with zero mistakes. One flaw or mistake in this investigation would be disastrous.

Even as smart and cunning as he was, he still wasn't aware that Germany was close to losing the war and very soon he would be a hunted man. His many bad deeds were about to be exposed for the whole world to see and judge; the agent had blinders on when it came to these current events. He believed everything the newspapers printed.

The agent lit a cigarette taking his time thus allowing Eli to finish his meal. He got right to the point asking Eli, "Who does she work for?"

Eli wanted to pay particular attention to the agent's reaction. He put his food tray on the ground, looked him in the eyes and said, "Colonel Von Ryan."

His eyes got bigger and it looked like the agent swallowed his tong. He knew this officer and he knew he would have to be very careful from that moment on. He wanted to get this information down properly as soon as possible. Keeping Eli alive and available was now a priority, just as Eli hoped.

The agent looked at the guard across the room and wondered if heard the Colonel's name. The guard seemed to not be paying any attention; but to be sure the agent looked at the guard in the same tone said, "Guard." The guard did not react. Then he said it again and the guard again showed no reaction.

Eli didn't know what was happening. "What did he do wrong?" He just sat there scared and wondering. The agent turned back toward Eli and placed a hand on Eli's arm. "You have done well today. We will take a break. You will tell no one what we have discussed. Do you understand?"

Startled, Eli replied with, "Yes sir."

The agent stood up, looked over at the guard and in a louder voice said, "I will leave for now." The guard heard this and stood up looking at the agent and Eli. "The prisoner is yours for now. See that he is well taken care of, he is important. No one is permitted to talk to him, do you understand?"

"Yes sir."

The agent exited the tent, entered his automobile, and drove off without discussing anything with the S.S. Captain. He felt everyone may know too much already and details he would not share at this time. He wanted to keep it this way for as long as possible.

After the agent drove away the guard inside asked the other guard to take his place and went directly to the S.S. Captain's tent. After requesting permission to enter, the guard removed his cap and saluted. The Captain returned the salute and said. "Report please."

This guard was handpicked by the Sergeant to be in Eli's tent because he possessed incredible hearing. "I did as instructed. I acted like I could not hear. I heard the entire interrogation sir."

The Captain smiled replying, "I want a complete report in writing ASAP and one copy only. You did very well I am pleased. Now go and write it while it is still fresh in your mind. Leave out nothing and tell no one about this. Dismissed."

Proudly, the guard snapped to attention and said, "As you wish sir!"

The Captain turned to his Sergeant, "I have to go away today for an important meeting. Keep me advised if anything else develops. Be careful what you say to me on the phone, and if it can wait, all the better. I will be back early in the morning."

*****

The Gestapo agent went straight to his office and started making phone calls to get files on everyone involved. He needed all the facts soon as possible. If there was a spy, she must be arrested immediately; lives were at stake. As an agent, he had the power to arrest her without any more information, but the involvement of the Colonel changed things. He had to be careful. He needed to accumulate a full and complete file before exposing anything. If the Colonel were innocent and the agent prematurely jumped to conclusions, in would be dangerous. He had to have patience and do this right. He could wait a day or two for the files to arrive, but not much longer. It may be that she was not a Jew or a spy at all. He needed proof. Accusing the Colonel without proof would certainly mean his death.

While waiting for the phone calls, the agent began dissecting his notes one sentence at a time. There was still a nagging thought that bothered him. Recounting details about Eli, the man, and the woman as he continually went over the facts. The woman was previously married to Eli and she had a daughter who was now forbidden to be contacted by Eli. As he was calling someone requesting Anna's birth certificate, the agent flipped over pages in his notebook and circled a date that Eli provided.

"Now exactly when did he tell me he left his wife?" The agent asked under his breath. He went back to his notes and compared all the dates. It was eight months before she was born. "She has this baby girl eight months after he leaves her. She just takes off with this other man and starts a new life. When the daughter was born, everyone assumed the couple was married and also assumes he is the father. The wife does not have to drive a car and has only the job with the new husband. When she is required to get proper papers, she is able to get them as she wants. She has a new life. Then this Eli shows up in her life and complicates everything." He wrote in his notes to check for an annulment or rarely accepted divorce documents.

The agent began wondering if Eli knew. Obviously, he didn't know and does not know that he may have informed on his own daughter. He suddenly decides that after he is sure Eli has told him everything and he has all the facts, he will then inform him. "The very woman he informed as a spy is his daughter. It will be an extreme pleasure to tell him. It will be fun to tell the rat traitor."

That agent stayed up late answering his phone and assembling the file.

*****

The next morning Eli was pale again and could hardly move. Bleeding off and on through the night drained his strength. Red streaks developed on both wounds during the night, signaling infection. His fever was now very high and climbing. Several times during the night he threw up all his food and was now facing dehydration, delusions and hallucinations.

There was no need for the ropes that now hung from Eli's cot. It was obvious to the Soldiers that Eli wasn't going anywhere on his own. Eli didn't acknowledge the agent when he entered the tent. He just watched him with a thousand mile stare.

The agent pulled a chair closer to Eli and sat down. "We have a lot to discuss today."

Not wanting to move Eli said, "I am ready as I will ever be, sir."

"What was the date you left your wife?"

Eli, noticeably aggravated, told him again.

Flipping the pages in his small notebook he replied, "That is what I have in my notes,"

Eli thought for a second, and then asked, "What is the importance in that, sir?"

"I will get to that in a minute. I have just a few more questions. This girl Anna wrote things she had heard in Colonel Von Ryan's house, right. She then sent letters to your friends telling them, is that correct?"

"Yes," Eli agitatedly answered.

The agent asked another question, "Anything specific that you can remember?"

"One thing only sir, the battle in the Ardennes. I thought I had kept that one, but I was wrong."

"That's good enough. You will get everything you have asked for and more." The agent later wrote in his file that the stupid bastard had not a clue as to what he had done. The agent smiled at Eli and said, "I have something you will be very interested to know and after I tell you this I will leave. You will be transferred to a camp as you have requested. Eli not knowing what was coming smiled back thinking he was going to hear something nice. He was just told he would get everything he asked for. "I will live long enough to see the end of the war. Then I will have a new life. What could be better than that?"

"Anna, the daughter of your wife and the supposed daughter of Otto, will be arrested today." The agent paused; allowing what he just said to sink in.

Eli with a puzzled look asked, "Supposed daughter. What do you mean?"

"Are you an idiot? Did you not think that this girl might be your daughter?"

Eli turned paler as all expression left his face with his mind racing to register everything. Numb, weak, burning with fever and with a cracked voice, he sheepishly mumbled, "Are you saying she is my daughter?"

The agent's smile got bigger. This was a real pleasure. He sat back in his chair lit another cigarette and said, "Yes."

Eli sat there stunned at what he heard. The only thing he could think of to say was, "What proof do you have?"

The agent then said to Eli, "I have her birth date and other information. Believe me she is your daughter."

"No, she can't be."

"Well," added the agent. "Unless before you left your wife, she was having an affair, then Anna is your daughter and the little boy is your grandson. Did you not ask how old she was or when she was born when you visited?"

Eli looked down at the floor. "No, the entire time we were together she wanted a child. She just never got pregnant. At least I thought."

The agent smiled again knowing this was hurting more than any torture. "Your daughter well, I will have fun with her then send her away. Her son will either go with her or be sent to live with a nice loyal German family. In any case you will never get to know them, ever."

Eli's started begging, "Is there anything I can do to help them please, anything?"

With a smug looked on his face he added, "I think you have done enough, don't you?"

Eli's eyes changed from sorrow to anger. His face started turning red with anger. The agent noticed and sat there smiling. "It was not so bad when you thought it was someone else's child and grandson was it? How does it feel? Hurts bad doesn't it? Now don't you go and kill yourself Eli. I will not have the pleasure of informing you what we are doing to them. Of course, it is going to please me to tell them everything and I mean everything you did."

Eli attempted to stand up only to fall off the cot. His legs were weak and the pain in the hip was too severe for him to stand. Not startled in the least, the agent was ready to see the anger and rage building inside Eli. The guard reacted; however, he went over and asked the agent, "Should I pick him up sir?"

"Yes and you do not have to be careful with him. I am done with him." The agent grabbed the guards arm and said, "He is to be sent to a prisoner of war camp in the morning. He is until then still to be isolated. You will have your orders shortly."

"Yes, sir" replied the guard.

Then the agent left the tent, started his car, and drove away.

The guard waited a moment looking down at Eli on the ground, crying and in pain, then spat on him. Picking him up, he roughly dropped Eli on his cot. "Getting what you deserve aren't you?"

The pain was terrible. The emotional pain was worse. He never even suspected that Anna was his daughter. The agent said he was going to tell them everything. It was bad enough to do such a thing to his two best friends. However, to do such a thing to his one and only child was now almost unbearable. Suicide was still an option, but then everything he had done would be for nothing, just as the agent said. As he started rationalizing thoughts, pain and delirium set in. Rational thoughts were now mixed with the irrational: "I will reunite with them if only there was a way to help them now. If they tell anyone what I have done then my life is over. I almost do not even care now. Maybe they will somehow escape and never be told. Then we can be together as a family. This is what I will think of and dream. I will raise little Max better than Anna, Otto, or Rianna would have; and yes it will be even better because of what I had to do."

The S.S. Captain returned to the camp shortly after the agent left, just missing him by a few minutes. Eli was to be transferred the next morning and all the paperwork was all in order. The Gestapo agent was sure he had plenty of time to continue his investigation without any interference. The guards couldn't hear anything. No one was allowed to talk to Eli. All he needed to do was type up his report and go arrest the woman with her little bastard son. He would report his findings early the next morning. It would be up to his superiors to deal with the Colonel and his family.

If the Colonel had known she was Jewish then that alone would mean imprisonment and possible death. The agent was sure he did not know because that would have been really stupid. Eli, her own father, wasn't aware of those facts. However, he had said something that she could hear of military importance and that alone was enough for the firing squad, or suicide demanded by Hitler.

*****

As the Captain returned to the camp, the Sergeant asked, "You look exhausted is everything alright, Captain?"

"No," he replied. "The meeting did not go well. We are ordered not to retreat under any circumstances." The Sergeant stood there listening as the Captain went continued, "We are low on ammunition. We mostly have old men and young boys. The Russians and Czechs press us harder every day. We are lucky to have been able to do as well as we have. The Fuehrer said "We are the only men protecting Berlin from the south and promised replacements of men and tanks soon. He is planning another surprise offensive and this time it is in our zone. This is to happen on his birthday,"

"Can we hold out until then, sir?" the Sergeant replied.

"We have to. If we must withdraw, I alone will take responsibility. I will answer to the Fuehrer alone."

The Sergeant changed the subject by asking, "About the traitor-prisoner sir."

"Yes."

"He will be transferred in the morning. The Gestapo agent just left and the guard is ready to report today's information with yesterdays report on your desk, sir. If I may say so, you will want to read it right away, sir."

"Very well, please sit down and wait. I may have questions."

The Sergeant sat down as the Captain read the report slowly making sure he did not miss anything. The Captain paused when he got to the part that had Colonel Von Ryan's name. He respected this man very much. The Captain knew that his country had lost another war; this one. The public might be fooled by the newspaper propaganda, but not him. He was privy to the best and most up to date information, except these new plans by the Fuehrer. The Captain looked up and immediately knew exactly what he wanted to do. With no hesitation he asked the Sergeant, "This retired general you spoke to me about. Do you know exactly where he is?"

"Yes sir" replied the Sergeant.

"Can you drive there and make it by tomorrow?"

"Yes sir I can."

"You handle it your way. We owe it to Colonel Von Ryan to help him any way possible."

Without any further explanation, the Sergeant saluted and left in a hurry. Time was now his enemy. It would mean certain death for both if caught. It was a risk they both felt was worth attempting.

The bond between the Sergeant and the retired general was tight. Men in arms have a special bond sometimes compared to a mother's love and dedication to her child. Same as mothers, they would sacrifice their lives to save the other. The Captain watched the Sergeant drive away and said out loud, "If there is a God, then God helps us now."

CHAPTER 9

Running Scared

The Sergeant drove most of the night in haste, worried, and trying to get there as soon as possible. He was covered in dust, in need of a bath and shave before arriving. Knowing time was being lost, he still felt it important to shave and clean up before approaching his friend and retired general. After a quick stop to clean up, he arrived at the home of retired General Kleist.

The brakes screeched as the covered truck rolled to a stop on the circular driveway directly in front of a two story brown brick building with two white columns wrapped in green ivy holding up a second level observation deck. On this upper deck, the sight of Berlin was amazing. The home was undamaged; unlike several other homes close by. Out of the respect he stood at attention and saluted the Army salute and not the hail Hitler salute as General Kleist answered the door. After returning the salute he reached out and offered a big hug saying, "Please come in. How have you been?"

"I have been better and also, as you know, worse, sir."

"It is so good to see you. We have a lot of catching up to do."

"I can't stay long. This is important and completely unofficial."

The general closed the door, took the Sergeant's hat and coat then turned away saying, "That does not sound good. We will sit in the other room, come."

The general sat in a stuffed chair resembling something out of the Victorian age and the Sergeant made himself comfortable on a small couch directly across. A male aid brought them coffee on a tray, setting it down on a coffee table between them. "Thank you," said the general. "You will please shut the door behind you when you leave."

They both took a sip of coffee and the Sergeant began his briefing quickly. "What I am about to tell you will put you in danger, however, I know you are going to want to hear this and I trust your judgments."

The general put his cup down looking seriously said, "I trust you too. Please go on."

It took about forty minutes for the Sergeant to tell the general the whole story. It was a very dangerous situation for everyone, now including the general. The Sergeant also told him details he may not have known about the war. The Russians were closing in from the east and the other allies were closing in from the west. The end was near. Speaking of these things was enough to get the Sergeant shot, but it was important for the general to have all the information.

Soon as the Sergeant ended the briefing, he asked the Sergeant, "What excuse do you have for being here?"

The Sergeant replied with a wink of the eye and said, "Tactics sir. I was sent by my Captain for your opinion on how we are to defend our area."

The general nodded in approval and replied, "That is good and as the commander of our trench defenses, I will advise you. That is a very good cover story indeed. So you do not have to lie my answer is: do not dig in. Do not fight a trench type war again. You must strike them hard then retreat and then do it again. Fight them on our terms. Remember this exactly as I have said if you are questioned."

They both smiled. The Sergeant stood up looking around for his hat and coat. "I have to leave now. If we should live through this, I will visit you soon as I possibly can. Then we will truly catch up. If I may be so bold may I ask you something sir?"

"Anything you wish Sergeant."

"Are you going to help Colonel Von Ryan, sir?"

The general held out his hand smiling. "Yes, definitely and I also know how."

"I am so glad I saw you, sir."

"Me too."

They firmly shook hands. "On behalf of the Captain and myself, I thank you again, sir."

The general didn't wait for the Sergeant to get out of the driveway as he put on a coat and hat on the way to his automobile. He was heading to Elsa's. There was not any time to waste - the Gestapo would be coming soon. If he decided not to tell her or delayed telling her, she would never forgive him. He was in love with her and wanted nothing to come between them in the future. The future he hoped was with her.

He knew she would help her grandson. Anna was another matter. She was now labeled a Jew and spy. She would have no pity for her. Over the years he had grown to love little Max just as Elsa. If he could have shielded her from the news, he would have. However, he did not have a choice. He must trust her and with his life also. Danger was something he was familiar with and missed it ever since retiring. Without any hesitation, he decided to help her.

He desired her so much. She was so different than most of the women he knew. He did not like her hatred for the Jews, but he understood. Earlier in his life, with all his duty and energies directed toward his Army career, women were put on his back burner. He loved the respect and honor that came with being in command. As a young man this consumed all of his time. Being in command of an Army during war was something he longed for constantly as a younger officer. It was his destiny. When his dreams came true, he dedicated all of himself to his career and sacrificed the love of a woman and a family.

Retired, he now missed being in the loop of knowledge and having to make serious decisions. Always having serious issues to solve and then moving on the next challenge was exciting. War was like a chess game to him. He was expected to know the enemies next move and be prepared to counter. In retirement, he decided to dedicate the rest of his life for other pursuits. He began writing his autobiography. Then he decided he had better not finish it; the way the state of his country was in made telling certain details not possible. He then decided to pursue someone to share the rest of his life and Elsa was that woman.

Now in possession of the entire story concerning Anna and her parents, there was little time left to plan what might happen next. How was she going to react and what would she do after hearing all the details? What would she do with this information? He didn't know. He loved her and hoped so much that she would do things that would make him proud. He liked being her confidant and friend. Deciding not to think about any possible outcomes was counter to all his training.

He drew a long deep breath before knocking on the door. He was the one she trusted. He was her confidante and protector. He was there for her now. He knew she did not love him back, but he knew she was going to need him more now than ever. After hearing his car, Elsa peaked out a window and immediately prepped her hair and checked out her looks in her mirror. She smiled at her reflection. She still looked good enough to have suitors and good ones too; men who had rank and prestige.

She liked General Kleist very much and knew he would use any excuse to come over to see her. This time was unusual. He always called first, politely asking her permission. This time he didn't and she sensed something must be wrong. If he did not even have time to call, it must be very important and urgent. The general was catching his breath on the outside and Elsa patiently waited on the inside for him to knock.

"Hello Elsa, may I come in? I have important news."

"Certainly, I will get us something to drink and then we can talk."

"There is not the time for pleasantries." He motioned for them to sit and reaching out and grasping both her small white hands he began telling her. She knew it had to be bad news for him to act this way making her heart skip a beat. He told her everything as quickly as he could; including that their country had lost. It was over. His life was now in her hands and what she will do might mean the end of both their lives.

She sat there stunned in disbelief. Her heart and mind were racing. She wanted to act, do something but he wasn't finished. He told her the Gestapo might be coming for Anna and little Max as he was speaking. The urgency of the moment was in his harsh voice. He squeezed her small hands as he finished.

She let go of his hands, pulled out a handkerchief and wiped away tears. He said so much so fast, she had a hard time concentrating on everything. She just sat there listening. It was hurting him to see her confused and crying. The tears were streaking down her face. All these years and all the tough decisions he was forced to make was not as hard as this. His eyes became glassy as he talked. It was the first time he had cried since his mother died. Burying his mother was the hardest thing he ever had to do. This was his second hardest.

As she wiped away tears she asked him, "What do we do?"

Sadly he looked her and said, "We have to help them. Whatever you decide I will support you. I know this is not the best time, but it is important that you know something else. I am in love with you. I will always be there for you no matter what you decide."

It was just what she needed to hear snapping her to attention. She stood up and said, "You are right. Go into the kitchen pull out food that will not spoil easily. I will get my largest handbag and some other things."

She dashed up the stairs as he went into the kitchen and began organizing items for Anna and little Max. There were lots of Army cans neatly stacked in a cabinet. He smiled knowing it was from him as he pulled several down and placed them on the counter. He had given them to her on several occasions as a pretext. It was so ironic now.

Some of his Army training kicked in as he chose certain items. He chose candles for light and heat. Matches would be needed as he pulled put his multipurpose pocketknife that he always carried with him. It could open cans and was as sharp as a razor. He knew they would need it much more than he ever did and placed it on the counter beside the cans.

Elsa quickly came into the kitchen scooping up everything the general had laid out. Seeing the knife and the General tear up again, she went into his arms. She wanted to hold him close for a second or two. She broke away from him again, wiping tears away; this time with her sleeve. "We do not have time for this, maybe later." They scooped it all in the handbag and headed out the door.

The general was a little confused. He knew she was going to try to give these things to Anna, but didn't she hear him? He thought, "I was sure I told her the war was lost and would not last much longer. Should I tell her again? Surely, she will bring them back and hide them? All she would have to do is ask and I will hide them too. I know she will do the right thing when the time comes."

As they reached her automobile, she told him, "You go home, I must do this alone. Will you wait for me there, please?" She grabbed both his hands, squeezed and said, "I will need you when I return."

She climbed into her car and quickly sped off. While driving and wiping the tears away she was trying to think. Her mascara was running down her face. In the time it took Elsa to drive over to the Colonel's house, she tried to plan what she was going to do. She had to find a way to give Anna the bag and time to escape. She never considered hiding them. She decided supplies and a head start were enough. She didn't realize she would have to live with these choices for the rest of her remaining days. They were Jews to be despised. Her attitudes weren't going to change that fast.

She imagined Anna knew all along and got madder at her for betrothing her beloved son. Allowing little Max to come over all the time kissing and bathing him made her sick. How dare her do this to her. She started believing that it wasn't her fault, but she did love little Max. She didn't know exactly what she was going to do. She just knew she had to do something for him and the hell with Anna. She wiped more tears away from her face and knocked on the Colonel's door.

Anna answered the door and was surprised to see her. It was not the right day for her to pick up little Max and she hadn't called first. She entered by pushing Anna aside and not saying one word. She put the overstuffed purse next to the door and promptly sat down saying, "I need to speak to the Colonel immediately."

Anna knew something was terribly wrong. "I will be right back." At that moment she had no idea how much trouble was headed her way. Her whole life was about to be turned upside down. That terrible deep dark secret was discovered and her parents were in Gestapo custody. As the Colonel and his wife entered the room, Elsa pointed a finger to the next room and ordered Anna out of the room. "You leave this room now."

Anna was not use to anyone ordering her around, not even the Colonel. Without objecting, she left the room not completely shutting the door and started listening. Something was terribly wrong. Elsa quickly began with telling them Anna was half-Jewish. Anna could not believe what she just heard and started to get angry and almost opened the door to confront Elsa, but something held her back. Elsa then told them everything about Eli, especially about him being her real father. Anna's heart sank to her stomach. Her knees went weak and she started sliding down the door. She grabbed the door squeezing the edges to hold her up and continued listening.

Elsa reveled that Anna had divulged confidential information spoken in this house to her parents in letters that the Gestapo now have in their possession. She was now considered a spy and they were coming to arrest her and them.

The Colonel turned and looked at his wife and saw she had both her hands in front of her face in disbelief and horror. His face was red with anger. He clinched his hands as if he was going to strike out at someone. Elsa wanted to stop talking and take a breather, but knew time was not on her side. She had to hurry. Then she told the Colonel and his wife about Anna's parents hiding Eli and all three being captured. Anna placed her hands on her cheeks and started silently crying. Little Max and the three girls were in another room playing, totally unaware of what was happening.

As a respected and high-ranking member of the Racial Purity Committee, she knew what to do to protect his family. She told them that was why she came over, she lied. He was furious, but still sat there listening as she told them to follow all her instructions and everything would be fine. First, they needed to sew yellow stars on both their coats and immediately march them publicly down the streets to police headquarters. They needed to say they had just received an anonymous telephone call informing them she was an undisclosed Jew. This would clear his family and Elsa at the same time.

Anna still listening and dazed started to rise up and collect herself. Her legs seemed to not move fast enough. She had to get little Max and somehow escape, run and hide. The Colonel quickly stood up and headed toward Anna. He tried to enter the room hitting Anna in the head with the door. Anna moved aside and the Colonel looked at her. It was obvious she heard everything. The Colonel was so outraged that he considered getting his pistol and shooting her. She had put his entire family in more danger than the threat of the Russians. He ordered her to get the material and sew stars on their coats immediately as Elsa had instructed.

He was like a rabid dog pacing back and forth. His wife said nothing as she watched everything unfold. He was furious. He loved Anna and little Max as if they were his own family. "How could she do this to them," he thought. For the first time since he could remember he was not sure of the right thing to do. Protecting his family came first. All of them were suddenly in so much unexpected danger. They were threatened by the collapse of the German government, Russian invaders, and now this. His wife had refused to leave with the children for a safer place. She wanted the security of the Colonel being able to get back to them whenever he could manage. She knew if she and the children were too far away he couldn't help. She believed the right thing was to stay in Berlin where the Colonel could assist if possible.

Anna was crying as she sewed on little Max's star first. Then her favorite black coat was next. It was a very warm coat and the bright yellow star showed brightly against the black background. Little Max came into the room several times only to be told to leave. He knew something was terribly wrong. His mother was crying, upset, and not paying any attention to him. All the other adults were mad and yelling.

When Anna finished, she wiped tears from her eyes and put Max's coat on him first. He was clutching his little nursery rhyme book and his little broken toy Soldier. She put her coat on and picked up

Little Max placing him on her hip. She took both items from him and put them inside her coat pocket making sure he saw her. With her free hand she turned his head so he was looking at her face. She smiled at him to reassure him. She took a deep breath, put a brave face and stood beside the front door and waited.

Elsa saw her chance. She asked the Colonel and his wife to go into the next room where they could talk in private. The Colonel and his wife looked back at Anna with hatred in their eyes. As soon as the Colonel and his wife left the room, Elsa scooted back to the front door, placed the overstuffed handbag on Anna's shoulder, leaned forward and in her ear whispered just one word, "run."

Elsa turned away from them and never looked back. Anna bolted out the door. Elsa entered the other room and proceeded to tell the Colonel and his wife the rest of her plan. She took her time stalling to give Anna and Little Max as much time as possible. "You are to tell the police that Anna admitted everything and you made her sew the stars on their clothes. You were getting ready to march them to the station when she bolted out the door. You then tell them you immediately called the police station, as you are going to do now. Her story will not match yours, but they will believe you and not her. I was never here. This should protect all of us."

Elsa left very quickly not knowing when the Gestapo would arrive and did not want to be caught. She headed straight for German Kleist. She was going to need someone to lean on now. He was that person. However, she was not even crying.

CHAPTER 10

The Book

Anna ran down the stairs and outside, suddenly being hit by cold air and rain. She placed little Max's face against her coat, shielding him as they began the run for their lives. Walking fast, sometimes slow with little Max in her arms, constantly shifting his weight, looking behind her and running as fast as she could, totally unaware that there were only five days that she would have in front of her before freedom. The cold rain pelted her like little cold projectiles stinging her face. Little Max was shivering while holding on to her tight as possible.

She didn't know what to do or where to go, she just kept running. Being mindful of the information the Colonel conveyed about the Russians, Anna felt it was a good idea to run away from that possible area of attack. Yesterday they had a nice place to live, food; and now nothing. The security living with the Von Ryan's was now lost and replaced by fear and uncertainty. Soon if not already, they were going to be hunted down like animals with little or no hope of survival. The cold rain and fear was now making Anna shiver too.

She stopped to rest under a gray tattered canvas awning flapping in the wind with the light rain dripping off the canvas on the sidewalk. Looking around and seeing no one was looking their way, she quickly turned her left lapel out covering the yellow star. She kept little Max close up against her body shielding him and his star from view. She quickly looked inside the bag for something to conceal his star and found nothing. She decided she would just have to hide it with her body for now.

It was a relief being sheltered from the wind and rain. The weight was hurting her shoulders. She took this opportunity to catch her breath. She could see their breaths in the cold air. The few people that were out and walking around were more concerned with trying to avoid the rain and staying warm than paying any attention to them. She avoided looking at anyone especially into their eyes, not wanting to be recognized or remembered. She wished she were invisible. The cold light rain was in some ways a blessing.

Little Max was a darling. He knew something was terribly wrong and was scared, yet he stayed calm without crying. He knew his mother would protect him. Many times she had told him he was her little man of the house. He knew it was the time to be quiet and brave. They were still together and somehow she will find a way to save them. She did not know how, but she knew she had learned many things in the past that were going to help. She knew she would have to remember everything.

Looking around, she saw some of the same people she had seen before and knew they needed to leave. If felt so good to rest. She took a deep breath, picked up Max and headed back into the misty cold rain. She kept pushing herself hard. The weight of little max and the bag seemed heavier. She was wet, cold and getting tired. The muscles in her legs were burning. She kept walking and walking, telling herself to take one step at a time and keep going. Each step away was another step closer to freedom and safety. It was beginning to get dark. She knew they would need shelter soon, but where?

She figured she would be able to develop a plan soon as she found some place for the night. Her second challenge was shelter and getting through the night without being caught. Little Max tried walking some of the time giving her a little break. However, he was tired and not able to walk fast enough for her. She continually scanned each and every building looking for a safe place for the night. She had to appear as if what she was doing was common place and not look panicked. She had to continually check and see that his star stayed hidden. Whenever she would see a possible place, she put Little Max down and looked around while appearing to be doing something else. She tried not to be noticed.

She had no one she could turn to or trust for help. They were on their own. Her mother-in-law made that very clear. She hated anything having to do with Jews. This meant she now hated them. "What a bigot," Anna thought. "First things first," she continually told herself. She had to stay focused on step two, and not let her mind wander. She stopped again under another canvas awning in front of a little café that was obviously closed for the night. She put the bag down. Little Max had fallen asleep so she couldn't put him down. The pain she was experiencing in her shoulders was now evident on her wet cold face. So tired, she did not know how much longer she could travel.

Diagonally across the street and only one block away she spotted the building at 108 Nine Straße. Damaged and appearing abandoned, a lamplight was visible from two upper windows. Dusk had arrived and daylight was fading fast. It was getting colder. The lights would be blacked out soon, so it was fortunate for her to be where she was at that moment. This meant at least some parts of the building had electricity and probably water.

It was a corner building at a three-way junction in the road. The junction was right in front of the building, giving a great view down all three streets which offered Anna more ways to see danger coming and escape. It would be perfect if she only had some electricity, water, and no people.

Forced to make a decision, she lifted Max and the bag and started walking toward the building. The streets were now deserted. Soon as she reached the building, she quickly ducked inside, shook off some rain and put him down carefully so not to awaken him. As she waited, she tried looking close around her. She was having a hard time seeing in the darkened building. She knew she really did not have any other choices. This was where they would have to spend the night. She quietly moved around and inspected everything she could see.

It was no wonder it was deserted. Upper floor beams had fallen down and wedged in at all different angles. Certain parts of the upper floor had collapsed and now were lying all over the floor. Furniture was broken and lying sporadically, upside-down, and on their sides. She wanted to avoid any contact with others much as possible. She had to be very quiet. Any noise at all might alarm someone and mean certain imprisonment and maybe death. She was very glad he was such a quiet and shy child. Even when hurt he rarely cried. She smiled at him lying there believing truly in her heart that someday he will be just like his father.

She found stairs leading downward. She slowly and carefully headed down the stairs one step at a time. It was dark and she could only see a few feet ahead. Feeling the walls with her hands and the steps with her wet shoes, she made her way down. Several steps creaked making her stop and listen. After ten steps she was on the ground floor. It appeared like a wine cellar slightly below ground level. She secretly wished someone left some wine. Right at that moment she stepped on a bottle twisting her ankle, almost falling down. She grabbed a beam and kept from falling. Reaching down and picking it up, she found it was a half full bottle of wine. Anna, always with a little sense of humor said softly, "Later tonight I am going to wish for something a whole lot more important than this."

She decided they would stay. It was good enough for the night. There was enough stuff lying around to make a small bed, a table, and there had to be more usable things she couldn't see yet. She quickly made the area ready for Max and carefully went back up the stairs. Attempting to make little noise as possible by stopping at each step and slowly lowering her weight, Anna made her way slowly. Still asleep, she touched Max's face and smiled. "Look at my brave little man. I am so proud of you."

Then she kissed him on his forehead, everything was so much heavier than when she started. She placed Max on the little bed and after shaking off all the rain on her coat, placed it on top of him. She was cold and rubbed her hands against her upper arms for warmth. She had to light up the room; it was going to be too dark to see soon. She needed time to figure things out, she would sleep later. Inside her bag, the first thing she felt was a candle and matches.

Barely visible and risky she had to quickly light the candle and throw something over any windows. She held the matches in her wet shaking hands, inhaled cold air and struck the match. It flickered and went out. She knew she had to calm down and get this done and soon. Taking in a calming breath, she struck another match and quickly lit the candle, throwing the still lit match on the floor and running to the only window. In her controlled panic she saw a drape partially hung over the window and quickly fixed it. She tried to quit shaking but she couldn't, so she climbed under her coat next to little Max and began warming up. She was cold, wet, and scared. Max was warm and asleep.

All she could do now was to wait. If discovered, she didn't have the strength to fight or run anymore that night. After a few minutes, she warmed up, breathed easier, and figured everything was fine. It was time to check out the bag and see what else was there. As she removed each item, she organized them on a table; five little candles with two packs of matches, six cans of Army food, a multipurpose Army knife.

She held up the knife to the light and examined it completely. It had a lot of handy attachments. With a puzzled look, she set it down. It was silver and red with engraved letters; G.K. "Where would Elsa get one of these and remember to include it in this bag? Then it dawned on her that it was from Elsa's retired German friend. Good at figuring out puzzles always pleased her. Now she knew where the information Elsa knew had come from. She wanted to cry and yell as she had when Max died as the thoughts of her parents returned. She grabbed her sides and just held it in knowing she had to be quiet. A few moments later Anna collected herself and continued her inspection. Bandages with iodine, two pairs of large socks, a small scarf, two forks, one spoon, a pencil and a handkerchief were all now unpacked and on the table.

She picked up the pencil and started wondering again. She assumed the bag was packed in a hurry and it must have been in the bag when it was packed. The pencil reminded her about his little book. She went over to her coat and pulled it out. Luckily it was dry and she carefully placed it on the table next to the pencil.

Elsa was one of the worst bigots she had ever known and could have refused to help. However, she did help. Anna just shook her head, "No, Elsa should have done more for her only grandson. Maybe not me, but definitely hide him. She was just too much a racist to change that quickly." Tired, Anna stretched out beside Max and under her coat again. It felt good. Anna stroked his short blond hair as she watched him sleep. All she knew and cared about was right there and they were still together. She put her head down, not intending to fall asleep.

When Anna awoke, she felt something tickling her stomach. It was Max playing with his toy. He put his nose touching hers and quietly said, "Good morning mommy."

She stretched out her arms and pulled him closer replying, "Good morning my little man."

Little Max always could get her to smile just by looking at her. He hated more than anything making her upset or mad. She slowly rose. Sore from the previous day, she gingerly walked over to the window and peaked outside. The window was so dirty that she couldn't see outside. She wiped out a small place in the corner. It looked different than she remembered. However, she believed it would be fine for a day or two. She needed to collect her thoughts and give him explicit instructions in easy terms he would be able to understand and follow. Things he can do and things he must not do. She would have to think of all possibilities including the possibility of being captured without him. That thought sent shivers down her neck and made her stomach turn.

She turned around from the window ran both hands through her hair and looked back at the table. She fell asleep with the candle still burning and it was gone having burned down to the table. She knew she couldn't let something like that happen again. She knew she had to consider even the smallest details if they were going to stay together and alive. She looked at the wine bottle and thought, "It has several uses, one being medicine. The wine would be useful as a sleeping potion too if needed. If either one of us cannot sleep, a little might just be the trick.

Turning toward the other end of the room she heard a soft constant noise. It was a constant tap, tap, and tap. She and little Max slowly walked over to the corner. There was a sink with the faucet dripping. She turned the knob and a slow steady stream continued to flow. She smiled at him and he smiled back at her. "You little man will have a bath soon." She set about quietly removing all the debris and cleaning the sink.

She found more useable items; two bowels chipped and a nice size empty metal can. "This will do nice I think. What do you think?" At the same time she said this she turned around to see if he was paying attention and he was standing right beside her as usual. She had such a soft and reassuring voice. She now would have to always speak softly encouraging him to do the same. She started softly singing a nursery rhyme and swaying while he watched her work.

Little Max was not much of a talker. The problem was the Colonel's three daughters just loved him to death and every chance they had spoiled him. If he wanted a glass out of the cabinet, all he would do is point and grunt and one of them would get it for him. He did not have to speak to get what he wanted. Anna had seen a doctor about this and he reassured her he was fine and would just grow out of it as soon as everyone stops spoiling him. Then he told her to be thankful he is a quiet child because when he breaks out, you will wish for that shy child again. She was thankful very much now about his condition.

Finished with the sink and placing the can to catch the water she smiled at him and said, "Time for breakfast sweetie. Do you want steak and eggs with toast?" Little Max looked at her with a puzzled look. Anna giggled and picking up a can of beans and said, "No steak and eggs but we have these real good beans." She used the knife to open the can and managed to place the can over the flame from another candle she lit. "These beans are going to taste so good."

As they silently watched the can, the air raid sirens went off. Frightened, little Max jumped right at Anna. She held him. Anna was also scared. Then she realized it was air raid siren and not the police. At the Colonel's house, they had to go downstairs to get into their basement. Here they were already in a basement and that was good.

She stood up still holding Max and walked to the window. She moved the curtain over just a little and peaked outside. People were running in all directions. While looking at the outdoor café a block away something caught her eye. The patrons left food on the table and ran away. She saw a boy grab some food as he passed by and no one seemed to notice or care. This is when she got her idea. She knew they did not have enough food for very long and she was going to have to find some. She squatted down to Little Max's level, looked right into his eyes and said, "The next time we hear the sirens your mommy is going to run out there and get us a proper breakfast or dinner. I will return as soon as I can. How does that sound my little man?"

He looked at her and just nodded a yes.

She said in a soft but stern voice, "When this happens I will have to leave you alone for a few minutes. I need you to be brave, be quiet, and stay until I return. Do you understand?"

He just looked up at her smiling and shook his head.

"If for some reason I do not return in just a few minutes do not worry. You are to stay here until I return. She wanted to say she might be gone for a long, long time, but she did not want to scare him. "You have to stay here or else mommy will not be able to find you. You cannot leave. Do you understand?"

He looked at her nodded then laid his head on her chest. She would have to tell him these instructions several times. However, for now this would have to do. "This may work out better than I thought." Then she began remembering important things she had heard at the Colonel's house. The war is lost to Germany; the end will be soon then everything will change. Maybe they will not have to hide that long after all.

The Russians are coming from the east and the Americans and British are coming from the west. Suddenly remembering how brutal the Russians were towards innocent civilians made her shiver. She knew if they got to her she would defiantly be raped and more than once. While thinking of these terrible thoughts she glanced at the knife on the table. If she did not have little Max to look after she knew what she would have to do. Little Max changed all of these thoughts. However she has the knife to use on them if needed. She will do anything or endure anything to save him.

Whenever she would want to change what she was thinking she would place big Max inside her head and all the bad thoughts would disappear. She began imagining that she was in his big strong arms and wished for those days again. She felt safe and secure with him. He would know what to do if he were here and everything would not have to be up to her. He was brave and strong. She now must be as brave, if not braver than she has ever had to be. She was sure of one thing. She would never give little Max up – never!

Looking at him she said softly, "I have an idea. I will fill this time we are together by telling you our story. I will tell you everything including things I have not before told you." She sat him on her lap. "I will tell you about our beautiful wedding. You will learn some music. You will learn everything about all your grandparents, the good and the not so good. You will remember these stories, forever I hope."

Little Max looked up at her and softly said, "Thanks mommy."

She knew he was too young to remember all the stories she was going to tell him. However, maybe he will remember some when he gets older. Anna then whispered back at him, "Maybe I will still be with you and I will tell them to your children." He gave her a little hug making her believe he understood completely. He seemed to know what to do, almost always.

Therefore, it began in earnest that very day and all through the night; Anna began telling him the stories of their entire family's lives. She started to take the stars off their clothes and changed her mind after thinking about all the consequences. If she was challenged and discovered they both could be shot on the spot by anyone for not wearing the star. This was a written law. At least if caught while wearing the star Little Max would have a greater chance of survival. A small chance and one she didn't like. So for now she decided it would be best to keep them but, hide them when outside.

She placed her coat on the stairs so she would be able to pick it up on the run when she heard the sirens. She knew she had to be quick. Grab her coat, run upstairs and out. Get to the café, grab what she could and return as fast as she could manage without being noticed. It was a gamble. She would not have to worry about any noise she made, the sirens and commotion would easily mask her noises. Leaving and returning would be the riskiest part.

It was not even a few minutes after thinking these thoughts when the sirens went off again. This time both Anna and little Max could tell the difference and weren't scared. Anna said quickly, "Stay as I told you."

She ran to the stairs, picked up her coat, and out she went. Her heart was beating fast and hard. She was not afraid - yet. She had decided what she needed to do and nothing was going to stop her. There was not enough food that would last and she was going to get more with every chance.

This time it was not a false alarm. Bombs hit down the street as she ran toward the café. People were running in every direction. She grabbed what she could from a table. Looking down she spotted two children on the ground. The boy looked right at her as she grabbed the food. She felt a little bad for the children for an instant, and then she turned around running back.

When she entered the abandoned building she was panting and could hardly breathe. She had done it. She smiled and bounced up and down with joy. Still with her wits, she watched outside while standing in the shadows. Everything had calmed down and the sirens had stopped. She could see the café and a woman was dusting off the children. They appeared fine. No one had noticed her except the little boy, it worked. She was so happy. She went to the stairs and quietly climbed down again.

Little Max was sitting right where she had left him. She went over and sat next to him smiling. First, she wanted to praise him for following her instructions. "You were such a good boy. You did exactly as I told you. Now remember if ever I should take longer you are to stay here no matter how long, understand?"

He excitedly asked, "What did you get for us mommy?"

She opened up her hand with fresh strudel squished inside. She laughed, then said, "I told you we would have a nice breakfast didn't I?" Without him realizing, she gave him most. Her trip was worth it, but took too long. She decided she was going to have to make a place for them to hide upstairs closer to the street. She needed to get out and back much faster. Even though it was stolen, she decided it was the best strudel she had ever eaten and licked the sugar off her fingers.

Her special time for reflecting and planning would now be whenever Max slept. Last night she dropped into sleep right after him. She did not have the energy to even try to stay awake. In the future, she knew she would have to do that part better too. She now considered sleeping a luxury.

She and everyone she truly loved were now branded as Jews to be hunted down and destroyed by anyone. There was danger everywhere. She went over to the sink, changed the full can of water for an empty pot then dipped a cup in the can and drank it. It was cold and good. This was a far cry from what their lives were like just a little more than a day before. However, they had escaped and all she had to do was take it one day at a time without any mistakes.

She concentrated on every detail over and over. "She heard that her parents were hiding a Jew and were caught. She was half Jewish. Why would they do that? Her letters to her parents were discovered and lead them to her. Why had they not destroyed those letters? A blood relative turned them in. Obviously Elsa didn't turn them in, so who was it? Little Max was and will be her only grandson, Elsa could have at least hidden him and kept him safe." Anna was glad for the supplies and the chance to run. However, since Elsa had time to get these things together, then she could have done more to help him.

CHAPTER 11

Two Days Left

She decided to write everything down that she had been telling him and more. Asleep with a little piece of food clutched in one hand and the other draped low, she couldn't help but smile at him. Whenever he slept, it was her time. Her eyes went back to the table and caught sight of a pencil. Her bloodshot and darkened eyes got larger with the sudden realization she could do just that; write it all down for him in his little book. He takes it everywhere. It was ironic that this book and pencil Elsa had given her would be the instruments telling little Max about her. Everything she did and didn't do.

It would help her pass the time. Writing things down always helped her with her thoughts. She wrote in tiny print everywhere possible. There was quite a bit of white space available. She had to think of a way to do this without endangering them should they accidentally leave the book somewhere or if they were caught. The print needed to be deceptive, appearing as if it were something else; something with little or no importance.

It was simple and brilliant. She decided musical notes would best tell her story that could later be decoded. If someone opened the book, it would look as though someone had written songs in the margins. Possibly believing they were children's songs or maybe even try to sing the music. Anna giggled at the thought of visualizing a Soldier or officer trying to sing the music.

She enjoyed the plan that she devised, but sought extra insurance, another barrier to hinder anyone from easily discovering the true meaning of the music. Something that was able to tell the entire story using fewer words. She wanted more than just the story to be told. She wanted little Max to later feel the desires and emotions she wanted to covey. Her education included learning several other languages, one being Latin. It is a simpler language with a hint of romance. Latin would suit her needs perfectly. Simpler words with more passion and an extra safety measure were exactly what she wanted and needed.

If one of the worst things was to happen and they were separated, she hoped Little Max would keep the book and somehow later in life decipher the coded story. This new project suddenly took on much importance. If something was to happen and she was not able tell him in person, this would have to serve the purpose. She felt an urgent need to start and finish as soon as possible. She stared immediately while little Max napped peacefully, still clutching the little piece of food.

Anna tip toed over to the table being careful not to make any noise. This was now a habit. She looked at little Max again and smiled thinking, "He would follow in her desires of education. He would also be talented with the same desire to learn drama and music. He will figure it out and be so proud of himself and her. I will tell him how his father loved and cared for us. I will even write down how he made love to me. He will someday understand how much we loved each other. He wanted me to tell him, he wanted to be there. It just was not meant to be and this may be true for me too."

It was now midmorning and one of the times the air raid sirens usually sounded. Before they went up the stairs, she gave him some quick instructions. "We are going upstairs and wait for the alarm. Mommy will go and get us some more food and you will have to stay and be quiet as a mouse."

Then she said something she would soon regret, "You are the man of the house now."

She had previously made a place in the shadows against the back wall, carefully placing other items around the space to conceal but still allow a full view of the street and café. It seemed perfect. If someone was to come out of an adjacent building, they were hidden from that direction too. They were huddled together in the back shadows against the wall. Anna stretched her legs out for comfort and little Max was on her lap. She felt this was much better than having to run up the stairs and lose valuable time. Now, when the sires go off and the panic begins, she would be outside in a flash and get back unnoticed quicker.

As a chilly breeze reached them, she buttoned Little Max's coat and proceeded to button hers. Out of another building across the street, two children emerged and headed toward the café skipping and playing. The girl was about eight and the boy about five. Little Max pointed to them obviously wishing he was with them and playing too. It was nice watching the children interacting. After a few minutes the two children headed back to their home on the same side of the road as Anna and Little Max's building. The little boy was eating an orange and dropping piece after piece on the ground while laughing. When they were directly outside, the little boy dropped the rest of the orange on the ground and they walked away, caught up in their own world, leaving the orange on the sidewalk.

Anna, still seated against the wall with her legs stretched out straight and comfortable, couldn't believe what happened. Without any warning little Max jumped off her and said, "I got it mommy!"

He dashed out so quickly that Anna couldn't say anything, grab him, or get up fast enough to stop him. Horrified, she stood up and watched him run outside into the daylight with the Star of David in plain sight. He reached down, picked up the sticky orange and looked up at the other two children staring at him.

"My god no," Anna muttered softly, now shaking with fear.

Little Max quickly dashed back to her. He held up the orange with both hands while sticky juice dripped from his palms. With pride in his voice he said, "See mommy I can help. I am the man of the house just like you said."

Anna could not help herself. She grabbed him by both his little arms and shook him, knocking the orange to the floor. "How could you do this? I told you to stay here! I told you I would get us all we need. I was the one that would run out when the time was right. Not you. You need to listen to me."

She had lost her temper and control. She continued shaking and lecturing him as if she would never stop. When she ran out of things to say to him, she took a breath looked away and tried to calm down. He was not saying a word. He just stood there with tears rolling down his sad face. She scooped him up in her arms and quickly went down the stairs. She had to get their things together and run again. She held him tight and started crying. She had temporally forgotten he was just a five-year-old boy.

*****

It was fun playing as children at the café. Only four days left until the end of the war and we were discovering so much. I knew it had to happen because of Mika dropping so many pieces and being so clumsy; as I expected he dropped the rest of the orange. Continuing our walk home without picking up the orange, both of us stopped about ten feet away so I could tie his shoe. As I bent down, we both saw the little boy with a bright yellow star on his coat run out of the building. He picked up the orange and looked right at us. Then he immediately ran back into hiding. We looked around and no one except us saw what happened. With bewildered looks on our faces we kept walking to our building. Mika whispered to me, "Wait until we are inside the apartment to talk."

I replied, "No problem, I am going to need a few minutes to digest what just happened anyway."

We climbed the stairs and opened our door. Our grandmother, Marion, immediately started praising us for getting home a little early and said, "There hasn't been any warnings or attacks yet, but soon I think. I am glad you are home now and rest of the day you two will stay here inside." She said this with a little nervousness in her voice.

I whispered in Mika's ear, "At least we have food and we are not like him."

Whispering back, Mika said, "Like whom?"

"You know, that little Jewish boy. I would hate to be him. You know, I was thinking he can't be alone. There must be someone in the building helping him, a mother or father. They also don't know there is only four days left until all this ends. They will be able to live not being hunted. Everything changes in just four days."

Seeing Marion looking at us whispering wasn't smart. So I whispered one more thing. "She is watching; we need to go in the other room."

We both giggled and went into the other room. Closing the door loud enough for her to hear and then quietly opening it a little. This way we could talk and monitor her too.

Mika said, "Maybe we could help them, without putting us in much danger. Drop food or something like that."

I could not help myself and reminded him, "Did you get what you wished for, or what? Remember you wanted an adventure. Now we have one."

Mika seemed to ignore me and went on to say, "Whatever we do, we must be aware of the dangers and all the ramifications. One example would be after we help them and they are caught, would they tell who had helped them? Then what will happen to our entire family, not only us but our children in the future too. I mean in the past. You know what I mean."

"I don't really want to expose ourselves to that much danger, but we have to do something." Then smiling I added, "What is adventure without some element of danger? There are so many questions we need to go over too."

"Like what?"

I looked at Marion who was busy reading the newspaper and then whispered, "Are we doing this or are our parents doing this? What did they do back then? Are we changing what happened sixty years ago? What if we are caught and killed? Will our children ever be born? Think about it?"

"I did not even consider those things. What do you want to do? Do you want to help them or not?"

"Of course we have to. We also need to consider everything." I replied.

"The least we need to do is drop them some food. We can slip in, drop food and exit unnoticed. I know we can do this, I know it."

Suddenly we heard our grandmother leave the apartment. We turned and looked at each other, puzzled. Relieved, we saw her come back in the room with mail. We sat still watching. She sat down and opened one carefully. She slowly unfolded the letter as if looking for something special. We could tell she was paying close attention to how it was folded. She said something we almost couldn't hear, "So that is where you are." Then she suddenly took the letter and crushed it up in a small ball. Then she opening it up to read it again.

Both of us looked at each other knowing what we had just witnessed. At the same time and said, "Code." She sat there quietly reading the letter.

Suddenly we were startled by a knock on the front door. It was a neighbor named Sophie. We were to find out later that Sophie would always come over at the time mail arrived. She would impatiently wait until Marion had retrieved her mail and retreated inside to come over. Then pry as much information out of Marion as possible. She had other reasons for finding out what was in the letters other than just idol curiosity. Sophie's husband was stationed in the same battalion as Marion's husband.

She and Marion almost always exchanged letters. Somehow our grandmother always knew more about what was happening than Sophie. All letters were personally read and scrutinized by sensors. If anything was written that was prohibited everyone involved would be arrested. Even if a letter had the appearance of something said that was not allowed, it could mean the end of a man's career and maybe a firing squad. Even with these dangers, many Soldiers risked everything to let their family's know more. It was these little unknown ways of informing their families that also might save their lives. The rewards outweighed the risks for many.

Before he shipped out, Marion's husband worked out a code that he believed to be foolproof. Every German Soldier was issued regulation stationary to be used. They were required to use this

179

stationary. On the upper left corner was a German Soldier holding their countries flag up high. He was standing on an outline map of their country. The plan was so simple and subtle. He believed no one would guess it or be able to spot it as long as she did not tell anyone and the letter was crinkle up immediately. He just folded the letter twice over the spot he was when he wrote the letter. She would open the letter and carefully look where the double crease intersected and that was his location.

It was the standard procedures to have censors inspect mail before approving pieces for delivery. Soldier would hand letters to them and wait. After the letter was inspected, the Soldier was allowed to fold and seal it in the envelope. Then, they were required to drop it in a box in front of the inspectors. This was a strategy to protect valuable information. After inspected, our grandfather would slyly fold the letter in such a way to inform Marion where he was at a given time. He hoped this method was foolproof.

Marion was against it at first and tried to convince him to not even try. He reassured her several times that it would be fine and not to worry. The first time he tried it, it would work perfectly. After she received that first coded letter, her tension about the plan eased and she was reassured. We now had added respect. There was so much more we were going to learn about our grandparents in the coming days.

Knowing the location of our grandfather helped Marion cope with so much that was not known. The anticipation of getting a letter each day was a joy. There was another code they had worked out. When he would tell her that there would not be a letter tomorrow, it meant something soon was going to happen. If he added not to worry, she was instructed to try and not worry. He was telling her it might be something as simple as he was going to be busy and would not have the time to write. If he did not tell her not to worry then whatever was going to happen worried him too and he felt she needed to know.

He decided the first sentence would set the tone. If it started out bad this would tell her things were not going well. If it started out happy then all was well. After the first sentence no more code except the last sentence. By then she knew where he was and if things were going well or not. The last sentence would tell her the probably of him writing the next day. If he said he would write to her tomorrow she knew she would receive another letter the next day or two. If he said in the last line that he will write as soon as he has time, then she would know something was about to happen and she might not hear from him for a while. He did not know at the time he would also indirectly be helping his friend's family too.

Sophie knew there must be a code. Even after reading Marion's letters she could not figure it out. She knew why Marion wouldn't take her in that confidence. It could mean death for her entire family. Whenever Sophie pried her, she would just say their souls were together even though their bodies were apart. At one time she simply said she just knew, and please quit asking. Our grandmother delighted in telling Sophie that she was going to get another letter or two the next day. Then it would happen and Sophie would be amazed shaking her head in disbelief. No matter how many times Sophie read the letters she just could not figure it out. We found out all these things later.

We were able to figure the most important items the first time we watched her handle the envelope and letter. She so carefully read the first line and skipping everything else to read the last line was strange behavior. We were the only ones ever able to see her do this having an edge over Sophie. We knew the history of the times also helping us to figure out their code. At the time our grandmother did not pay any attention to us watching her. She figured we were just children and what would we know. Wow, was she wrong.

She kept repeatedly reading the letter. She even held it to her chest daydreaming. Oh, how she loved and missed him. Even after all these years they were still in love and missed each other very much. It was so evident. Every letter told her how much he loved and missed her, every single one. She told him many times to never stop telling her. She needed him, and said, I never get tired of hearing you say this," Everything they wrote was somehow important. He asked her to write every detail about Mina and Mika every day, including what they ate. He told her he needed to read her letters and imagine he was there, escaping his predicament. She knew he needed her and she would be there for him. She had not missed one day while he was away.

Marion called us in the other room to read the letter to us and Sophie. Sophie sat down at the table with her hands holding up her head and listened intently paying close attention to every detail. When she finished Sophie abruptly changed the subject and asked Marion, "Have you read today's paper? It says we are winning the war and both fronts? I guess you would know if it was true or not." She said this with a little jealousy in her voice knowing Marion would not tell her. "These bombings are just a last attempt to get concessions when they surrender to us. What do you think?"

Marion, while wiping her forehead with a towel, told Sophie, "The bombing was too close today. I was scared we were going to die. Mika even got hurt this time. It was only a small cut and nothing serious. It could have been a lot worse being caught out in the open like we were." She also added, "It was unusual this time because most of the attacks have been at dusk or after dark." Letting the children get out was a little safer when the raids were regular, but now she did not know if she was going to let them go out and play at all. At least until the attacks stopped or went back to a regular schedule. After she told Sophie these things she added, "I just do not know how much longer this thing is going to last or how much more I can stand."

Sophie leaned toward Marion, twisted some hair around her finger and asked, "You know something don't you? Sophie prodded her for more information. "What do you mean saying how much longer going to last? Sophie then took one of Marion's hands and said, "You need to watch your mouth. Saying things like that could get you in bad trouble." She motioned for her to look our way. We took the hint and went into the other room.

Still holding Marion's hand tightly she said something very interesting, "Did you hear what happened to Colonel Von Ryan's maid?" Without even waiting for a reply she went on with, "It seems the Gestapo is investigating all servants even more completely since the attempt on the Fuehrer's life. They have found several Jews living with some of the most important people I have heard of, and now the very important and influential Colonel Von Ryan."

Both Marion and Sophie let go of each other's hands and lit cigarettes both looking our way. We could see them through the crack in the door, but they couldn't see us. Sophie drew on the cigarette and exhaled and then said, "The Gestapo does not even knock on the door; they just knock down the door and take everyone away. That is everyone and not just the Jews. Then they take them to headquarters for questioning. Sometimes the host families return scared and quiet, but most times they are never seen again. There are rumors. Some families are so frightened that even if they simply suspect their servants have lied to them and have Jewish connections they place the yellow star on their servants and family members and parade them to police headquarters. That way they are in less trouble. However that is not what happened to Colonel Von Ryan's servant and family."

Marion contributed, "I have heard about him. He lives across town. He has three young girls and a woman servant with her young son living with them. Sorry for interrupting. Something went on with the servant and her son?"

"From what I heard, his servant is a Jew. Somehow she was discovered and escaped. Can you believe escaped, where would she go? They were made to wear the yellow star and were going to be paraded to police headquarters when she bolted out the door with her young son in her arms. When the police got there, she was gone and on the run."

I looked at Mika. He was already looking at me and we knew. I whispered it to him, "I will bet you that little boy is who she is talking about."

Mika whispered back, "That means the person hiding him is his mother."

I felt my heart sink. "You are right, no matter the consequences we have to help them."

Mika just smiled back at me. Marion then said something shocking. Marion looked Sophie dead center in her eyes and said, "I do not know if I could do what you just told me some do. My children's wellbeing is the only important thing to me. However, I really do not believe everything I have been told about Jews."

"Shush," said Sophie. "You can tell me that but you must not ever say that again. Looking around and not seeing us she added, "If your children should here and repeat it to someone else, well, you know what I mean." Sophie picked up the letter. "Out of these few sentences you know where he is and everything else."

"I have never said I know for sure," was the quick snappy reply from Marion.

As she slowly took another drag she lowered her voice and said, "Just think about it for a minute, we are being bombed or shelled almost every day. Some are artillery shells and not just bombs. That means two things. Our enemy is getting closer and to defend us our husbands are closer also."

Sophie the asked, "How close are they?"

Marion shook her head no. "The enemy is about twenty miles east. Our husbands are about five miles closer. Because I say these things do not mean there is a code in the letters. I wish you would never speak of this again. It is just too dangerous to speak of these things. We might be somehow overheard."

"Ok, ok I get it but please keep letting me read them, I will stop I promise," begged Sophie.

Marion gave her a re-assuring look and lit another cigarette. She didn't notice there was another one burning in the ashtray. She handed the pack to Sophie as she exhaled her smoke. Both Mika and I looked at each other and simply smiled. We stretched out quietly on the floor behind the door and continued to listen. It was fascinating.

"Anyway," Sophie continued, "The Jews carry all those diseases. I am glad they are almost all gone." She took another drag on the cigarette and continued talking while blowing out the smoke.

Marin got up from the table and headed toward the kitchen, partially to get away from the accumulating smoke. It appeared to us she did not want to hear what was next. Enjoying Sophie's visits with adult conversation was refreshing since she had us all day all-night all the time. So even thought you could tell she knew what was next and did not like that subject she still asked her to continue. "Please go on."

Sitting up straight in her chair and acting proud Sophie said, "If I were to know where some Jews were still hiding, I would turn them in without even thinking about." She snapped her fingers as she said this.

Mika and I did not speak a single word during the whole conversation.   Marion and Sophie assumed we were busy quietly playing and could not hear, much less understand what they were talking about. Then Sophie changed the subject and told Marion, "You are so much luckier than me."

Marion leaned against the kitchen sink and sucking on the cigarette again asked her, "Why do you say that?"

"Well, you have two young and beautiful children to care for every day."

"Oh this makes me luckier than you? Marion walked back to the table and sat down. "I need to hear more."

"It is like this. You have more things to do in a day keeping you busy. Most of my day is waiting for the mail and then being able to talk to you."

Marion smiled raising an eyebrow and said, "Please go on you have my attention."

"You get up in the morning and make them breakfast. I only have myself to cook for and cooking just for me isn't as much fun as when I cook for others."

"I can understand that but this is every day" She held up her hand as to stop her and said, "Sorry please continue."

"You get to dress and bath them. You have someone to take care of, love, and be loved. I have no one. I miss my husband so much."

Marion exhaled smoke and smashed the butt in the ashtray. "You know Sophie; I sometimes don't look at it that way. I am glad you said something. This has made me feel better."

Sophie went on saying, "Before I forget, I will tell you something I have never told you before. My husband and I tried to get pregnant before he left. He really wants a boy. I know he wants someone to carry on his name in case he is killed." Sophie put out her cigarette and then said, "It obviously has not happened yet. We are so afraid he will be killed before I get pregnant. We want a child so bad. Now do you see why I think you are so lucky?"

"Well let me tell you a thing or two about my children. You need to know just how hard it is. There is the stretching of money for food and just the few little extras. If I could I would made them stay indoors and safe all the time. Then I have the dilemma of letting them go outside and play or make them stay inside with me all the time? They do get on my nerves some time. I just want to scream sometimes. This sometimes makes me think I am a bad mother. I go out most of the time with them, but sometimes I just need some space. Adult time without the children is one reason I value our time together so much in spite of your nagging. Then when I let them leave without me I worry the whole time they are gone. There is another thing we must talk about it and I think now is the time."

"Oh no, this sounds serious." said Sophie.

"First, I know you have heard some of the same rumors I have heard. Marion looked at our door and what seemed like right at us. We both started to get up then she turned away. She picked up her almost empty pack and offered it to Sophie. They both lit cigarettes again.

*****

Anna had to keep reminding herself that little Max was only five years old. They were holding each other and crying. She knew they needed to change hiding places immediately. The ordeal was affecting her. No longer was her curly brown hair looking proper. It had straightened and had serious knots. Her beautiful eyes now were blood red with large dark circles completely around each eye. She was weak from lack of food. She had to ration what they had left.

She placed him on the makeshift bed and scooped up the supplies into her bag. On the bed and crying she wanted to comfort him but there was not much time left. She would have to deal with that before they left because his crying would attract unwanted attention. Nervously her mind raced as she was trying to figure out how much time they had left. She guessed it had been ten minutes since he was spotted. The children would be home now and explaining what they had seen. Allowing five minutes to tell the story and make their mother believe what she was hearing and another five minutes for the phone call made the time start now. Fifteen minutes for the police or Gestapo to react and get here meant at the most they needed to be gone in less than fifteen. Ten minutes would be safer. She didn't know where to go, only keep going west. She needed to hurry.

She glanced at her watch and figured she would have enough time to stop his crying and calmly she sat down next to him. She pulled him into a sitting position and smiled at him while wiping his face. He was so hurt that he did something wrong and made her mad. Looking at him she said, "Honey, you will always be the man in my life. You never have to do anything to prove this to me. Mommy is just upset because we must leave now."

It was working. He stopped crying, sniffled a little and put his small arms around her with his head on her shoulder. She looked over her shoulder at her watch and knew they needed to leave and now. She pulled away from him. "I need to look outside before we go. You were so brave for what you did." Wiping a tear from her eye while he was not looking she got up and walked to the dirty small window. Slowly she pulled away the curtain. After she did, her eyes got huge and she gasped. What she saw was the back of someone's polished boots standing in front of the window blocking their exit. Did he know? Did he hear them? Was he there standing guard? Looking at her watch she had do something fast.

The boots were from the young Nazi boy. Her heart was racing and beating so hard that she placed her hand over her chest to calm herself down. Then she heard it in the distance; it was the siren of the Gestapo with their distinctive up and down shrills. Her heart sank and the hair on her neck stood up. Anna knew they were coming for them.

She rushed over and picked up little Max in her arms. Her tears streaked down her face. There was no time to hide or run, they were caught. As the cars got closer the sirens got louder. She could feel him shaking. He knew too. She kissed him on the cheek and tasting the salty wetness of his tears said softly, "I love you so much. I am so sorry I failed you."

The police car, with its blaring sirens, was in front of their building.

*****

Sophie took a drag on her cigarette. "It obviously has not happened yet. No matter what you have said, I still think you are so lucky?"

Marion said, "I am now going to say some things I may regret." She paused a moment and looked directly at Sophie saying, "I know as much about you as you know about me. I am glad we can confide in one another." Marion took hold of Sophie's small hands and said, "Back to the rumors. If we are losing and are conquered what will happen to us?"

"I have not really thought about that? What are you trying to say?"

Marion looked a little teary eyed. "I also have my children to protect and worry about."

Marion then said something we had no idea she knew. "If the Americans or British get here first, I believe the children and I will be fine. If the Russians get here first, I have heard horrible stories of rape and murder. I don't want them to see any of these terrible things. I am hoping my husband gets here first and he will know what to do and protect us. In the mean time I think we need to talk some more and get a plan together. We need to do this soon there is not much time."

Sophie replied, "If you are right we will talk tomorrow and figure everything out.

Mika and I knew this new development was special. Marion knew about the Russians. The end was near and she knew we needed to leave and head toward relative safety, toward the western allies. She also was not a racist and bigot toward people of Jewish decent.

Sophie scooted back her chair, stood up and said, "I have to go now. I will talk to you tomorrow. Please be careful what you say."

As she left the apartment we all heard the police sirens heading our way.

*****

They were crying and holding each other as the siren approached. Anna knew it was going to stop in front and there was nothing she could do to help except hold and comfort little Max. She was going to miss him so much. Maybe he will be spared somehow. She knew she was going to possibly be raped, tortured and sent away. However, her main thoughts were about him.

She fully expected the cars to stop in front and Soldiers to exit as the cars reached the front. Soon they would enter the building screaming and shouting. They would tear up everything until discovering them hiding. Then forcing them into waiting cars for whatever would happen next.

The cars with their loud sirens passed by, not slowing down. They were going somewhere else. Anna's knees were weak. She almost fainted. Pulling a little away from him so she could see his face, she said, "It is ok baby. It is ok. We are going to be fine."

This time her tears were from unexpected joy. She held him tight sitting down on the bed with a grip of never letting go. She knew she had to collect her thoughts and get back to the reality of danger still around them. Relieved, Anna wondered what exactly just happened. She took a deep breath as she set little Max on the bed. She tiptoed slowly over to the window. The Nazi boy was still in front, obviously not aware of Anna and little Max. He was talking to some other people oblivious to what had happened a few feet away. She snuck back to Max and happily said, "I do not know about you, but I am hungry. Let us eat and celebrate a little, ok?"

With shaking hands, she opened a can of food not even looking to see what it was. She was still shaking uncontrollably. She looked at the bottle of wine and said, "I can't think of a better time to drink some." She looked directly at him and added, "You too."

Little Max wiped off his face with his sleeve and said, "Me too mommy."

"Of course honey. We will always do everything together, including your first taste of wine."

While eating, Anna relaxed and stopped shivering. She believed if these two children had reported them that the cars would have stopped and they would have been caught by now. Tonight they should be fine. She decided not to attempt to capture any more food today. The risk was too great. She wanted more time with little max and was exhausted. What had just happened was to be recorded in the book, including how she felt as the sirens passed.

Everything happened so fast. One minute everything was quiet and fine, then the sirens or something else. Everything now meant danger. Anna continually reminded herself that the end was near and all she would have to do was survive maybe just one more day. She could do that.

*****

When the sirens passed, Marion asked us, "Are you both hungry?"

She went into a cabinet and brought out some food to fix for us. We both saw where the food was and nodded at each other. We knew what we were going to do next. It was a little late and we were tired. We went into the other room to talk and retire for the night. We had a lot to discuss. We talked about everything we had experienced. We knew several important things. We knew there were two people needing our help; a five-year-old child and his mother. We knew something they did not know. We could not tell them. They would not believe us even if we did. There was only four days left. Who would believe an eight-year-old girl and five-year-old boy? Dropping off food was about all we could do for now if our grandmother allows us to leave. We talked quite a bit before falling asleep.

*****

Anna and little Max played with his toy Soldier together. She did everything she could think of to help him forget all the bad things that had happened that day. She knew she had made the right decision not to venture out. It was their night. The air raid sirens went off twice and she did not even get up and look around. Before long, he fell asleep for the night.

Anna thought about how she was going to write the story and where to begin. She started with earnest. Occasionally she would stop and take a break, but not often. She would drink some of the water and change the pots and cans catching more water, and then she got right back to writing. She made up her mind; they both were getting some sort of bath tomorrow and somehow she was washing her hair. It would make them feel better.

She could not help herself, she kept writing and writing. It was so important and she was in a zone. In the morning she woke up on her side with the book and pencil clutched in her hands, not remembering falling asleep.

*****

Knowing only three days of danger was left, helped us sleep. Off in the distance, during the night, we heard what sounded like distant thunder. It was so faint that we could not tell the distance or tell the difference between bombs or thunder. It seemed that for that moment, the war was all around but somehow forgetting about us. This is how it may have seemed to the people of Berlin at the time. Believing the war was somehow sparing them. This could not have been further from the truth. This and more is what Mika and I knew.

We could smell breakfast cooking. It smelled delicious. We got up and went into the other room where Marion greeted us with, "Good morning sleepy heads."

We stretched, yawned, and replied, "Good morning."

This was the day we may have been waiting our entire lives. We were getting prepared to risk our lives and our entire family to help two strangers. We knew this was the right thing to do. We hoped our parents had helped them before or maybe in the past they did not help them and regretted it and we were there to fix things. Maybe this was the family's shame. Maybe somehow we were sent to correct things.

191

We decided we would just have to do what we knew was right and hope for the best. We were overanalyzing everything.

Marion went out the door for a brief period and Mika ran quickly snatching two cans and stashing them in the other room. He then returned to his seat before she came back. When Marion re-entered, she had not noticed anything different. We smiled at each other. First step completed.

We quickly finished our breakfast. I went in got our coats and put his on him first. Marion seemed to start to stop us but said instead, "You two are sure in a hurry today."

I answered her with a lie, "We will have more time if we leave now and Mika wants to see his German again today. He said he would be back about now."

"You tell the German hi for me too. You two only have fifteen minutes, understand?" Then she turned completely around and watched us getting ready said, "You two are growing up so fast. Remember our rules."

I answered, "Yes mom," as we closed the door behind us.

Mika smiled and looked at me and asked, "What rules?"

I smiled back at him shrugged my shoulder telling him I did not know either. We chuckled and started down the stairs.

*****

Anna didn't sleep well. Restless and couldn't get things off her mind to relax made for a long night. Little Max was stirring; he slept all night without moving one bit. She realized she fell asleep while writing, book still open and pencil on the floor. When she opened the book, she was amazed at how much she had written. There was a lot more done than she realized making her smile. She stretched out and it felt so good. This was also bath day and they were going to get a good cleaning. It was nippy down there but she knew she needed to keep him as healthy as possible with a good cleaning. If he were to get to sick it would be all over for them both ensuring he was totally dry and warm. Then she would take care of herself. She was tired of looking so bad. She knew her health was just as important. He was totally dependent on her.

She went over to the sink, poured enough water in to do the job and smiled at him saying, "This is going to be a little cold but little fellow you need this bath. You still need to be real quiet, ok?"

He looked at her with his blue eyes and all he said was, "Yes mommy."

"Then we will eat some breakfast and wait for something good to happen. Today I will only go out once, I promise." When she was finished, they both went upstairs to wait for the sirens.

*****

It was chilly, mid forties and going to warm up nicely in the afternoon with partial clouds, so maybe no bombing raids might happen during the daylight hours. As we exited our building into the street, we saw him standing across the street. He was just standing there in his Nazi uniform, all of about sixteen. His black hair slicked back looking so much like a littler version of Hitler. If he was old enough he would grow that ridicules moustache and be Hitler's little double.

He knew he looked like him and loved it. The color of his uniform was light brown signifying youth league. He wore it with pride. He was not a typical teenager wanting to have typical teenage fun. He was a serious teenager desiring his chance to be the Fuehrer's man. The Army was calling up all seventeen year olds and allowing older men to join. He believed all the propaganda. Especially everything printed about Jews.

He wore four honored ribbons on his chest. They were like battle ribbons that the real Army awards for being in battle or doing something deemed important. Two of these ribbons had a small yellow Star of David on it in the middle. It was awarded to any Nazi youth that found Jews in hiding and either captured them or reported them to authorities.

"We need to be on the lookout for him and anyone like him. We need to know when he is and be careful. He is on the lookout for anything strange or different overlooked by others." I had to tell Mika these things. Immediately as I said this he looked at us and started to walk toward us. We just froze. There was something so cold and unnerving that it just stopped us right in our tracks and we had those two cans in Mika's coat pocket. How would we explain that if he noticed?

I saw Mika place his hand in the same pocket. He was thinking the same as me again. We were holding hands and squeezed them at the same time, signaling. We held our breaths and began shivering. We did not know if it was the actual cool air or the situation. It was as if we were seeing pure evil walking toward us. He seemed to not even blink. His dark eyes were hiding something. His eyes were so dark and deep.

Did he see something unusual? What made him decide to come over? What are we going to say? Mika must remain quiet and let me do most of the talking. Mika must hold his temper. If Mika was his usual size, I know he would slug him. We must play this part of two innocent children. If we mess this up just what are the consequences? There was not enough time for me to even tell him to be quiet. We were just frozen there staring at his approach.

He stopped about three feet away and said, "Hi Mina. Is there something wrong?"

Without waiting for a reply, he looked at Mika and said, "Hi Mika."

I thought at the moment, "Oh my God he knows us! What am I going to say? Without thinking I said, "Oh, I am just a little cold, how about you?"

"I am doing real well." Then holding out his chest for us to see said, "My commanding officer just awarded me another ribbon the other day."

Mika was holding my hand so tightly it was beginning to hurt. I knew I must keep Mika quiet. I could feel through our hands his temper building. He was getting ready to explode and I knew it. I felt the responsibility of everything was mine. He said he wanted a little adventure now we have one; a large and real adventure with life and death consequences.

Mika squeezed my hand twice letting me know he was about to do something. Oh no, I have to stop him. He let go of my hand and looked me right in the eyes. I could see his hatred for the little Nazi. Then he just gave me a little smile and placed his finger to my chest and said, "Tag you're it." Then he ran toward the café. I quickly said to the Nazi boy, "I have to go sorry," and ran after Mika. It was brilliant and I was worried. It was so unexpected. It was exciting and thrilling. We both loved the excitement with our hearts beating so fast.

Mika looked at me and whispered, "I knew you would like some excitement too. Something we will always remember."

I replied, "We will have to drop the food when we go back."

Mika said. "We will have to wait for him to not be around. Good thing we saw him before we tried." With an even bigger smile he added, "See, fate is with us, everything will be fine."

*****

Anna and little Max sat in the darkened corner and watched the same two children they saw yesterday as they exited their building again. She thought, "I know they saw him. Why didn't they report it?"

Anna's heart felt better as she kept him closer and watched with her other eye. She pulled him closer and whispered, "You see the brave thing you did yesterday did us no harm."

The smile on his face reflected much happiness. Still, he felt a little different. Maybe she will trust him a little more in the future. He so wanted to be a little older so he help more. Anna sensed the difference in little Max. She held him close and whispered, "Never to do anything like that again."

Anna did not want to spoil the moment by indulging too much information. When the time is right she will tell him, but not now. They sat there content just watching the people in the street. She knew maybe someday when this nightmare was over, little Max might have a normal childhood again. They could no longer see the Nazi boy. He seemed to have left.

Anna continued to whisper in Little Max's ear, "Remember if the air sirens go off, I will take off running. You are to stay here and be a quiet as a mouse no matter what you see."

They were down to one small can of food. If she gave it all to him and drank plenty of water, she figured she could hold out for two or maybe three days. She would have to try every day for more food and sometimes more than just once. She did not want to go out more than once a day if she could help it. As she contemplated her plan, Anna wondered why the two children crossed the street and headed their way. This was strange and slightly alarming. Anna stood up holding little Max with both hands. She looked toward the stairs hoping to retreat. Something did not feel right.

*****

We decided the time was right; the Nazi boy was nowhere to be seen and only a few other people around. Our plan was to duck inside quickly without being seen and drop the food where the strangers would be able to find it. Little did we know that even the best plans are sometimes flawed. Just before we ducked inside, we carefully scanned the area. We both rushed inside and were startled to see the two strangers standing in the corner. There was just enough light for us to see a woman in a dark coat with the little boy standing in front of her with her white hands on both his shoulders. We surprised her too. Her chest was going in and out very fast with her breaths visible in the cold air. She was visibly frightened.

We glanced at each other. We had no contingency for this unexpected confrontation. Mika nervously reached into his pocket and pulled the cans out. He gently placed the cans on the ground and without saying a word, grabbed my hand and hastily pulled me out of the entrance and away from the building. We crossed the street and entered our building. Mika spoke first. "Why did you not say something?"

Take back by his question, I answered. "You have a mouth and a big one. Why did you not say something?"

"I was so surprised. I became dumbfounded."

"Me, too," I replied in a softer tone as I lowered my head. "Oh well. It is done now."

As we looked up the stairs, Sophie was looking at us.

"Now what are you two up to?" she demanded.

"Our usual games Ma'am," I answered as we slowly climbed the stairs.

We awkwardly entered the apartment with Sophie close behind.

*****

Anna replayed the brief interaction in her mind as she analyzed the situation. The two children ducked inside quickly as if to avoid being seen. They seemed surprised to see us standing there in the dark corner. They did not scream or run for help. Anna's heart started racing. This brief moment seemed to unfold in slow motion. The little boy, no older than little Max, placed two cans of food on the ground not saying a single word, and then just left. These two children must have suspected we were here and planned the clandestine delivery of the food. Anna looked down at little Max. He looked up at her and smiled. He felt a delightful connection to these children. Anna stepped into the light of the entrance, briefly looked outside, and picked up the cans.

Down the stairs, Anna sat down next to little Max and began opening one of the cans. A single tear escaped from her eye and slowly rolled down her face. Anna could not comprehend why people that she did not know would risk their lives to help them. These two children did almost as much as Elsa. They have nothing to gain and everything to lose by helping. She now knew she would not have to go out and get more food at least that day. For now, this made her feel safer. This had to be written in the book soon as little Max fell asleep.

Anna also debated trying to talk to them should another opportunity arise. She would have to decide what she wanted to say. Gradually she was comforted in knowing they had helped. Joy and hope now were inside Anna. This was so unexpected. This feeling was brief. As she was getting ready to light a candle, she heard someone talking outside the window. She looked at little Max and put a finger in front of her lips, "Shhhhhhh."

She tiptoed quietly to the window. As she pulled the curtain slowly and carefully away, she saw him again. The little Nazi boy was standing there talking to an adult. She heard him say, "I am going to look around anyway."

The adult replied, "Go ahead. You will not find anything. I am sure."

The adult started walking away but the boy turned and went into the seemingly abandoned building that had so graciously harbored Anna and little Max. Anna quickly went over to hold and keep little Max quiet. She looked over at the darkest corner. If he comes down the stairs he would spot them for sure, so she moved them both to this desperate hiding place. If they moved or made a noise, the threatening Nazi boy would definitely come down in order to investigate. She held her breath and listened.

Anna heard the boy moving things around upstairs. Only a few minutes before they were there and would have been captured if it hadn't been for the two children leaving the food. She wondered if they left anything giving away their presents; a piece of trash, anything and were the two children seen. She hoped it was not obvious how she had arranged objects to hide behind. It was not fair. One minute everything was fine, and then something happens like this that changes everything. They both started shaking with fear again and holding each other tight as they heard him starting down the stairs. Same boards creaked that Anna had noticed before, so she knew exactly where he was. He stopped and listened. Anna put her hand over Max's mouth and silently shifted her head back and forth saying no. They were listening for any noise from him and he was listening for any noise coming from them.

*****

As the three of us entered the apartment, Marion greeted us, "Good I am glad you are home. I will fix all of us some food. Want to eat with us Sophie?"

Sophie sat down at the table and as usual lit a cigarette. "Sure what are we having?"

Marion looked in the cabinet. She moved several things around looking for the missing cans. Our eyes shifted towards each other. We scurried into the other room, partially closing the door as we had done before. We could hear her mumbling to herself, "Now what did I do with those cans?"

Mika looked at me and whispered, "It won't matter we only have two more days at the most."

"We will only take one tomorrow that will be enough."

He agreed saying, "We are also going to take a small coat for him. I saw one in the closet I want to give him."

"That was exciting. It felt good and right."

"I thought so too. I also know we are doing the right thing. It has been a long time since I have felt this good."

"It will be another drop and run with less time. I can't wait for tomorrow."

Marion sat at the table lighting her cigarette and they both started talking at the same time, only very softly - obviously wanting us not to hear. It did not seem to matter to us. We felt happy knowing that tomorrow we would execute another good deed. There was such little time left. We knew they would make it and we would have been one reason why.

We moved into the kitchen to get water when we heard Sophie say, "You can catch it from just by being around them. I also blame them for this terrible war. Hitler was right when he said they need to be exterminated like bugs. I know he did not say that, but it is what he implied. I hate all Jews, even children." Sophie looked right at me and I got a bad feeling in the pit of my stomach.

*****

They were frozen in place; scared to move. Anna with her cold hand over little Max's mouth and listening, they knew the little Nazi boy was standing on the stairs listening too. Time seemed to stand still. She was so afraid that little Max might start crying, sneeze, or cough.

Then she heard it. He turned away, stomping his feet on the stairs as he left. She heard his boots on the pavement as he ran away from the building. She did not know if he knew something and was leaving to tell someone, or just changed his mind. She was tired of running, hiding, and making decisions. She held little Max close and decided to chance it and stay. She would again spend the entire night adding more stories to the book and hope she had made the right decision again. Besides she had help now. Only time would tell. She stayed up all night worrying and writing.

CHAPTER 12

Change of Heart

April 30, 1945

We knew what the significance of this day. Underground, within a few short miles, Adolph Hitler and Eva Braun would commit suicide plunging Germany into leadership turmoil. For some unexplained reason, there were no air raid warnings during the night; only an eerie silence. It helped us fall asleep - unlike everyone else. We knew in the morning there would only be two days left.

The morning arrived and little did we know just how this day would change our lives forever. Things were going to happen so fast that decisions would have to be made almost without thinking. We were to make life and death choices never dreamed we would ever have to make. Our happiness in thinking we had made the right judgments were now going to be challenged.

We quickly ate and stole another can of food as planned. We had the routine down to a science. In what seemed like a flash, Mika put on both overcoats, hid the food in one pocket, and we were out the door. Our little hearts beating fast with anticipation. As we descended the stairs, we heard Sophie open her door to either look or call us. We didn't even look back.

*****

Anna didn't sleep at all during the night. She should have. She wrote all night as if everything she had lived for depended on her writing this masterpiece. Carefully to add what the two other children did for them. Extremely tired, she was about to make several mistakes. She washed her face and made a cold breakfast for little Max while continually peaking outside. The sun was shining and people were moving about in the street - more so than other days. Anna decided they needed to wait upstairs. If a chance happened, she wanted to talk to the children. She breathed a sigh of relief not seeing the little Nazi boy. He must not have seen anything to report.

Hurriedly she told little Max to be quiet and follow her. Upstairs she looked around and didn't see any potential problems and promptly sat down with him on her lap, proceeding to wait. Little Max was quiet and continually smiled at Anna. She always smiled back at him. She was warm, comfortable and so tired. She kept her head up and resting against the wall believing she would not fall asleep in that position. She was wrong and slipped into sleep.

*****

We looked around and there were more people than usual. No one paid us any attention and the little Nazi boy was absent. We looked at each other, smiled and both nodded yes. It was time for adventure again. We felt confident because of what we did yesterday. We couldn't wait to do it again. We walked directly across the street, not even trying to disguise our actions. In our excitement, we forgot to do this and we would regret it. We went into the front of 108 nine Straße. As we entered the little boy was waiting for us, we did not see the mother.

Mika took off his extra coat and placed it on the little boy. I told him, "We can't be here long, have this. We have to go now."

Mika and I walked out the building happy in what we had just done. We were about twenty feet away when I looked back. What I saw shocked me. Mika looked back and saw him too. The little boy, with our coat on, was behind us about three feet away. He had followed us outside without us noticing.

We rushed back to him and as we approached, we saw the little Nazi boy come around the corner. We knew we could not take him back right then; we had to take him with us. I held one of his little hands and Mika grabbed the other. All three of us headed toward the café. Our hearts felt as if there were beating through our chest. This was unexpected and we knew we were in much danger.

*****

Anna did not mean to, didn't even realize she had. She was up all night and exhausted. She sat down hoping not to fall asleep. It did not work; she was just too warm and comfortable. She never heard Mika and Mina enter. She did not feel or hear her little darling walk away from her. She woke up and immediately knew something was wrong. She looked around for little Max in a small panic. She closed her eyes for a few seconds; he couldn't have gone outside again.

Then the hard panic set in as she saw all three holding hands and heading away. She put her hands over her mouth and said, "Oh my god no." She put the lapel over her star and started to go and get him. Then she saw him, all spit polished in his brown uniform. She looked at little Max and then back at the Nazi boy several times. There was nothing she could do except step back into the shadows, watch, and hope.

The Nazi boy stopped in front of her building and placed his hand over his eyes straining to see into the darkness. Anna stood there frozen in fear. Then he turned around snapping his boots together and stood at attention in front of her building. She knew these actions meant something was terribly wrong. All she wanted to do was go out there scoop up little Max and run. However, she knew she could not just yet. She knew not to move or make any noise and pray. She could see the love of her life playing and having fun; oblivious to the danger.

*****

I told Mika, "Try and not look back at him."

"Not a problem. Let us play like nothing is wrong and hope for the best. When he leaves, we will take this little guy back and everything will be fine."

I smiled at the boy and he was smiling and looking so happy. He had no idea. I asked him, "What's your name?"

"Max. I am named after my father."

Mika then said, "Nice name and you need to follow everything we tell you, ok?"

He just smiled back at both of us with bright blue eyes and dimples.

I said, "Let's play tag. Do you know the game, Max?"

He smiled and touched me and said, "You are it," Then started running toward the café.

I smiled at Mika and said, "I like him, he cheated already."

We both laughed and ran after him. The old German was there at the café. Max went right up to him as if he recognized him, until he got close. Realizing it was not Colonel Von Ryan, he froze right in front of him. The German smiled and offered him a piece of pastry. "Bitta," Max shyly obliged.

The German went to lift little Max as he had done to Mika but Max was a little too quick for the German. Max turned and ran toward us. He held up the pastry for me to see. I smiled at him, placed my hand on his little shoulder, and said, "Go ahead and eat it. Everything is fine." Then I looked back and saw the little Nazi boy standing at attention in front of 108 Nine Straße and motioned Mika with my elbow to look.

Mika immediately glanced and turned back around. I could see in his eyes that he was worried. I looked down at little Max. The outer coat had come open and anyone looking could see the yellow star. I quickly turned him around and pulled him close to hide the star. Mika saw this and came over to help me get Max's coat straight and buttoned up tight again.

We looked at each other and he whispered to me, "What next?"

Off in the distance, we heard it. It was distant sirens of police or Gestapo heading our way again. It made the hair on my neck stand up. My stomach started turning. My knees went weak. I knew they were coming for us, I knew it. I have never been that frightened before. Now our family would perish because of us. There was only one day left and we failed. Not only would this little boy perish, but our entire family too.

Mika looked at me, placed his hand in mine. He felt it too. He whispered, "Nothing we can do now," as the sirens up and down sounds got closer and closer.

All three of us started slowly walking hand in hand back to Max's building. It was all over. At least we had tried. The police car came around the corner and headed right for us. Then it went right by us. Mika looked surprised as I, and we both exhaled a deep breath of relief. It was short lived. The Gestapo car stopped in front of 108 Nine Straße. The little Nazi boy opened the back door of the black sedan. Then he raised his arm and saluted in the Hail Hitler salute fashion while at attention. Then he turned and pointed inside the building.

*****

She watched in horror as her little darling went straight over to the high-ranking officer. She knew he probably thought it was Colonel Von Ryan. What would he do when he realized it was not him? Her heart was pounding and she felt a pit in her throat. She could do nothing. When the German reached for little Max, Anna lunged forward as she prepared to go out and save her son. She then bent down to see if the little Nazi boy was still there standing guard. He was. If she could sneak out somewhere else, maybe then she could take her little man by the hand and simply walk away. She started to devise a plan as she heard the sirens. It was far away but the distinctive sound was headed her way.

She put her hands together as if she was praying. However, she knew there was no time to escape. The warm tears started to run silently down her soiled face. Despite everything she had done, they were caught. The help from the two brave children created hope only now to be dashed. She still had hoped the cars would pass as before. She watched as all three holding hands looked helplessly her way. She could tell they knew. When the police car passed them, she let out a sigh of relief. It was quick lived.

Two of the cars stopped in front of the building. Time did not slow down this time. It sped up. Gestapo were on her in a flash. Someone grabbed her arm spinning her around and ran their hands all over her; searching. They were yelling and barking orders too fast for her weary mind to process. Confused and defeated, she said nothing. She did not know what to do as she was pulled and pushed out of the building into the daylight. She looked over at the three of them standing there.

They were standing still, watching like everyone else. She realized the police did not know about little Max and they were not going to get him yet. Momentarily she was relieved and tears of horror changed to ones of joy. The Gestapo and police didn't know the difference. She was able to give all three a special smile before she was pushed into the back of the car. As they pulled away she watched from the small oval window in the back.

*****

Max, Mika, and I just stood, stunned and watching. Immediately the woman was escorted out, being pushed and shoved. She looked right at us. Her dazed look was instantly replaced with a sweet gaze. She turned and watched us as she was driven away, with a little smile on her face.

Max then said, "Mommy."

My heart sank. I placed my arms around him and scooted him inside the nearest doorway covering his mouth with my hand. I needed to keep him quiet. Mika was there helping me shield him from view. We knew we had to keep him quiet and keep him out of site, especially from that little Nazi boy.

"Now what are we to do?" I said to Mika. "We cannot leave him here. We can't leave him across the street. We can't take him home. We have to keep him from being discovered for just one more night and some of the next day, maybe. What are we going to do?" I was lost.

Max was crying and shaking. Mika looked back and saw the little Nazi boy shaking hands and talking to others. Then he said, "We need to get out of here."

Looking around I said, "Where?"

"Anywhere out of sight and hearing distance," there was a tone of panic in his voice.

Max was crying repeatedly, "mommy." It was sad and dangerous. I started crying too. Consoling and quieting little Max wasn't easy. We were staying too long. We needed to get away and soon. Even at his young age, he understood that his mother was now gone. We were trapped.

Mika peaked around the doorway and told me it was no good, "The little shit is still there looking like a cat that caught a bird. He is talking to two or three other people, all adults. I will bet he gets another ribbon for this."

After hugging Max tighter I said, "Not for this one."

Mika looked at me intently. "Not if I have anything to do with it either."

Then he held out his hand. I placed my hand in his and squeezed. We were in this together. I asked, "Do you think he saw Max or knows about him?"

"He saw him. I do not think he knows the connection just yet. He is busy and we might be able to sneak away."

"No," I said. "We have to be sure he does not see him with us again. He might then put two and two together."

Mika squeezed my little hand again as he said, "If I was only a little bigger. I would have no problem snapping his neck. I don't think it would bother me."

"Well, we have to do something soon." I pointed at Max and continued with, "Someone is listening."

Max was sobbing intensely at this point and it appeared as if he might throw up at any minute. His mother had told him if anything like this was to happen, she would do her best to get back to him soon as she could and to stay, but this was different. She hadn't prepared him for this. She tried as much as she could to prepare him for as many situations as possible, not thinking of this one.

"What is the Nazi boy doing now?" I asked.

Mika peaked around the brick corner in the doorway and said, "Same thing; he is just talking and looking around. I think he is looking for us. You have to keep him quieter."

I replied sarcastically, "Sure thing, I will just put my hand over his mouth 'till he stops breathing. If it were you, do you think someone would be able to quiet you?" I tugged on his coat pulling him back.

Mika looked at me scared. "Too late, he just started walking this way."

"When he gets near," I said, "I will run up and start talking fast. I will distract him enough for you to take Max around the block to our apartment. I will meet you there later."

"That won't work. We cannot take him home."

Frustrated, I exclaimed, "We can't leave him here or alone. If you have a better plan now would be the time." Just as I said that, the air raid siren started to blow.

Mika looked back and smiled. "He's running the other way for a shelter." There was excitement and relief in his voice.

"Let's go, this is the perfect time" All three of us ran toward our building. There was nothing else we could do. As we approached the building where Max and his mother had been hiding, max's hand slipped out of my fingers and he ran into the building with us right behind him.

Mika yelled at him, "No, we have to go to a shelter in our building."

Little Max just kept saying, "My book, and my book," as he quickly ran down some stairs. We were directly behind him every step. Dark, but still able to see, we witnessed the scene of their hiding place. He quickly picked up a little book and a small toy Soldier which he tucked in his little pocket. This time Mika grabbed his cold little hand and pulled him up the stairs, across the street, and down in the basement with me following.

Marion, Sophie, and several other people were already there huddled together. Marion took our hands and made a place where we could sit next to them and be somewhat sheltered. We saw the relief on their faces.

I looked for Max and saw him being held by Sophie. He must have gone right to her. He was already on her lap with her re-assuring him. It was dark with flickering candles that made eerie shadows and movements dancing on the walls. It was cold and musty, much colder than outside.

We could hear the blasts from above and with dirt falling after every thunderous blast. We knew this was not a false alarm and the bombs were close. Mika and I knew that we were being carpet-bombed. This was intense and real. We could die here. I saw an intense fear in others' eyes that echoed after each explosion as they watched the quivering ceiling. With every sudden burst, we flinched and hid our heads. Marion was trying to shield us both from any possible harm by covering us with her frail body. This was something special, and if I live I will never forget.

There was a calm moment during this storm that Mika and I looked over at Sophie with little Max snuggled up tight in her arms, holding on for dear life. Sophie was quietly singing something. At one point I heard her say, "I am here, don't worry." As I leaned a little closer, I recognized the melody as a nursery rhyme. I was amazed she knew the song so well without having any children. Someday she just may become a good mother after all. I nudged Mika to look at them. After, he turned back around and smiled at me. Here was the bigot that we both knew and she was holding this little Jewish boy with care.

The bombing went on and on for what seemed like several hours. Marion was markedly more scared this time than when we first awakened into these bodies. Somehow Mika and I have to get her to believe that the war is lost and to not stay in this part of Berlin. This part of Berlin, the Russians will possess in just a few hours; not days or weeks. We knew if we could move south or west, we might make it out of the pending Russian territory and be safer.

The sirens announced an all clear and Sophie spoke first. She surprised us by saying, "I will take this little fellow with me. Evidently, he was separated from his family and somehow made it here. Do you know who he is Marion?"

"No," she replied. "But it is too late to search. We do not have any other choice but to take him home with us."

"We will find out where he belongs in the morning." He had somehow fallen asleep in her arms. "I want to take care of him tonight."

Oh no I thought, "What about his jacket? It has the star on it; she will surely see it and that will be the end of him. She hated all Jews, even children. I whispered to Mika, "We have to get his coat."

Marion looked at me and said, "What are you two whispering about?"

Then turned to Sophie and said, "We need to talk where little ears cannot hear. It is very, very important. It can only wait 'till we get home."

Sophie stood up with sleeping Max in her arms and said, "Ok the children can stay in your place and we will go to mine for a little talk."

"Whew", I thought, "That was close. This will give us time to get his other coat off." As we entered our building and went upstairs, we didn't know what to expect. Many of the hits were louder and closer this time. When we opened the door to our apartment, we saw that the kitchen window was broken. Dark now with light snow blowing in the window, Marion and Sophie quickly went to the window and hung a blanket over it. We could see our breaths as we exhaled. The only damage seemed to be the window. We all looked in the other room and it seemed unscathed.

Sophie gently placed Max on our bed, carefully placing a blanket over him, and returned to the kitchen.

Marion told us to, "Bundle up in the blankets and stay warm, I will be back in just a few minutes. Sophie and I have to do some adult talking. We will keep our doors open so you can see us."

Sophie and Marion, true to her word, cracked both doors open and left. Struggling to get the coat off, not be seen and not to wake little Max was not easy. However, we did it and just in time too. Marion and Sophie were coming back and still talking as we finished. Their talk took little time, but we knew it was important. We could tell what the subject was by what Sophie said next. "We can go south to my sister's place. It is about ten miles southeast of here."

Marion said, "We will have to travel light with mostly just food."

Sophie replied, "I trust you. You have always known what was happening and have always helped me. We will figure everything out in the morning. I will take the little boy tonight and clean him up and feed him in the morning. I am going to enjoy this so much. Then we can drop him off on the authorities while we travel. His family must be going crazy."

I whispered to Mika, "We have to somehow stop her."

Mika asked, "Why?"

"When she cleans him up she will see he is Jewish."

"Oh, yes." Both of our minds were racing to find a way to keep him with us. There was so little time left.

I spoke up to Marion and Sophie saying, "He is asleep, it would be better if he stayed and slept here."

Sophie snapped at me. "No! He is going with me."

Marion said, "We will get up just before dawn. It is going to be a long day. Sophie you get back here then, ok?"

Sophie went over and carefully picked up sleeping Max. As she carried him toward the door, Marion clapped her hands together and said to us, "Children it is bedtime. We are going to have a very long day tomorrow."

We climbed into the bed and as Mika looked at me and whispered, "We did all we could do. We will just have to pray and hope for the best."

I replied, "One good thing is we are heading tomorrow in the right direction. Our grandfather must have told her we all needed to leave and what direction." We said our prayers that night, making sure we spent extra time including this little boy, Max, in our thoughts.

CHAPTER 13

Chimera

May 1, 1945

Only one day left until the unofficial surrender

It seemed like we had just fallen asleep. We were still exhausted and wanted to stay warm under the blankets. Lit candles in the other room allowed us to see our breaths. It was terribly cold. Mika was looking at me as I was woke up, obviously wanting to say something but waiting for me to fully come to my senses. He whispered in my ear, "It is almost daylight. She's making breakfast. We have not heard from Sophie. I wonder if she gave him a bath. If she had, she would have come over right away - probably screaming.

"I fell asleep so fast; if she came over I slept through it. Were you awake for a while?"

"I fell right asleep too. I do not think she came back here last night."

"We are leaving here today and finally I think we can be of some real help with what we know."

Mika then added, "I am sure we can. I wonder what dangers are in store for us today. Then what's going to happen? Are we stuck here forever?"

"I don't know. I was just thinking about his mother. She only had two days at the most. This is the last full or partial day. Why did that have to happen?"

Mika softly said, "I do not know. Everything happens for a reason and maybe she will live and they can be re-united."

We smelled the eggs cooking. Marion went to our door and softly said, "Ok children, I hear you whispering. It is time to get up. I will need your help all day today. We are going to travel and stay for a little while with Sophie's sister."

Mika asked her, "Where is that mommy?"

"It is a little far and we will have to walk. This is going to take all day. We may get lucky and someone may give us a ride. However, if not, we will be walking all day. She walked over to us and sat beside us on the bed.

"This is the time you two are going to have to just grow up a little. Today, and even tomorrow, may be tough. I know it is the right thing to do and we will be just fine. Now get up and get dressed. Get into your favorite clothes and put on several extra layers, as many as comfortable."

The sky was now beginning to lighten. Several holes in the clouds allowed light rays to scatter through. A knock at the door startled us. Max was in Sophie's arms and smiling at us as they entered. It was as if he jumped out of her arms and into mine after stretching out his little arms. I was so glad to see him too. He was clean. I looked at Mika and said loud enough for everyone to hear said, "She cleaned him up and he looks so handsome. Probably looks like his daddy too."

Max looked at me and said, "Everyone say I look like my mommy too."

It choked me up a little.

Marion asked Max. "Did you have a good night and isn't Mrs. Sophie nice?

He smiled as I held him and answered, "Yes."

Mika looked at Max and announced, "We are going on a trip today, and everything will be fine."

Little Max replied, "Mommy said if she leave me to stay so she can find me."

It was a heartbreaking moment since we knew the truth. I was just thinking, "How much does he understand? How much should we tell him? If we say the wrong thing what will happen?" I chose my words carefully.

"You are right, you should stay if possible. However, you cannot stay here by yourself. We are leaving and you need to come with us. We will leave her a note so she can find us later. We will find her, I promise."

Mika added, "I will get something to write the note." He went into the other room and removed Max's little book from his coat getting ready to rip out a page. As he opened it he saw all the music that was hand written in every available space. Mika changed his mind and later told me he felt this little book was special. He felt an odd energy emanate from the open pages. With no one watching, he scribbled something in the back and handed it to Max with a large smile. He found another piece of paper and handed it to me.

I took the paper and pencil to Marion and Sophie asking them, "Max said we need to leave a note for his mother so it would tell her where to find him."

Marion took the paper and said, "I will do it." She then added, "You go over there and tell him I will take care of it and we will be with him soon."

Whispering in the corner, hoping not to be heard, Sophie told Marion, "I know who the little boy is!"

Marion replied, "You do? That's great! We can drop him off and be on our way."

Sophie looked over at us believing we could not hear and said, "It is a little more complicated than that. He is an orphan."

"How do you know?"

"You have your secrets and now I will have mine."

"Now Sophie, don't get mean. I have two good reasons for needing to know everything."

"I know and that is why I am going to keep it a secret."

We could see Marion starting to get flustered. "Are we in any danger because of this secret?"

Sophie hesitated in answering and stared into Marion's eyes as she searched for a response.

"You have to tell me!" Marion exclaimed.

Sophie didn't want to tell Marion the truth. She knew Marion would not give up so she tried to bargain, "If anyone asks you anything about him or me, this is all you know. We are neighbors and friends. Not close friends, but friendly towards each other. Max is the little boys name and he is my son. This is all you know about me understand?"

Mika and I looked at each other a little stunned. She knows his story?

Marion reached out taking her hands and softly said, "Not really. I understand what you said. But I need to know more, trust me."

Sophie looked serious at Marion and added, "I do not care what may happen to me. He is mine now. I am keeping him and I know what I am doing."   Whispering to Mika, I said, "It looks like Sophie wasn't exactly what we thought. Maybe there is a caring and thoughtful woman under there after all."

The moment seemed so right. Mika and I went over and gave Sophie a hug.

She quickly got control of herself and said to us, "If anyone asks anything about me or Max. He is my son. Do you understand?"

I replied with, "If anyone asks, Max is your son and we love you for it." I hugged her tighter and saw tears coming slowly out of her eyes.

Sophie wiped a tear and said, "I do not have anything for him Marion, can you please help me?"

"Sure. I have some things that should fit." She stood with her arms crossed smiling at the new Sophie and said, "You are welcome to anything you need."

At this moment, we could not have been prouder of our grandmother. As Marion headed toward the other room she said, "I will go and pick out some things for him." She re-entered our room with Max's coat and a terrible look on her face. She held up the coat in front of her with the yellow Star in plain sight and said, "You need to tell me everything you know, now."

Sophie put both her hands in front of her face and sort of collapsed on the kitchen chair. Mika and I just stood there watching. We did not move or utter a word. We did not know what was next. Sophie composed herself and softly said, "Ok, and now I'll tell you everything I know."

Marion said, "Ok, but you are not going to change my mind about what I know I have to do. I will not endanger my children any more than they are already."

Sophie pointed toward the other room. "Children you need to go in the other room with Max. Your mother and I have to talk again."

I quickly replied to Sophie, "We already know and we will tell no one."

Marion looked at me with eyes a little more open than usual and said, "I doubt that. This is adult stuff that is way over your head dear. Now go as Sophie said and shut the door."

I could have tried to explain what we knew, but Max was also listening and I did not know how much he could or did understand. So, for the moment, we three children went into the other room and shut the door. We needed to talk privately. We needed to make at least two plans. One was to convince Marion that we knew the whole story or as much of the story that we did know. Then we needed a plan on how we would help all of us to get away to safety.

We talked and did not know at the time if Sophie and Max were going to be staying here or be going with us. At the very least, we could tell her the whole story about us. She would be shocked, but we could try. We also knew time was running out for all of us. This is the last day and we must head out south or west and soon. We were wasting valuable time.

Marion told Sophie, "I don't know what you are thinking. We can't go with you now if you insist on taking him. It would be too dangerous."

Sophie looked at Marion with disappointment in her eyes. "I know. I will stay here with him. If you are to make it there in daylight, you have to leave very soon, if not now."

"I don't know where she lives. We need to go, including you. The Russians are coming. I know these things."

Sophie reached out and touched both of Marion's hands before gently wrapping her fingers around her palm. "I do understand but I am keeping him."

Marion tried to reason with her and said, "Ok, let's just say we all go and along the way we are lucky enough not to be discovered. What happens when we get to your sister's home?"

Sophie replied, "She is a younger sister. She has always done whatever I have said. She will do whatever I tell her. She has two children of her own. I know everything will be just fine when we get there."

"I am glad you are that confidant in your family, but we are not family and the risk is just is not worth it for us." Marion replied.

"You don't think that little boy isn't worth it?"

Their voices kept getting a little louder and louder as the conversation went on. We cracked the door to listen. The two were so intense in their conversation that they did not even notice the escalation.

"Yes, he is worth some risk; maybe by you, but my family; no," Marion explained.

Just two days earlier Sophie hated all Jews including children. Now she's willing to help one survive with all the risks. Sophie then calmly dropped her voice and slowed it down. "I know more. He is the son of the woman that the Gestapo took away from across the street yesterday. He is alone now. He has no one except us to protect him. He is helpless. If we turn him in or turn him loose, he will die."

"I know and it is chocking me up too, but …"

Sophie broke in and added, "Just listen to a little more Marion. Do you remember the story I told you about Colonel Von Ryan's house keeper and her son?"

"Oh my god, are you telling me that is him?"

"I didn't remember the little boys name until last night. Yes, that's him."

"So now, not only is he Jewish and an orphan, but somewhat famous. This means when we are out there someone might even recognize him. Just think Sophie, this little boy knows all the top brass. He might not know them but they do know him. He was for all practical purposes his son; the son of the high-ranking confidante to the Fuehrer. He is surely going to be seen and recognized. They are required to report everything. There is no gray area here. If seen and recognized he will be turned in and die. So will all of us including our husbands. Do you think after all your husband has been through he will understand and approve?"

Sophie raised her head and proudly said, "Yes I do."

Marion then said something that astonished us. It filled Mika and me with much pride and joy. She shook her head as if to say no and said, "What can I do to help?"

Sophie jumped out of her seat and hugged Marion.

Marion refocused and announced, "Ok we need to change our plan and get going."

With tears of joy and relief, Sophie agreed. "Yes! You are right."

Marion started rattling off another plan. "Your story that he is your son will not work. We also need to travel together with space between us for safety."

Quietly the three of us joined Marion and Sophie in the living room. Max climbed into Sophie's lap and put his head down on her chest. She stopped talking for a moment and smiled. "All I know is that I have already fallen for this little fellow as if I had him myself. All those things you told me about having children, I understand. Something has awakened inside me. I am different somehow and I like it."

"It's called motherhood," Marion said sarcastically, "And you will never be the same. It is something so wonderful. It was how I felt giving birth to Mina and when we adopted Mika."

Mika looked at me and whispered, "Well that explains a lot. Our parents grew up together and then married. It was shameful for the times but not incest. That is why everyone hid everything from us. What a sudden realization."

Marion wasn't listening to us and kept talking. "We will travel ahead, and you keep us in sight much as possible."

"This way if we are stopped or meet a checkpoint, you will see and have a chance to hide, right?"

"Right."

At that juncture, everything had become clear. Mika and I were fascinated as we listened. Our grandmother was calmly talking about walking out into complete danger without any doubt that she was doing the right thing. She was amazing; a true hero. We were proud to be part of this family.

Marion then warned Sophie. "About your papers; they say nothing about you having a child."

"I will just tell them they were destroyed in an attack on our building and I am waiting for new ones."

"No, that won't work. Whatever excuse you have for not having them will not be good enough. It will only raise suspicion."

Sophie was lost and depending on Marion for advice, then asked, "What am I going to do?"

Marion calmly suggested, "When you are asked about Max, you tell them he was separated from his family last night in the raids and that you are taking him to a station to drop him off. You ask them for directions."

"What if we are heading the wrong way?"

"Act confused, ask for assistance. Tell him you're lost. It will work. Then just go out of site, around a block or two and we will wait for you to catch up."

Sophie nervously said, "I hope we aren't stopped. I do not know if I can do this. I am getting scared."

"You will be alright. When stopped, just catch your breath. Act as if you are out of breath from walking and carrying him. You might even hand Max over for him to hold. This would help you catch your breath, hide any fear, and focus."

Sophie smiled at Marion. "You are so smart. I would not have thought of that. Still, I hope we are not challenged."

Marion took a deep breath. "I think we can bet on that we will be. Do not worry, after the first time it will be a lot easier."

I decided it was time to speak. "You know the little Nazi boy that seems to always be in the street sometimes handing out pamphlets?"

"Yes we know him," Marion replied as she bent down to get closer.

"I think he was the one who turned in Max's mother and he saw Max with us. Yesterday when she was picked up by the Gestapo, the Nazi boy was taking credit for her being caught. I don't know if he knows anything about Max, but he started to come over to us when then sirens sounded."

Sophie looked shocked and said, "That does it for sure. We have to leave right now."

Marion stood up. "Thanks for tell us. You do not have to worry about him, we will be gone soon. We must look out for him. Thank you Mina."

Sophie and Marion both got up from the table and started taking out cans of food. They were getting everything together and trying to plan at the same time. They were two nervous and very brave women. Several times each of them lifted the blanket, draping over the broken window, to look outside.

I looked at Mika as he whispered to me, "They are checking for the little Nazi boy."

"I know. How much time do we have left?"

"We need to leave now. In fact, it may be even too late."

"What time is the surrender?"

"In some places the war is already over, just not here yet."

I said, "We are doing the right thing aren't we?"

"I believe so. The further away we can go, the better," Mika whispered.

Sophie and Marion cared less about us whispering. They were trying not to forget anything and still planning. They went over and over their stories several times as they packed. Marion told us to get our coats on and help Max. We put on our coats first and then helped Max. Mika showed him his little book before he tucked it inside Max's coat. Believing he was putting max's toy inside his coat too, he accidentally put it in his own coat instead. We forgot about the star on his coat.

Marion looked out the window one last time. Everything was packed and they really hoped they were doing everything right. Marion turned around, looked disappointed and said to Sophie, "He is out there."

Sophie looked out and then said, "We will have to wait a while." It was cold in the room. We were bundled up nicely but it was still cold. It seemed even colder with the Nazi boy outside.

Marion said to us, "When we get outside, you are not to pay any attention to Sophie and Max. They will shortly be following us. We will see how he reacts and I will signal her when she may leave. You are not to look their way unless I tell you. Do you both understand what I am saying?"

Both of us just nodded yes.

The Nazi boy was standing at attention directly in front of our building. There was no other way out, except by him. We were getting ready to leave when shivers of hair stood up all over me again; even before I heard the sirens. I would always get a sick feeling in my stomach and my knees would get weak thinking they were coming for me.

Little Max heard it too and bolted right up to Sophie grabbing her. He was holding her tight and shivering with fear. She picked him up and said, "Do not worry little fellow, everything is going to be fine, they are not coming for us."

As the sirens got louder Marion and Sophie looked out the window together and waited. Sophie was holding Max and swaying back and forth to calm him. The cars stopped at the street right in front. Two armed Soldiers jumped out of the car and ran past the Nazi boy as if he was not even there. We could hear them opening the downstairs door and heavy boots running up the stairs. We all listened to all the approaching sounds. The loud band on our door startled us. All of us stood frozen in fear. We were holding each other's hands and squeezing hard.

The door burst open and there stood the two Soldiers with rifles slung over shoulders. Marion was standing behind us with her hands on our shoulders. Sophie had little Max in her arms. Mika and I looked at Sophie and Max noticing the yellow star was out in plain sight. The solders saw this too.

CHAPTER 14

Tomorrow

When I opened my eyes, I was confused. It seemed that all movement was in slow motion and a bright white hue filtered objects and people. I felt like I was spinning. I was frozen in place but still moving. I was being wheeled around on a gurney. As my senses started returning, I heard people talking. I was in a hospital. I asked someone in a white overcoat walking beside me, "My brother; how is he?"

The young doctor responded, "He is right behind you. Do not worry he is going to be fine too." I felt relieved, he said too. We were rolled together in a big bright room as the staff worked on both of us at the same time. I could see my brother lying next to me. He was no longer a child. I had forgotten what my brother looked like as an adult, at least for the last five days. I stared at him as I my eyes focused.

I moved my right hand to touch my torso but there was an intravenous line inserted in the back of my hand that obstructed movement. I tested my left hand which freely found its way to my waist. I swept my fingers down over my hip. It was the hip of a woman. I then noticed the bandages on my head. The itchy band gauge around my temples felt constricting. I felt nauseous. I focused my vision again on my brother.

A medical professional was examining Mika's hand. From my perspective, the wound looked identical to the one he sustained in the vivid dream from which I had just awoken. The dream was still clear in my mind. I had a horrible headache felt dizzy and nauseous. I noticed that Mika was now looking at me and smiling.

"My head hurts, and you?" He asked.

"Yes and no. I feel strange; different and a little sick."

As medical staff cleared the room, the young doctor stood between us and our sides. "You both are very lucky. You both have a slight concussion." He looked at Mika and added, "No other injuries except your hand and that is not bad. You will be fine. We are going to put you both in the same room for observation."

Mika asked, "How long were we out?"

"You both were unconscious until you arrived here, maybe thirty minutes. It is not uncommon. Don't worry; we will do some x-rays and watch you. However, from my experience, you both will be just fine in a few days."

When we were alone Mika spoke first and asked me, "What is the last thing you remember?"

"We were at an outdoor café and a car seemed to hit us."

He looked at me with a puzzled look and said, "That is not what I mean. I know you were there too."

"Oh, my god, it was real and not a dream?" Searching my thoughts, I grasped for the last moment of the experience and mumbled, "The soldier looking at Max's star in the doorway."

Mika laid his head back down and said, "Hooya, me too." Then rolling on his side and stretching out to reach his coat, he reached into a pocket and pulled out Max's toy soldier. "I knew it was real," as he I laid back down holding it in the air for both of us to look at. "The hand is the same too. Did you notice that?"

"It was the first coincidence I noticed."

We talked for hours. Our experience coincided perfectly. There was no way it could not been a dream. It was more. The proof was the toy. We knew we had to do more. We would leave tomorrow and find out what happened to our family and sweet little Max.

Mika said, "We know so much more. We can stay here and follow up. We may even find people that remember the same things we experienced. Some of these people may still be alive. I won't leave till I know everything."

"We might even be able to track down the Nazi boy, so you can punch him smack in the mouth. We can start at the café, or the apartment building."

We did not want to sleep. Maybe it was just a little fear that we would not wake up again and be somehow transported back into the experience. We felt awakened. A goal and ambition that had been lacking in our lives was replaced with a new burning desire to complete this journey.

He agreed with me and also decided that no matter what, he would not leave without knowing all the answers too. We could not go back home and continue with our lives not knowing what became of these people we encountered. Eventually we both slept.

Morning started too early and I could no longer understand the foreign dialect so easy. Clattering carts, paper flipping over charts, and too much random conversation amplified the pain in my head. My head pounded. The pain was incredible. I allowed myself to weep in order to decrease the pressure, but the ache in my heart was more severe than the throbbing in my head.

As I started to cry, the memory of the experience flowed through me. My grandmother, Sophie, little Max, his poor mother, even the Nazi boy. What suffering. What needless and drawn out suffering. How could these women cope? Could I cope in such a situation? How was my brother coping with the memory of this experience? As I looked up to face him as he approached my bed. He looked at me cockeyed with a smirk on his face. "You are such a girl," He said.

"How are you coping with these memories?"

"What are you talking about?"

"Aren't you affected by the suffering our parents and grandparents experienced?"

"What are you talking about? How much medication did they give you this morning?"

The most humorous aspect of my brother's response was his sincere inability to get it. My head felt lighter and I sat up in bed. I was now slightly annoyed that my brother was up and Adam and ready to go. I was down and Eve, and wondering when the handsome young doctor might return. A nurse came into our room and announced that we had a visitor.

Mika glanced at me before informing the nurse that we did not know anyone in Germany. As she walked out, a gentleman walked in. He was finely dressed and appeared to be about sixty years old. There was something familiar about this stranger. I could not help looking in his bright blue eyes. His eyes looked like identical to those of little Max. I quickly covered my mouth and fought back the tears. My brother gasped out loud while he caught his breath. He was not able to look away from the man's eyes either. With distinctive traces of yellow, it had to be him. Under the man's arm was the little blue children's book faded with age, but obviously well kept.

Without saying a word, Mika picked up the toy soldier off the table and held it up like a gesture or a question. "Max?" he asked

The gentleman nodded his head and smiled, exposing his dimples. "Yes, yes I am.

"How do you know us?"

Little Max explained that he had read about the accident in the newspaper. It stated there were two Americans hurt and gave their names. The article asked if anyone knew them. He wondered how two Americans with the exact names he remembered from so long ago could be here and now. He said he was drawn to come down here and see us for himself.

Mika suggested that we get out of the hospital before we are all committed. "I do not understand this at all. We have a lot of catching up to do and I am so hungry I could eat a bear."

Max said, "Why not the outdoor café? The sun is shining and it is a beautiful day."

Mika smiling shrugged his shoulders and answered, "Why not, except I want to be close to the door if you don't mind."

"Sounds perfect," I said, as we chuckled a little.

We got dressed and left the hospital with little Max and headed for the familiar café. Over hot coffee and fresh strudel we shared out phenomenal experience with little Max and learned what happened on that fateful last day. Max did not seem bewildered as we spoke of our experience. I asked him why he seemed to accept this as rational. Max advised us that phenomena are natural and, while this one is unique to him, we are not the first or last to have such an incident.

Mika added, "We learned so much about ourselves and our past family members. I learned just how important loyalty and love is in my life. I have truly loved only two women in my life, other than Mina and my mother; my ex wife Deborah and Sue. I also learned that we were not cowards. Even as children, we stepped up to the plate and actively made a difference. I can't explain how good that feels."

Max never stopped smiling. "I think I do. Your actions have had a much larger effect that you know. However, you will soon know. Your brave acts that changed my fate are now being passed on. I was able to find out everything about my parents, grandparents, Colonel Von Ryan, and even some about your parents." He opened his book and asked us, "Do you remember what was inside?"

Mika quickly said before I could, "In every available space were musical notes. It looked like songs. I would guess nursery rhymes."

"That was what it was supposed to look like, but it isn't. My mother wrote it every night as I slept. If I was captured or lost the book, the message had to be written in code to protect us. She hoped someday that I would find a way to decode it. Max stopped for a second to sip his coffee. "The notes are letters and words in Latin; not songs. Many times when I was a young adult, I tried to play the songs. It was awful. I like to think that she knew I'd try and laugh. I would just put it away and try again later. I repeatedly tried, determined to never give up.

I knew it was important but could not get past her obstacles. The notes or songs did not make any sense to me until my third day in

Latin class. It hit me like a ton of bricks. I recognized some of these words. I was so excited; I could not wait to get home. I knew then what she had done after all those years. It was so simple and brilliant.

I spent all night and several days in my room decoding her work. I couldn't stop until I finished. She had written about everything she could think of in the few days before she was captured. I cannot tell you the joy I felt. Almost every line made me tear up, these were her words. She wrote them down for me. I was able to accomplish what she wished. It was amazing and exciting. It is our story; her life and mine, told with emotion. Things I may have been told and couldn't remember. I so needed this, you have no idea." He wiped a tear away.

I touched his hand and said, "I am sorry. I wish we had known her." I could see Mika in the corner of my eye. He was nodding a yes.

Max told us about his mother and father and their love for each other from the book. He told us Sophie and her husband raised him as if he were their own. They put him through school and they were wonderful. They tried to find his mother. It was chaotic in the following days and records were destroyed or mishandled. "The two soldiers at the door were Sophie and Marion's husbands. The Army had arranged for a police escort whenever possible. There was urgency in them returning to their families.

Mika looked at me and Max and said, "We thought that was the end of you."

Mika then said something that shocked me. "Did you get the message I left for you?"

I looked at Mika and asked, "What message?"

"Remember me handing Max his book in our apartment on the last day? I wrote a note in English in the back."

Max said, "Yes, but first I have so much to tell you." He explained all the people in his life and their fates. He started with Otto and Rianna. They were together to the end. They were driven to a well-known field used for executions and burials. They were holding each other face to face when they were shot as recorded in the report. There was no record of Anna's arrest or what had happed to her. There were the Gestapo records before her capture and nothing later.

General Kist could not believe what Elsa would not do for Anna and little Max. Simply giving them some escape items was not enough. He lost his desire and respect for her. All her property and assets were seized by the Russians. She was poor and without friends and family dying after several years of loneliness and desperation.

Max looked up at us and said, "Records about my real father, Eli, detailed his interrogations and stated that he died several days later in a liberated prisoner of war camp. He lived just long enough to see the end, but not long enough to enjoy the benefits.

Max then said to Mika, "For the longest time, I could not understand your message. It said in English, buy IBM and you will be rich. It meant nothing to me until I saw an advertisement for International Business Machines." He then said, "It was written in my book in 1945 way before I.B.M. existed. I had to pay attention and bought as much as I could scrape up. Boy, you were right."

He took a deep breath smiling, "It made me enough money to pursue a dream of mine; a dream that I get so much joy and pleasure from every day." We could see the gleam in his eyes as he was telling this to us. "I founded a charity called The Max Schelling shelter for war children. It is international now. We do not care about their religion. We care not about skin color or the shape of their nose. We get these displaced and sometimes orphaned children out of danger. We do everything we can to re-unite them to their families. We do whatever we can with each situation being different. We ask only one thing from these children."

Mika and I were spellbound as Max kept talking. "We send letters with them to keep and when they grow up and become responsible, they are asked to do something important. It says if you want to truly fulfill your destiny then save a child's life helping us. No greater pleasure will you ever receive."

He put his book down and looking at both of us said, "It is the product of your bravery, strength, desire, and love that kept this one child alive for five days. I thank you so much."

The End

EPILOGUE

I was once told that people are smarter than you might think. Do not treat them as if they will not understand everything. However, I do not like assuming.

Life's lessons I learned because of this story are real. You do not really know what your parents have sacrificed for you unless you try and step into their past shoes. Even parents that were not around as much as you wished may have sacrificed more than you will ever know without attempting to find out.

Racism and bigotry will eat at a person eventually destroying any possibility of having the joys of life he or she deserves. Nothing good can come from the destructive power it possesses. One person can make a difference, you.

Made in the USA
Charleston, SC
23 October 2012